DracuLAND

COME FOR THE ATTRACTIONS.

STAY FOR THE APOCALYPSE.

DracuLAND

George W. Young

CELESTIAL ECHO PRESS

ROSLYN, PA, U.S.A.

2022

Cover art and design: Dan Smith

Editing: Gemini Wordsmiths, LLC

Published by
Celestial Echo Press
An imprint of Gemini Wordsmiths, LLC
P.O. Box 1191
Roslyn, PA 19001
celestialechopress.com

For L. Frank Baum, the real Wizard of Oz

"And the great dragon was thrown down, that ancient serpent, who is called the devil and Satan, the deceiver of the whole world — he was thrown down to the earth, and his angels were thrown down with him." - Revelation, 12:9

Praise for DracuLAND

"This charming read of the Dracula trope is made even more clever by a lack of vampires. *DracuLAND*, however, is such a compelling read the shopworn neck-biters aren't missed at all. Plenty of good undead bad guys in a wonderful new take on the Romanian legend."

--Dan Smith, Director/Writer, *Savage Sistas*

"George W. Young is the Bob Ross of letters. He starts with a blank canvas and somehow sketches a masterpiece in *DracuLAND*. Plus, he's scary funny."

--Joe Becker, Director/Writer, *Please Do Not Disturb*, *The Fixer*, and *Muerte: Tales of Horror*

"*DracuLAND*, like the theater, transports its audience to another world, but unlike the live show venue, there's no guarantee the experience is the one anticipated or expected."

--Joe Giuffre, Director/Writer, *The Mirror Never Lies*

Foreword

The film industry is made up of a collection of talented, quirky, and in many charming ways, unhireable-in-any-other-business individuals. And that's the beauty of it. Somehow via a pathway of dead ends, blind alleys, and missteps, we find each other.

Filmmaking is also a joy ride.

The working relationships are temporary, but intense. Both of these qualities make it a career of connections. Interdependencies due to deadlines and the ephemera of creative product are the focus of your life. But like the special effect of a vanishing person, or alien, or creature, or animal, they are gone before you blink.

And you move on to the next professional and important connection.

George W. Young, author of *DracuLAND*, and I had one of those connections on Tim Burton's *The Nightmare Before Christmas*, a movie which still captures the imagination today. An entire generation, not even born when *The Nightmare Before Christmas* dropped on Halloween 1993, watches its annual release with a cult-like fascination.

The Nightmare Before Christmas still holds that same fascination for George today. Its creative grip led to the writing of his second novel, *DracuLAND*. The book engulfs the reader in a classic good-versus-evil trope.

Will the good guys prevail?

Do the bad guys win? What happens if they come out on top?

The novel, despite its titular pedigree, features no vampires. It does, though, include Dracula, or Vlad Dracul, as is his formal Wallachian (Romanian) name. The infamous, or famous if you are so inclined, leader of the people of Romania makes several appearances in this novel, but not as you would expect. He does not glide down a long stairway. Nor does he spend any time pursuing Mina Harker.

No. But he is in *DracuLAND*, in—dare I say it—spirit. His malevolent life force is once again in play in the final battle between good and evil. Without Vlad Dracul there is no *DracuLAND*.

As a forty-year veteran of special and visual effects for the film industry, I, and my company Fonco Studios, have worked on countless films and television shows in the good-versus-evil genre. We have been fortunate to contribute to such brilliant entertainment for so long.

Each story starts with a great idea. Without that great idea, everything is simply window dressing and not compelling. Our finest production work always built on that concept.

A great idea as the anchor leads to an enrapt audience, one that *cannot stop* watching or listening. You have hooked them, and Fonco Studios has been fortunate to contribute to some great hooks.

DracuLAND has that great idea.

A New York City real estate developer buys Dracula's Castle, an, ahem, creepy and long-ago abandoned structure on a precipice in the Carpathian Mountains in Romania. The protagonist is convinced the world's greatest theme park should open there. And eventually it does.

But not before a few things happen first.

And not many of them positive.

Therefore, the good-versus-evil trope. The battle to preserve the Age of Man. The Second Coming. The Apocalypse. Little things like that.

I am delighted to add *DracuLAND* to *The Nightmare Before Christmas* on the list of intense and beautiful professional relationships shared with George.

Hey George, let's not wait another thirty years for the next one.

--Fon H. Davis, Creative Director and founder of Fonco Studios (foncostudios.com)

The Headline

The New York International Dispatch

<u>**Dracula's Castle for Sale!**</u>
July 15, 2017—Bran, Romania

Romania's former royal family put "Dracula's Castle" in Transylvania up for sale Monday, hoping to secure a buyer who will respect "the property and its history," a U.S.-based investment company said.

Bran Castle, perched on a cliff near Brasov in mountainous central Romania, is a top tourist attraction because of its ties to Prince Vlad the Impaler, the warlord whose cruelty inspired Bram Stoker's 1897 novel, **Dracula.**

Legend has it that Vlad, who earned his nickname because of the way he tortured his enemies, spent one night in the 1400s at the castle.

Bran Castle, constructed in the 14th century, served as a fortress to protect against the invading Ottoman Turks. The royal family moved into the castle in the 1920s, living there until the communist regime confiscated it from Princess Ileana in 1948.

After being restored in the early 1980s and again following the end of communist rule in Romania in 1989, it gained popularity as a tourist attraction known as "Dracula's Castle."

In May 2006, the castle's ownership returned to Princess Ileana's son, Archduke Dominic Habsburg. Habsburg, a 69-year-old New York architect, had pledged to keep it open as a museum until at least 2009, but offered to sell the castle last year to local authorities for $80 million. They rejected the offer.

The Theme Park

Elizabeth Astor slapped *The New York International Dispatch* on her desk. After all the years of holding paper and ink in her hands, she could not tolerate the online version. Her 27" computer screen displayed the same article. She leaned back in her chair and spun around to look out the window. She whipped back to face front.

As she did her chair tilted over and Elizabeth, all 98 pounds of her, crashed onto the floor. Her reading glasses, unnecessary though stylish, skidded across the carpet to the front door of the Southwestern-style office. They smacked into the stiletto of her admin, Rebecca. Rebecca placed the glasses on Elizabeth's desk.

"Everything OK, Ms. Astor?" Rebecca's tone weary from investigating the clumsiness of her boss.

"Fine," snapped Elizabeth. "Get out!"

Rebecca's substantial figure turned and stomped out, deliberately slamming the turquoise double doors behind. Elizabeth hissed and got to all fours. She shook herself like a wet hunting dog, righted the chair, and put herself back into the seat, once more behind the computer and hard copy of *The New York International Dispatch*.

Elizabeth's office building, Astor Plaza, had been known as the Flatiron Building, until her purchase. Located at 23rd Street and Fifth Avenue, and away from the hustle of midtown and Wall Street, she could not see any of Manhattan's famous skyline, which suited her fine.

"Never liked Pedro, anyway," she mumbled.

Pedro, the name Elizabeth had given the Charging Bull, the iconic statue in the financial district, was nowadays confronted by a brass and stone likeness of a young girl.

"But I hope Pedro gores the little twit."

Elizabeth rocked from side to side using her heels as pivot points. She dropped her head and pressed the tips of her fingers together, a habit from her student days.

Her right elbow shot out when she leaned on it too much. The worn suede elbow patch of her favorite suit jacket slammed into a sculpted miniature of Sedona, Arizona. It shot off the desk and dropped to the floor. A chunk of Red Rock Crossing snapped on impact.

Elizabeth heard movement outside her door.

"Don't even bother, Rebecca!"

The movement stopped. Then Elizabeth's mumbling resumed.

"Dracula's Castle. Dracula's Castle."

She moved her feet in a front-to-back motion and pushed herself further into her chair.

Her cellphone rang. Elizabeth grabbed the offending device and tossed it in the trashcan.

"Worst invention since the silent dishwasher." She picked up the newspaper, and read the headline once more. The disposed cellphone rang again. Elizabeth reached down and pulled it out of the trash. Her partner and twin brother, Garrett.

"Garrett, you useless winner of the Chromosome Lottery," she said. "When can you get here?"

"Not even a 'Hello how are you,' from my beloved sister?"

"Hello. How are you? When can you get here?"

"You're kidding, right? I called to tell you that I'm finally kicking Joanne out. I can literally, or is it figuratively, see the door hitting her admittedly shapely posterior on its way to the elevator. I guess, given her shapely posterior, it would be, uh, figuratively?"

Garrett cleared his throat.

"Uh-huh, sure."

"…although it hasn't happened yet, mind you."

"Of course, it hasn't," said Elizabeth. She picked up the top of Red Rock Crossing and the Sedona miniature. She laid the sports page of *The Dispatch* underneath, and fished a well-used tube of Krazy Glue from a desk drawer.

"What did you break this time?" He noticed the long delay, scratching sounds, and Elizabeth's off-key humming.

"Ah, kiss my … speaking of Joanne's shapely posterior."

"You are kidding about coming into the office?"

"No, I'm not kidding," she said. Elizabeth glued Red Rock Crossing back together and turned it over in her hands before placing it on the desk. She lifted it to move the miniature to a safer position, and ripped the sports section where her jacket attached itself via some renegade Krazy Glue.

"Oh, so the Sedona model hit the floor again," he said. "Don't tell me. Worn out suede elbow patches?"

Elizabeth ignored the comment but couldn't resist asking him about his wife.

"So, you're finally kicking her out? I'd say I'm sorry to hear that—but only if *you* are."

"I'm not sorry, and like everything else in her life, Joanne has been slow to actually *do* something that she said she would do . . . like leave."

"Sure."

"Elizabeth. It's been a long time coming. No one will be happier than I . . . well, maybe Joanne will be just as happy."

"Garrett, I love you, but Joanne is going to be ecstatic, especially after the divorce settlement gives her half of what you own."

Garrett blew out a breath between clenched teeth and spoke.

"What's your rush on this latest project?" he asked, and added, "Maybe I'll come in. It'll take my mind off this mess."

"Right." Elizabeth laughed.

"It *will* take my mind off this mess."

Elizabeth tapped her right index finger next to her keyboard. She'd let Garrett wait now that he had agreed.

"I read something in the news today," said Elizabeth. "I think it's time to shake it up here at Astor Holdings. We've been sitting on our proverbial laurels too long."

"Sure we have. What's it been? A whole week since—"

"Swim or die, Garrett. Swim or die."

Both breathed into their phones.

"All right, do you want to tell me about it?"

"Nah," she said. "Tell me more about Joanne's imminent departure."

"Nope. Don't want to talk about it with anyone except Joanne, which I will do now and get to your office."

"Typical male. No reason to talk it over."

"I would expect you to say just that, and how soon should I be there?"

"As soon as possible."

"Got it. No point in pursuing the original purpose of the call. I'll jump in a cab. Give me thirty minutes. Oh, and make sure there's a roast beef on rye for me when I get there. You're making me change dinner plans from the sound of your voice. My blood sugar is already going south."

"God, you are such a wuss. Are you sure you're the *male* twin?"

"Click," said Garrett, mimicking an old-fashioned telephone hang up.

"See you in a bit," said Elizabeth. She eyed the phone's cradle.

"Hold on there, Baba Looey," Garrett snapped. "Give me something to google before I get over there. I want to be prepared."

"Search today's news for Romania." Elizabeth hung up.

Garrett walked into the executive offices of Astor Holdings.

"Mr. Astor," said Rebecca, who greeted Garrett in the waiting room of the executive suite. "She's only had two accidents so far today. *And* we didn't have to take her to the emergency room."

Garrett nodded. He walked through the turquoise double doors into the executive suite populated by his twin sister, two of her admins not named Rebecca, and Astor's chief counsel, Larry Winters.

Larry's presence in the executive suite signaled a serious undertaking by Elizabeth.

Larry and Garrett shook hands. The admins acknowledged Garrett's presence with perfunctory waves. Garrett stepped back and shut the doors behind him. He embraced his sister. Elizabeth handed him a sandwich bag.

"Enjoy! You keep eating those and I won't have to worry about sharing too many more deals with you."

Garrett snatched the bag and ripped it open.

"You wish," he said, already chewing. "And can't we do something about the doors? The loud artwork? That cigar store Indian?"

"I like the motif, but if you promise to stop clogging your arteries, I'm sure we could compromise on design elements." Elizabeth walked from the front to the back of her desk, a single piece of treated wood resting on two fragile-looking chrome tripods. One slim drawer cut into the middle for the vital Krazy Glue and a nail file. "Take my desk for example."

"Yes, you say minimalist Southwest. I say no such thing," said Garrett. "Just love the roast beef from this place," he said between a chew and a swallow.

Garrett sat in one of the chairs in front of his sister's desk, while Larry and the two admins occupied the sofa just off to his left, Elizabeth's right.

"Should we get on with why we're all here, or do you two want to continue discussing diet and interior design?" asked Larry, as he smoothed the remaining strands of hair crossing his scalp.

"I want to buy Dracula's Castle," announced Elizabeth. She tripped over a dent in the animal-skin rug, which served as a floor protector for the chair. Elizabeth recovered as quickly as a gold medal finalist in gymnastics after a faulty landing.

"No, you don't," Garrett choked out, and grabbed a Coke from the torn bag.

"Yes, I do."

"Larry?"

Larry Winters, a short, chubby man, looked up from a legal pad. Elizabeth described him as a man who wore fine suits, but wore them with no idea as to how much he looked like an unmade bed. Larry had an annoying habit of clearing his throat before speaking. But no one in a courtroom cared how he dressed. Larry was a top-tier corporate attorney.

Larry cleared his throat.

"Oh, so I get to be the only grownup in the room again?"

"Bran Castle, as it is also known," said Elizabeth, ignoring Larry.

"*Bran* Castle? So what? Tell me something about it," said Garrett, after a healthy swallow of Coke. He turned toward Elizabeth. "At least what makes it worthwhile to pursue a development deal."

Elizabeth paced behind the desk.

"It's a huge tourist draw. Gets close to a million visitors a year. Located in a small town in Romania called Brasov. Access will have to be improved. The area needs a better highway system, and a short-haul airport nearby."

"That sounds easy and inexpensive," said Garrett. "Actually, if I may, that sounds like a lot of bribes, kickbacks, delays, and the usual amount of interference by the dolts that run foreign governments."

Larry cleared his throat.

"Garrett, we've had about a half hour to look into this," said Larry. "It's all preliminary research. We'll know much more in a few days."

"Anything else? How about a Chunnel from Paris?"

"Ease up, Garrett," said Elizabeth. "Like Larry said, we're just beginning to look into this."

"I know what that means, and you have no intention of 'just looking into this.' What's the end game? Surely you're not just buying this as some charitable gesture to the Romanian royal family," said Garrett.

"Uh, no?" asked Elizabeth. "Is that a real question?"

"It's what I gleaned from the financials I found on the drive over here," said Garrett. "They haven't turned a profit in decades, despite the crowds. I have a feeling those cute, cuddly Romanians are already on the take."

"And?"

"And nothing. Come on Elizabeth. You do know they'd love to unload this white elephant because they're in debt up to their dark Romanian eyes. They're looking for a payday. I don't like this idea. Not one bit," he said. "But, given my capacity for *your* self-indulgences, why don't you tell me *exactly* what you want to build on the site of Dracula's Castle."

Garrett moved out of his chair toward Elizabeth, and leaned across her desk. She placed the palms of her hands on the slab of Scandinavian pine. Elizabeth stuck out her jaw and got as close to him as possible. Garrett set his mouth in a thin line.

"Let's go, you two," said Larry.

"*DracuLAND!*" Elizabeth proclaimed, drawing an exclamation point in the air for effect.

"This is your brother you're selling here. I'm going to need a little more information than just some catchy . . . oh, no. Not that. Not there."

Elizabeth made fists with her hands and planted them on her hips.

"Come on, Garrett. It'll be great. A theme park. We've talked about building one for a decade."

"*What?*" He exploded. "*You've* talked about it. Not *us!*"

"*We* are Astor Holdings," said Elizabeth, pointing an index finger back and forth between her and Garrett. "It's not just you *or* me."

Garrett waited for a response from Larry, who pointed *his* index finger first at Elizabeth, then at Garrett.

"Elizabeth. Garrett. Happy to weigh in as soon as you two stop with the childish competition."

He cleared his throat again. Elizabeth winced.

Garrett turned his attention to Elizabeth, who stood behind the buffer zone of her desk.

"Allow me. We *hate* foreign holdings, Elizabeth, especially entertainment properties. Building laws, while restrictive enough in America, absolutely, pardon the schoolboy language, *suck* in Eastern Europe. Governments change them capriciously. They nationalize industries. They're fascists when it comes to compliance. Do I need to remind you about our Bulgarian ski resort? We're still digging our way out of that one."

"Digging our way out," laughed Elizabeth. "That's actually funny. I'm surprised Joanne would leave a man with such a great sense of humor."

"Now we're going to involve Joanne?" asked Garrett.

"Why not? She's going to have a lot of our money soon, so—"

"All right, you idiots," shouted Larry without clearing his throat. "Garrett, why don't you *add* something to the proceedings. Hang on, Elizabeth."

Neither moved from their tactical positions.

Garrett continued the assault.

"If memory serves, English ain't the national language of Romania, just as it wasn't in Bulgaria. Just a guess."

Garrett leaned back. He gestured to Larry, who pushed himself up off the sofa and cleared his throat.

"Would you stop doing that!" Elizabeth shouted. "Ahem! Ahem! Ahem!"

Larry sat down. Both admins, who had been furiously typing notes on their tablets, stopped.

"I'm sorry," said Elizabeth. "Call it the Astor factor. Go ahead, Larry."

Larry shifted on the sofa. The admins went back to their tablets.

"The land around the castle is inexpensive, especially when compared to the other properties we've researched for a theme park. Also, Romania isn't on the euro. The country is still on the leu. It's cheap money over there."

"Have we spoken with the government?" Garrett asked.

"Investor Relations is on the task," Elizabeth answered. "And Larry will contact the country's attorney general, or the equivalent of it."

"Fine," conceded Garrett.

Elizabeth continued. "The biggest draw for them, other than our purchasing the castle, is our willingness to help fund the superhighway from Bucharest *and* build the short-haul airport. We'll know a lot more in a few days. My guess is they're motivated to sell."

"I'll bet they are," said Garrett.

"Enough with the *Glengarry Glen Ross* imitation."

Garrett dropped his head forward. Elizabeth kept her gaze on her brother. He raised his head and they locked eyes.

"All right, Elizabeth," he capitulated. "What would you like me to do?"

"I want you to go there with me and do the initial site survey. Believe it or not, I feel as reluctant as you to deal with a foreign government. If we don't like what we're hearing, we'll drop the project."

"That's such a crock!" Garrett shouted. "Elizabeth, when you don't like what you're hearing, you change the rules and proceed anyway. Why should this be any different?"

Elizabeth strutted around the room. Garrett watched the act. The two of them, in an homage to genetics, placed their hands on their hips at exactly the same time and in exactly the same manner.

"You really want to deal with some third-world—"

"Garrett," interrupted Larry, "Romania does not qualify as third-world. That's an unfair statement."

"Well, it ain't northern Virginia." He drew on a fake cigarette. Blew the fake smoke out. He tossed it on the carpet and crushed it with his toe.

"And it's not Calcutta," barked Elizabeth. "If you don't want to be part of this, just say so. I'll do the preliminary work without you because *I'm* CEO, but once you're out . . . you're out."

Elizabeth closed an eye and fixed the open one on Garrett.

Her brother met her single-eyed stare. Elizabeth blinked first, and slapped her hand on the desk.

"Don't go, but like I said, when you're out, you're out!" She raised her volume. "As soon as we complete the arrangements, we're off. The Romanian government is prepared to send representatives to Bran Castle the day we arrive. I want to get there before someone else sniffs this deal. Clear your schedule for at least the next week."

Garrett crumpled up his sandwich bag and searched for a trash can.

"Or not." Elizabeth spat out the words.

"I cleared it after we closed the deal last month," said Garrett. "Of course, I closed it for reasons other than heading off to Romania."

"Try to think of it as a vacation," Elizabeth added. "Something else bothering you?"

Garrett looked over at the sofa. He jerked his head in the direction of the door. Both admins and Larry left the office.

Elizabeth sat back in her chair and exhaled through her nose. A sneeze followed.

"Is this about Joanne?" she asked. "Maybe you're not ready to go after some new undertaking right now?"

"Nah," said Garrett. "Nothing about Joanne is playing into this. Don't know, Elizabeth. I might be weary from battling my soon-to-be-ex, but yes, there is something about this I don't like. A foreign language. Parts of Romania *are* on the brink of third-world status, despite what Larry says. Except for the eastern side of the country bordered by the Carpathians, the country is not in great shape, economically or politically."

Garrett's voice trailed off. He located a trash can, tossed the paper bag, and walked toward the office doors.

"Garrett?" Elizabeth asked, her serious tone gone.

Garrett stopped just outside the turquoise doors.

"Not afraid of vampires, are you? Do you still hide next to the TV when you're watching *Creature Feature* on Saturday nights?"

Garrett pulled out a pen and a notepad from his jacket pocket and scribbled. He walked over, tore off the page, and handed it to his sister. The doors shut behind him.

"Dear Sis," she mumbled as she read. "Should you have any spare time today, I would suggest that you find a little private room and go—"

She crumpled up the paper, and burst into laughter.

The Wrong Castle — July 25

Elizabeth sat behind the worn, chipped antique desk in the Presidential Suite at the Brasov Intercontinental Hotel. She leaned back in an ornate French Renaissance chair with her hands laced behind her head, face flush from a day spent poking around Bran Castle. Eyes narrowed to slits. Elizabeth's right hand pressed the bridge of her nose.

A migraine. The result of wasted time.

Garrett, also a participant in the unsuccessful real estate tour, sat across from Elizabeth in the French chair's twin. He studied the flocked walls and a tapestry that served as an area rug on the hardwood floor. Their suite classic, but care-worn.

"A joke," Elizabeth said. "And not a good one."

"Well, *you* wanted to buy Dracula's Castle, Elizabeth. Now that you've seen it—"

"Dracula wouldn't have stayed in that gingerbread fiasco for all the whatever the commodity is in whichever country has the monopoly on that commodity," she retorted. "It's a great big 14th -century joke."

"That was the 18th century. The original castle *was* constructed during the Dracul's reign, but Vlad didn't deem the property strategically worthy of occupying to fight the Ottoman Turks, so he abandoned the place. It fell into disrepair until the royal family of Romania rescued it in the 1800s, which is the vers—"

Elizabeth raised her hand.

"I've had enough history for one day, Garrett," Elizabeth said and despite the headache, smacked her forehead on the edge of the table, an almost comic move which brought Garrett's Romanian history lesson to a close.

"Someone on my staff could have told me about Bran Castle before I schlepped out to Romania. It ain't a quick trip."

Garrett snorted.

"Elizabeth, your staff did try to inform you, but of course, no one can tell you *anything*."

She fired one of the hotel pens across the desk. Garrett ducked the projectile.

"And that's how *we* ended up in Romania, and, that's how *you* ended up realizing that Dracula's Castle isn't some gothic Hollywood construction. That it wasn't filled with vampires and ghouls and ghosts and headless Turks. And that it's actually in the town of Bran, and sits *near* a tourist trap called Brasov. We are here, Elizabeth, because no one can tell you a darned thing."

Elizabeth rose and slapped the palm of her right hand down on its surface. The sound echoed through the room.

"Oh, I see. That is how *I* ended up schlepping out to Romania!" She shouted as she pointed her index finger at Garrett, then herself. "No one can tell *me* anything?"

Garrett glared at his sister. His eyelids twitched.

The contentious siblings halted their discussions at the sound of a sharp double rap on the door.

"Everything all right? I heard shouting."

The door opened and the dark-haired, local bodyguard Elizabeth hired for the trip entered with two strides. Elizabeth moved away from her latest confrontation with Garrett and toward the 6'5" Romanian, Max Capitanou. She stopped just past the desk, leaned against the floor-to-ceiling window, her petite, athletic figure silhouetted against the late afternoon sun.

"Everything is fine, Mr. Capitanou. You'll have to understand that my beloved sister —"

"—is a little upset over the fact that Dracula's Castle wouldn't frighten field mice?"

Max, briefed for hours regarding the venture prior to his employ, smirked.

"Yes."

"You are not the first to complain about this, Ms. Astor," said Max.

"I might, however, be the first to have offered to purchase the castle for one hundred million euros or lei, or whatever Monopoly money is being used here, before being let in on its little secret!"

"That is such BS, Elizabeth!" shouted Garrett. "You would have come anyway because you don't trust anyone's eyes but your own." He got out of his chair, and stomped to the window. "Pay them the kill fee and be done with it. The Romanians get a nice little windfall and you can go back to New York and work out something else for the theme park. Where do the Frankensteins live, by the way?"

"Funny," she fumed. "And no! Absolutely not on the kill fee. I came here to buy Dracula's Castle and I'm going to buy it. The good Count must have lived somewhere in Romania, so let's find out where that is and go there."

"We know where it is, stupid," said Garrett. "Our CMO informed you of the ruins of Poenari Castle before we left New York City. He even showed us pictures. You 'refused to be dragged out,' I believe were your exact words, 'to examine a pile of Romanian rubble.'"

Elizabeth gave his comments a dismissive wave of her hand, and turned to the bodyguard.

"Where is Poenari Castle, Max? And have you ever been there?"

"It's in Curtea de Argeş, Ms. Astor," said Max. "And I have been *there* a number of times."

"All right, just where is Curtea de Argeş?"

"South of here. I have to warn you that it is not easy to get to the ruins of Poenari Castle. It sits on a cliff five hundred meters up the Carpathians, a militarily strategic move by the Draculs. No enemy breached that natural line of defense for centuries. Not the Romans, not the Saxons, and not, for many decades, the Ottomans. The Turks eventually overran Poenari Castle and executed Vlad the Impaler in 1476."

"Wow! Anything else?" Elizabeth asked, her eyes on Max.

"Well, yes, if you would like to know. Vlad the Impaler was betrayed by his own half-brother, Radu, during the siege of Poenari. Vlad gained his revenge by killing Radu in the main hall of the castle keep after the Ottoman Turks broke through the inner defenses. The Sultan of the Turkish Empire, Mehmet II, to whom Radu betrayed Vlad, beheaded the Impaler, and left the torso to rot. He took Vlad's head back to Istanbul."

"That's impressive, Max," said Garrett.

"Credit your admin, Rebecca, Ms. Astor. She was quite thorough preparing me for this assignment."

"Go on. I'm getting all tingly," said Elizabeth showing more interest. "What about the castle after its conquest by the Turks?"

Max forced a smile, and stood straighter. His face took on a serious aspect.

"Abandoned. Poenari Castle is cursed. Few people visit it. It has a damp and cold feel to it, even during the sunniest and warmest of Romanian summers. Legend has it the Draculs haunt the castle." He took a breath. "Nothing good will ever come of Poenari . . . according to the locals."

"Really?" Distracted, Elizabeth laughed, her voice hoarse from travel and stress. "Any nighttime visits by caped B-movie actors? A dungeon in the castle? Iron maiden? Uh, not the rock group."

"Ms. Astor, I can only tell you what I know as a Romanian plus the information Rebecca gave me."

"Elizabeth. You're not in Manhattan," offered Garrett. "You might want to pay attention to what Max is saying. Sounds like there might not be a lot of support for your venture and you know what that means."

"So what? Teamsters scare me more than any of these legends, Garrett. Poenari Castle sounds perfect. Think of it. DracuLAND. It's a theme park like no other. We don't have to invent any myth or legend. The landmark has the pedigree, and it's supported by superstitious Romanians." She turned to the bodyguard. "No offense, Max."

"None taken, Ms. Astor," said Max. "The country of my birth surprises me at how attached it is to these events of our past, particularly the Draculs."

"Here's a bonus for you, Sis," said Garrett. The register in his voice dropped. "Did you know there used to be a thriving manufacturing site where the castle's tourist parking lot is now? Yes, even during the Ceausescu era, Curtea de Argeș supplied a good deal of Eastern and Western Europe's medical supplies."

"And?"

"It closed after a few years. Workers had disappeared and were never heard from again. Speculation and rumors abounded. Recently, a couple of tourists have gone missing, their abandoned cars found in the parking lot."

"Even better!" yelled Elizabeth.

"How did you come by this information, Mr. Astor, if you don't mind?" asked Max.

"First of all, please sit, and I think you should call us by our first names," said Elizabeth.

"Yes," said Garrett. "We aren't royalty."

"I am not used to that, but this is my first assignment with Americans," said Max, looking down at the floor. He took a seat in another of the room's chairs.

"Give it a whirl, Max. You might like it," said Garrett. "Now, to address your question about the information, I vet all of Astor Holdings' ventures. I unearthed the missing tourists' information without help from the local authorities, because they don't want any of it to become public. The episode is especially troubling—innocent people disappearing? Not good for Curtea de Argeş. And not good for Romania."

"But it could be good for a theme park based on—"

"I hate when you do that," said Garrett.

Elizabeth ignored him and spoke directly to Max.

"Poenari Castle sounds like my kind of place. How soon can we get there?"

Elizabeth crossed her arms over her chest.

"I guess there's no sense speaking further about the trouble and the obstacles. It'll only motivate her more," said Garrett to Max.

"Well?" She turned toward the bodyguard.

"If we leave soon, we could be in Curtea de Argeş late tonight, and gain entrance to the castle tomorrow. I will call the local officials from here to make sure we can have access tomorrow. It normally is not an issue, but there's a caretaker, actually more of a ticket taker on site who sometimes closes the footbridge, the passage that leads to the castle."

"Sounds good. Make the call." She looked at Max. "Ticket taker? There's a charge for looking at that rock quarry?"

"Yes, ma'am. I'll also arrange for overnight lodging in Curtea de Argeş."

"Thank you, Max," said Elizabeth.

Max smiled, stood, and walked out.

Garrett waited for Max's footsteps to disappear. Elizabeth eased back into the chair, and tilted her head. She touched both index fingers to the bridge of her nose.

Garrett approached his sister.

"Elizabeth, are you really that unaware of your surroundings? I'm standing right in front of you."

Elizabeth broke her concentration and looked up from the desk. Said nothing. She didn't have to. Her smile said it all.

"All right," said Garrett. "Our Eastern European adventure continues."

Curtea de Argeş and Poenari Castle — July 26

The next morning a blue town car entered the parking lot at the base of the Carpathian foothill home of Poenari Castle. The sun broke the cloud-covered horizon coloring the castle with red light. Once the car stopped, Max hustled out to open the doors for Elizabeth and Garrett as he usually did, but brother and sister beat him to it.

They had dressed for a hike up the side of the Carpathian foothill, the only way to access the castle. Along with backpacks which contained rock-climbing gear, they wore sturdy boots, cargo pants, long-sleeved shirts, and zippered jackets for an extra layer of comfort against the rumored chill of Poenari, though the calendar said July.

The rock-climbing gear brought to survey the back of the foothill upon which Poenari Castle sat.

Max shouldered a backpack, as did Elizabeth and Garrett.

"That's not going to happen," said Garrett, referring to Elizabeth's pack and the gear inside.

"Is that right? We'll see, won't we?"

They turned when another car pulled into the lot.

Oskar Naguschewsky, the park's lead designer, and Gregor Anghelescu, the municipal liaison from the nearby city of Curtea de Argeş, joined Elizabeth, Garrett, and Max.

After introductions, Gregor, a small and slender man with pronounced chin, ears, and nose, took the lead. He guided the party toward the bottom of the wooden stairs opposite the entrance of the empty 200-car lot. The stark blackness of its tarred surface and white dividing lines displayed little wear and tear from visitors the last few years.

Before the stairs, a couple of white sheds in need of fresh coats of paint displayed souvenirs from Poenari Castle, the usual collection of miniatures, cheap plastic likenesses of Count Dracula, and wooden stakes.

Gregor stopped the group in front of a sign to the left of the first wooden step. The hiking party read the history of the castle. Written in both English and Romanian, it provided information about the Dracul's occupation of Poenari in the 1400s.

"Fifteen hundred steps," said Gregor glancing up the hillside. "It will be a beautiful climb." He smiled and displayed a mouthful of white teeth, shining in the morning sunlight.

Max led the hike, his head on a swivel.

As they climbed, Gregor explained more of the history of Poenari Castle.

"The Wallachian rulers of the early 14th century built the original Poenari Castle. The Draculs, aware of its strategic position, commandeered it in 1420, specifically to repel the Ottoman Turks. Three generations of Draculs ruled from 1421 through 1476. One legend is Vlad the Impaler died defending the castle's keep from the Turks in 1476. Yet another is he was ambushed during a planned attack on the Ottomans. As you can imagine, the Romanians prefer the first tale.

"During this final battle, Mehmet II, the Ottoman leader, beheaded Vlad. Some say the Turks gained the castle through the treachery of Vlad's half-brother, Radu, who got them inside using a variation of the Trojan Horse."

"Yes, Max took us through the story of the last day of the notorious Vlad the Impaler," said Elizabeth. "But what would that variation be?"

"I do not know exactly, Miss, but I believe it had something to do with the trust Vlad the Impaler had in Radu. To breach the iron and wood door of the castle's keep required more treachery than force."

Gregor continued his lecture, though the higher they climbed, the more breaks he needed between sentences.

They arrived at the top step. The castle visible in the distance, its stone bleached by harsh weather and beating sun. A footbridge crossed a dry ravine, with a wooden shack just in front. The last of the morning fog clung to the ground.

Gregor now trailed the pack. When they stopped, he trudged to the front, and spun around to face them.

"Let's cross the footbridge, please."

Gregor went on.

"It never again enjoyed the notoriety it had when the infamous Vlad lived here. The conquering Turks occupied it for less than a year. Poenari fell into disrepair for more than three centuries.

"In the late 1800s, the royal family of Romania, under King Carol, initiated repairs. They were not completed. The castle appears today as it did then. Poenari gets few visitors each year. The government doesn't keep records."

Gregor swept his arm across the front of the castle.

"The castle sits on a plateau on top of a Carpathian foothill. The castle's rectangular foundation, with the longer sides facing east and west, occupies a precarious section of this plateau. Erosion caused most of the back of the hill to fall down to the valley level and parking lot level. Please try to not venture away from the confines of the castle proper."

He walked the group closer to the front, then turned left and walked everyone past the remains and to the back.

"The sheer drop in back made attacking the castle possible only by the wooded area we where we just walked. A slender piece of the foothill remains here in the back, but is almost as difficult to climb as the sheer wall. I've only seen some of the wildlife do it. Overall, the Wallachians found the rugged terrain surrounding Poenari Castle nearly impassable. Something not lost on the Draculs."

Gregor looked at his audience. To a person, they stared at the sheer drop.

"One interesting side note is that during the Communist era, foreign visitors had the option of spending a night in the castle. There were more than a few takers. Many left during the night."

He led them back to the pathway, and then to the front entrance to all that remained of Poenari Castle, the foundation and parts of the first floor.

In front of the access ramp from the footbridge that led visitors onto the main floor, two mannequins of Turkish soldiers impaled on spikes looked as real as the Ottoman warriors impaled by Vlad more than 500 years ago.

Their costumes hung ragged, as did the mannequins. With the castle as a backdrop, these icons of brutality and death garnered the attention of the site survey party.

Gregor noticed the group's focused stares, their fascination with the display. When he spoke again, he broke their concentration.

"The castle had three floor-to-ceiling, stained-glass windows on both the west and east walls. Today, there is nothing but—"

Elizabeth who trailed behind, finished a call. She caught up to the group, clueless about the mannequins, and cut him off.

"Gregor," said Elizabeth, "I've called back to have bedding and supplies brought up. Your lecture has inspired me. I think we should spend the night. Won't that be fun?"

"Ma'am, I—"

They toured the interior sections of the main floor. Parts of which, and the foundation, contained huge gaps. Sections of the walls also contained as many holes as stones.

"Oskar," Elizabeth said, pointing at the foundation when they exited. "We're going to redo the foundation, aren't we? Looks shaky. Can you render a sketch of what the castle looked like when the Draculs occupied it?"

Oskar, who looked like a Hollywood misconception of an Eastern European, husky, ginger-haired, full mustache— pulled a laser measuring tape from a jacket pocket.

"Yes, ma'am. Started working on it. I'd like to take measurements and a series of photos. Might take several hours."

"Get to it."

Elizabeth dropped her backpack on the ground and pulled out rock-climbing equipment.

"While we're waiting for dinner and overnight gear, Max and I are going to take a look at the valley that opens up behind the castle."

"Ma'am, this is most irregular," protested Gregor, his voice breaking.

"Not a chance, Sis," objected Garrett. "Step aside."

Elizabeth did not move away from her climbing kit. Garrett stomped over and grabbed her backpack. A tug-of-war ensued. He released his hold. Elizabeth toppled over and landed on her back. She got to her feet.

"Not going to happen," insisted Garrett. "I'll go. If you want some photos, I'll take 'em. You've injured yourself brushing your teeth."

"It's my idea and my rigging!"

"Then I hope it's been checked thoroughly."

"Garrett."

"Elizabeth."

Garret tossed Elizabeth's backpack to Oskar.

"She gets hold of that, it's on you, Oskar," he said. "Max? Let's go."

Max walked to Gregor and placed his hand on the man's shoulder.

"I know this is a bit irregular but please bear with us. *You* don't have to stay the night. When I return, I'll release you."

Max anchored a piton into a rock at the top of the drop. He looped two ropes through it, securing his and Garrett's. The bodyguard glanced at the horizon and calculated the sun's trajectory.

"We'll have just a couple hours of light, Mr., uh, sorry, Garrett," said Max.

"Plenty of time," said Garrett, adjusting his harness. "Since the majority of the park is going to be behind Poenari, not in front of it, Elizabeth wants us to explore the back of the castle."

"Yes, sir."

"Anything else?"

"According to legend, Mr. Astor, this is the side of the castle from which Vlad's wife threw herself when she saw the approaching Turkish Army," said Max.

"You're such a fun guy, Max! Is that supposed to discourage me?" Garrett laughed. "Or do you hope we run into her bleached remains on the way down? Perhaps that will talk us out of it? Not a chance. Let's take a selfie with Mrs. Dracula between the two of us. What do you say?"

"Other than coming across Vlad the Impaler himself, I'm looking forward to making Poenari home for the next couple of years . . . God willing."

"That's the spirit, Capitanou. Let's go. The sun isn't setting any slower these days."

The two rappelled 50 feet down the wall. Then each drove a secondary support piton in and descended further.

Garrett pointed to the gorge as they descended. "Elizabeth's idea is that the castle proper will be the entrance point to the park. I think we're going to have to put in two sets of people movers. Large elevators to take them to the castle, then down to the park. I've got our engineers in talks with the construction concern that built the towers in Abu Dhabi. They've got multiple buildings taller than 1500' with service elevators to get to the top. Plus a tunnel through the foothill from the back side to return them to the parking lots using shuttle buses."

"Why both?" asked Max.

"Because there's no reason to funnel them through the castle both coming and going," said Garrett. "It would create an unnecessary choke point given the crowds we anticipate. The castle's main floor should only require a one-way flow for guests."

Garrett lifted the binoculars that hung around his neck. He scanned the gorge.

"I'm taking a closer look."

Garrett rappelled another 50 feet. He pulled out his cellphone and hit the record app.

"Gorge feels further down than estimated. Need exact measurement."

He took photos of rock outcroppings, and central portions of the valley floor, which was rimmed like a cul de sac by Poenari Forest. He dropped further down and away from Max to get additional photos of the gorge.

A gust of wind slammed him against the foothill.

"Max!" he shouted and sucked in a breath. "Afternoon wind is picking up. Let's get back. I've got enough for now!"

No response.

Garrett looked up and spotted the limp body of Max Capitanou. The wind had thrown him hard against the foothill. One of Max's additional pitons, pulled out by the force of the wind, dangled next to the bodyguard. Garrett's supports creaked with the added weight. Only the primary piton at the top and a couple of secondary ones supported them.

Garrett inhaled and let his breath rush out. He grabbed a hammer from his belt, took another piton, and began banging away.

"I'm not sure how much good this will do when Max's two hundred and twenty-five pounds come rushing past me," he mumbled as he worked. He looked up, and shouted Max's name again.

He put the hammer back into his belt and checked his cellphone.

"No signal, of course."

Garrett ascended.

He secured himself by placing pitons every 15 feet. After placing a half dozen, Garrett unclipped his body from the primary support piton, and worked his way toward Max.

At the 50-foot mark from the top, he pulled even with Max, but the arduous climb had taken 30 minutes. The temperature dropped and the shadows grew long across the face of the wall. The valley turned a cold, muddy gray.

Elizabeth ran to the edge when she heard the anchor piton straining against the rocks into which it had been placed. An attempt to take out her cell and view the area below as she approached the edge caused her to trip and spin around like an injured ballet dancer.

"I'm calling Garrett's cellphone! Can't see anything below! There's something wrong!"

"We should go back to the castle and stand on the top of the remains of the main floor," said Gregor. "Cellphone reception is better —."

Elizabeth shot by him and sprinted to the castle.

"Get a hammer and secure that piton!"

Gregor grabbed Elizabeth's backpack.

She'd neglected to include a hammer with her rigging.

Max's body faced the cliff. An outcropping of rock obscured much of his torso. Garrett could only see the outline of the man, boots dangling in the wind.

"Max! *Max!*" Garrett shouted above the wind. He gripped the rocks, strength fading, as he worked toward the bodyguard, hammering in pitons as he moved. He arrived at the rock that hid Max.

Garrett looped a second safety rope through Max's harness and took two pitons from Max's gear. He drove them into the hillside, and tethered Max to them. If the primary went, he had secured Max ... perhaps. Garrett resumed the climb.

Thirty feet from the top, Garrett heard the primary piton scrape against rock. He increased his effort and at the summit another blast of wind, more powerful than the first, pounded him against the wall. He lost consciousness. The jagged ridge gashed his forehead. Blood seeped into his eyes, waking him. He squeezed his eyelids and cleared the fluid. Garrett pulled himself over the edge. He collapsed at the top and shouted for help in English and then in rudimentary Romanian.

"*Opreşte-te! E* Garrett Astor! *Max este rănit! Urmaţi-mă!*"

The four members of the supply team shouldering the food and bedding ascended the last of the steps. They made their way across the footbridge to the castle. The leader saw Garrett, dropped everything, and ran to him.

The balance of the supply team also crossed the ground to the back of the castle, and hustled to the blood-covered Garrett Astor. Just as they reached him, the primary piton, weakened by Max's weight and Garrett's extended climb, pulled out of the rock and shot down the foothill.

Garrett disappeared over the edge, yanked by Max, who dropped another ten feet down, his weight pulling out some of the additional support Garrett placed.

Garrett Astor bounced down the cliff as the pitons he'd hammered in earlier failed one at a time. He plummeted to the bottom of the valley.

The scouting party, walking Castle Poenari's main floor, heard Garrett's shouts. Elizabeth flew down a stairway and traversed the access ramp, which connected the castle to the back of the foothill. Oskar and Gregor worked their old bones into something of a run and covered the short distance as quickly as their middle-aged selves could.

Elizabeth caught a glimpse of someone going over the precipice.

"Oh, my God," she cried. "Please don't let that be Garrett, or anyone who closely resembles him."

Oskar saw where the primary piton failed. He spied the caretaker/ticket taker's shack, located a hundred feet away.

"Please have some rope. You're a caretaker," Oskar murmured as he sprinted to the shack.

Oskar kicked open the door, which roused a hungover Nikolai Asilimov.

"Nikolai?!" Oskar shouted into the man's face. "Right? Nikolai? I need some rope. Heavy duty. You must have some."

"Closet," Nikolai mumbled, and pointed.

Oskar ransacked Asilimov's closet, grabbed a couple of badly wound coils of rope, and dashed back. Elizabeth leaned over the precipice. She held a flashlight in one hand and binoculars in the other, both from her backpack. She found a place that gave her an unobstructed view of Garrett and Max. She turned her head and addressed Gregor.

"They're both down there. My brother might be moving. I can't tell. Max is not."

The primary spike clanged off the rocks and lodged in a crevice about 15 feet down. That and the additional supports stopped Max, who slammed against the hillside again. Garrett did the same a moment later.

He composed himself, and continued his movement. Garrett stopped a few feet above Max and watched the nearby spikes shudder and pulled out his hammer to secure them. A blast of pain jerked his arm. The hammer dropped into the valley below.

Garrett's ribs were broken. The simple act of lying motionless in the harness sent signals of pain to his brain, but not enough to stop lowering himself toward a still-limp Max. This time when he arrived, he did something he hadn't done before. Garrett checked for a pulse.

"Come on, Max! Show me something!" he shouted at the bodyguard.

A pulse. Garrett's ribs pressed against the rocks, as another gust pushed him against the hillside.

"Now. That. Hurts." He bit off his words one at a time.

His breath came in shorter and shorter spurts each time he pressed against the rocks. The wind increased. Above him he could hear shouting. He felt a slap against his head. His damaged ribcage limited his movement. He reached around his head and grabbed … something.

A rope with a heavily knotted seat dangled next to his ear. Garrett, breathing in bursts, grabbed the seat, which consisted of Oskar's tying and re-tying rope pieces together in a latticework, and slipped Max's legs through.

Garrett secured himself to Max's tethers. Once he distributed Max's body weight in the seat, pressure released off Garrett's ribcage.

He tugged three times on the rope and shouted as loud as his ribs allowed. Garrett watched Max ascend.

The sun set by the time the scout team dragged the unconscious body of Max Capitanou over the precipice. One of the Romanians who brought the overnight supplies left prior to the rescue attempt to get medical assistance.

Oskar unwound the harness from Max. After checking the knotted seat, he tossed it down the side of the foothill to Garrett.

Garrett, in shock, lapsed into a semi-conscious state. Above him, Elizabeth pulled on Max's rigging.

"What are you doing?" asked Gregor.

"I'm going down there, and nobody's going to stop me," she stated. "Garrett won't know if we drop the basket down again. He's not conscious."

"Wait! You'll need a hammer." Oskar handed her Max's.

Petite Elizabeth looked even smaller against the fading light. The resolve in her voice trailed off, as she looked over the side at a blackening gorge. Her hand trembled when she took the hammer from Oskar. She dropped the first two pitons she pulled from her belt.

Another strong gust of wind caught her just as she stepped toward the edge. Her feet tangled up and she lunged toward the edge.

Oskar grabbed her. Elizabeth sat down.

"Wait a second," said Oskar, "let's not lose two of you."

Elizabeth ignored him, and got to her feet. She gripped the hammer and piton. She pushed Oskar away. He grabbed her arm.

"There's one thing we can try before anyone has to go to Garrett. If it doesn't work, you can go down there, Ms. Astor. Two minutes."

Oskar sprinted back to the shack, as fast as his 50-year-old legs would go. Against the wall a single hose lay coiled on the weed-filled grass. He tested the flow from the spigot, pinched it shut, and dashed back. He leaned over the precipice and released the flow.

The water splashed over Garrett, but he'd already drifted off to sleep.

Garrett walked along the beach in Cape May, New Jersey. When he and Elizabeth were young, their parents took them there, eschewing the more crowded areas of Long Island. A mild, sunny day greeted him, and the waves broke on the sand, covering his feet with warm water.

Garrett waded in. Soon it reached his waist.

At first, he walked parallel to the beach, then deeper and deeper into the surf, until the ocean pressed against his chest.

Garrett turned toward the shore. His parents, seated on a beach towel, shouted and waved their arms—at first in excitement, then in panic.

He smiled, turned, and walked further into the Atlantic. The warm, comforting water up to his chin.

Garrett's head dropped over his right shoulder. The tip of his nose dipped into the inviting sea.

A swell hit the side of his head, his ear and his nostrils filled with water. He exhaled through his mouth and slid forward. Stabbing pain bit into his lungs. Brilliant light seared his eyes through shut lids. Garrett's head led the rest of his pain-wracked body into the waters of the Atlantic Ocean.

Elizabeth, more bravado than common sense, pounded the support pitons into the rock at the top of the cliff. Oskar held the rope for the basket, which she tied to her tool belt. Darkness had fallen on Poenari.

She looked up at Oskar.

"You got a better idea? Now's the time."

Oskar swallowed.

"Sixty feet. A support piton every fifteen. You're going to have to—"

"Yeah. Yeah. I know. I'm going to have to drop below Garrett in order to put him into the basket. I'm not supposed to do anything requiring my lack of upper body strength."

"Let gravity do the work," said Oskar. "When you get his feet through the loops, tug on the main support ropes."

"We're wasting time."

She placed her feet against the sheer wall and rappelled.

Less than halfway to Garrett, the wind, which increased as she descended, rattled her tool belt of pitons. They clanked together. Elizabeth fought with all of her 98 pounds but had little force to drive the supports into the rock more than a couple inches . . . at best.

"It'll h-have to d-do," she whispered through chattering teeth, though the temperature had not dropped in the last hour. It was just the wind, which sang an aria from the underworld as it howled along the rocks.

"P-p-p-please God, i-if you let me rescue my brother, I'll never buy another castle for the rest of my l-l-life."

The wind pushed her away from the wall. It slammed her, head first, into the rocks. Oskar had taken one of Nikolai's bike helmets along with the rope. He insisted she wear it.

The force cracked the helmet.

"Oh, Garrett, dear brother, where are you?"

And then she was next to him. Elizabeth shook him a couple times. No response. She didn't bother checking for a pulse.

"Let's g-g-get out of here."

She rappelled a body length below him, reached into her pack, and came up with nothing.

The basket was gone.

"Wha—no?"

She found and switched on a flashlight. It slipped from her grasp, shot out in front of her and hit the wall. It bounced back and Elizabeth caught it under her chin. She deliberately wrapped the fingers of her left hand around it and scanned the area. No sign of the basket.

"Maybe I can loop the support rope between your legs and under your arms? You won't be able to have children, but maybe that's a good thing? The team above can haul us up together."

Elizabeth pulled herself to Garrett's waist and started to figure out the pretzel logic of the best way to tether him when something scraped across her helmet.

Garrett's gloved hand?

No.

The basket.

Elizabeth let out a whoop. It died as she saw the maximum length of the rope was a foot or two short.

"That's not enough to stop us. Not now."

She placed one boot heel against the wall and with both hands, bent Garrett's right leg at the knee. She ignored the wind, which whipped her around every time she got the toe of his boot into one of the loops. On the eighth try, his leg slipped through.

"Lack of upper body strength, my keister. One down."

Above, Oskar and Gregor stared at the support pitons like nervous parents. From below they heard a deafening scream, which cut through the winds now swirling in, out, and around Poenari Castle.

"No. Please, no." Gregor said. Oskar embraced him.

Then a tug on the pitons.

42

A Return to Poenari Castle — August 30

"Yes, and I'm not sure I believe what Max said. Remember, he'd been buffeted by the same winds as Garrett. He hit his head, a few times."

More than a month after the climbing accident, Elizabeth and Garrett returned to their Astor Plaza office. Once again, the company attorney, Larry Winters, sat in his favorite place, the executive office couch, a large blue binder in his hands.

Elizabeth continued.

"And I do not want to discuss the accident any further. It's behind us," she said. "I want to talk about DracuLAND. Come on, Larry. Look at the numbers. Look at the sketches. This is a great idea. It cannot fail."

"Elizabeth, *nothing* you do fails," said Larry. "But that may not be the point."

"Rarely fails. At least nothing, ah, of consequence." She mimicked her brother by taking a quick hit off an air cigarette, and then struck a '50s film noir pose, left hand on hip, right hand holding the air cigarette.

"Not a time to be joking, Elizabeth," said Larry. "Garrett could have died out there. Max too. This doesn't bode well for work crews. The back side of the foothill the castle sits on is going to be dangerous for construction."

He turned to Garrett. "But I have to ask, have you thanked your sister for climbing down to rescue you? If not for Elizabeth—"

"Oh, she's getting her money's worth on that one." He tapped his knuckles on the ribcage support vest he wore under his suit.

Larry opened the blue binder, and flipped through the full-color renderings of DracuLAND. The people movers. The touring groups. The employees. The overnight accommodations inside Poenari Castle for VIPs. He exhaled.

"Granted, on paper this is a great idea. On paper this is a moneymaker. On paper no one loses. But no one advising you *likes* this venture." Larry almost cleared his throat. "You don't *need* to do this. Astor Holdings doesn't *need* to do this. And Max's statement upon waking?"

"Oh, come on, Larry," yelled Elizabeth. "I've considered what Max said, and it's a bunch of superstitious bunk. Max hits his head and sees the decapitated torso of Vlad the Impaler dressed in full battle garb, mounted on a horse? The Impaler warns him to stay away from Poenari. Are you kidding me? This stops me from making a great real estate deal?"

"His MRI came back clean," said Larry.

"He's a freakin' bodyguard from a country that just discovered the wheel, when? Last month?" Elizabeth fired back. "This is crazy. If you had information that the permits were millions of dollars. Or work crews couldn't live nearby. Or this isn't a one-year build, but a two- or three-year build, I'd listen. But a dream or a nightmare from someone with a head injury? A *premonition?* Hold on, let me check my calendar and make sure it's the new millennium."

"Elizabeth. That's enough," demanded Garrett.

"Why? I don't think I'm finished pointing out the stupidity in—"

"Ah, why don't you kiss my—"

"Shut up, the both of you!" Larry, not known for emotion, shouted at the twins.

Elizabeth and Garrett stiffened into military-like postures. Their faces changed from angry, pinch-faced and aggressive, into those of humiliated children.

"All right, let me grant you that he 'had a vision.' Maybe, just maybe, that vision was a figment of his imagination, or a dream, or whatever. Whether you understand it or not, Elizabeth, you are breaking ground on one of the most historic sites of Romania. I'm not worried about vampires and legends. I'm concerned about real people who may not like us demolishing part of their proud past."

"Larry, Max did not say he saw an attorney with a notice of eviction or a mob of angry gypsies holding pitchforks and torches. He said he saw a headless, medieval soldier warning him *not* to remain at Poenari Castle. Think about that," said Elizabeth, whose demeanor shifted back to one of confrontation and resolve. Her mouth tightened around each word.

"About what?"

"First, how does a *headless* person warn you about something? Did he use sign language? Jesus. Does Max understand sign language? God, this has already passed *stupid*. It's . . . this is ridiculous! Why are we even discussing it? I'm buying Poenari Castle. We're developing it into a theme park called DracuLAND. European and Asian tourists bored to tears with Disneyland Paris will flock to the place. We're building a superhighway from Bucharest to the park, and a short-haul commercial airport that can accept flights from as far away as Frankfurt. That is what we are doing."

Larry said nothing as he stood, and headed for the doors of the office.

"Larry," said Elizabeth.

The attorney turned.

"You know I respect your opinion," continued Elizabeth.

"Which means about the same as it has always meant," Larry shot back. "That you will listen to my opinion, as you will for most people close to you, and then do *whatever the hell you want*. All right, Elizabeth. Let's do this. I have no evidence that you shouldn't, but like everyone else, I don't feel good about this venture. I just don't."

Elizabeth walked back and sat behind her desk. She picked up one of her cellphones and texted Robert Brancatelli, the company's American bodyguard who worked with the Astors and Astor Holdings from time to time over the past several years. With Max's absence open-ended, he also would be called upon to take part in DracuLAND.

And given recent events, the Astors decided they could use both of them.

A few minutes later, a sinewy man with handsome Roman features appeared in the office. Known as "RJ" since childhood, he undid the only closed button of his Armani suit.

The suit jacket opened.

When RJ slid his cellphone back into his pants pocket, the handle of a metallic green handgun showed just inside the left lapel of his suit.

"You, uh, texted?"

"We are going back to Poenari, RJ and Max will meet us there, now that he's out of the hospital and back on his feet."

"Outstanding. In spite of the mounting evidence of evil spirits, bad karma, the maloiks, the presence of the Willies, and an ancient Romanian gypsy curse upon you and your household, you're going ahead anyway? Smart move, boss."

Elizabeth tried not to, but laughed. RJ also broke into his version of, as even he referred to it, the Pirate Guffaw. Garrett raised his right eyebrow at the two of them.

"Sorry, Madame President, but I couldn't help myself." RJ paused and half closed his right eye, and continued, the traces of his Staten Island childhood bleeding through in his speech.

"I'm going to need you both."

RJ had an impish habit of looking at his boss with only his left eye and cocking his head, all part of the pirate persona he cultivated. Elizabeth had never gotten used to this, but it reassured Garrett.

"I said," reiterated Elizabeth, "I'm going to need you both. Capisce?"

"Ho capito," said RJ. "Since you just met with general counsel, who did not look happy when I passed him in the hallway, I'll assume you've been advised to have extra security. Therefore, my presence in Romania along with Max?"

"This is my idea, RJ," interrupted Garrett, pointing his right index finger at RJ. "Just start the arrangements. You and I can talk with Max tomorrow morning on the phone. Sure it's unusual to take two bodyguards, but everyone is giving me grief and I've had enough. This is one of the few concessions I, we, will make."

Garrett paused.

"This isn't going to present a problem, is it?"

"No, sire."

"Good. Then get out."

RJ patted the handle of his weapon that he had named Louise.

"Louise and I will be back tomorrow to fill you in, chief. I'll keep Max in the loop. And I will make an appointment with the minion at the front desk."

He rebuttoned his jacket and left the room, his muted cackle, another trademark of RJ Brancatelli, trailing. The telltale pirate laugh just loud enough for Garrett to hear, and like Elizabeth, he could not suppress a laugh.

"All right," she said. "I'll go first."

"There's a shocker."

"What's that supposed to mean?"

"What do you think?"

"I see no reason *not* to return to Poenari, do you?"

"Other than your continued use of double negatives? No."

"Funny. Then it's settled."

"I'm almost positive it was settled before you said it was settled."

"Garrett, you know you don't have to do this."

"Sure, Sis. Just like everything else involving more than one Astor. No sense of obligation there."

"And what's that—"

Garrett was already out the door.

Kodiak, the Sentinel Dog—Late Autumn

The same survey party that initially scouted Poenari would be doing a second inspection of the site of DracuLAND with two changes. RJ Brancatelli would accompany them, but Elizabeth would not.

"One Astor on a second trip is plenty," Garrett had said to RJ, when pressed for a reason. "We do have other projects going on, and Elizabeth is, well, starting to act a little squirrely about this."

"Oh," said RJ, arching an eyebrow.

"Yes, and I have no idea why."

The sun rose over Curtea de Argeş, throwing a wash of tepid yellow light across the Carpathian foothills. Garrett's rental car pulled into the parking lot at the base of the climb to Poenari Castle. Brilliant red and deep orange leaves adorned the trees on the hillside, but to RJ's eyes they appeared dull and muted, like an old photograph stuck in a scrapbook.

Max and the survey party arrived in a Mercedes town car, which he parked next to what few souvenir shops remained. He insisted on driving wherever they were going.

Fog held its beachhead at the base of the foothills. The sun hid behind a layer of mist and the light over the foothills disappeared. The wind picked up as Garrett exited the car and a gust chased the low-lying clouds off the lot. The sun returned and the chill, along with the fog, evaporated.

"I'll take that as a good omen," said RJ, as the brilliant sunshine returned. He donned a pair of Maui Jim's and cracked his knuckles one at a time. RJ joined Oskar, Garrett and Max outside the car.

Max winced with each knuckle.

"That," said Max, "cannot be good for you."

"Wearing sunglasses?" teased RJ, but before Max or Garrett could reply, a four-cylinder vehicle leftover from the Soviet era entered the parking lot.

Gregor Anghelescu, the twitchy government liaison from the nearby city of Curtea de Argeş, arrived. His face did not have the same beautiful smile as at the first visit. His lips pressed together, his eyes not as bright. Ever the dutiful official however, he agreed to take the Astor Holdings representatives on another inspection of the property despite the events of the previous scouting trip.

"I bet he drove here on his own, just in case you ask him to stay overnight," said RJ.

"No doubt," replied Garrett.

The owners of two remaining souvenir stands walked outside their shacks, arms folded across their chests. Awakened early, their body language communicated a "squatter's" attitude.

"Haven't made them an offer yet?" asked Oskar.

"We have," said Garrett. "They're trying to gouge us for more. We want to be fair, but I don't take to extortion."

The two men, features weathered from standing outside waiting on what few customers bought their trinkets, took in the long, sleek sedan. One of them made a hand sign that Gregor recognized. He hustled toward them, and conversed in a quiet, but animated tone. All stood in front of the shops. Gregor's hands danced through the air, while the pinch-faced men listened.

RJ watched but after he spotted one of the men reach out his right hand and stab Gregor in the chest with his thumb, the bodyguard double-timed to the group.

"RJ," said Max. "Where are you going? Let me do this."

"I don't think they're being very hospitable to Gregor," said RJ over his shoulder, as he closed the distance to the souvenir shops.

The man who poked Gregor broke away from the group and met RJ halfway between the survey party and the shops. Before Max could intervene, the man lay on his back, RJ's grip on the fellow's badly bent right wrist.

RJ stood over the man, and spoke in Romanian. Max edged closer.

RJ helped the man to his feet.

He ran back to his fellow shop owners and spoke to them, hands, including the injured one, performing a mime routine. Gregor listened to the account and returned to the group.

"They're going to accept your offer, Mr. Astor," said Gregor, his voice weak. He turned and watched RJ trek to the base of the hiking trail.

"And why is that, Gregor?" asked Garrett.

"I'm not sure what RJ said to them, but one of the shop owners said he wanted to be nowhere near anyplace that Mr. RJ would be working or living," said Gregor. "I told him that he would be here for the construction *and* opening of the park."

"Is that right?"

"Yes, sir. I think they will all be cleared out and off the premises in a day," said Gregor. He pushed a non-existent pebble around by shuffling his feet. He did not make eye contact with Garrett. "You will still give them some compensation, yes?"

Max looked at Garrett.

"Of course. Let's go," said Garrett. "RJ has a distinct style. I'll have a talk with him."

The four members of the survey team approached RJ who waited at the trailhead. Max led the way. RJ covered the rear behind Gregor and Oskar.

Garrett caught up to Max and put his hand on the bodyguard's shoulder.

The group halted. Garrett addressed Oskar.

"We can't do this by air? There must be a way to get a helicopter to castle ground? I like exercise as much as the next guy, but hiking up and down takes two hours out of our day."

"Garrett, the wind shear is too powerful from the rear of the castle," Oskar explained. "As you know from your experience. Once we have the construction elevator in place, we'll be able to move men and equipment faster, and we can airlift up the *front* side of the foothill. I can engineer the helipad away from those crosswinds, but we're months out."

Garrett stretched his calf muscles on the railroad logs which served as steps in the series of switchbacks that led to the castle. He set his jaw.

"All right. Let's press on, but I'm all for a little double-time. Gentlemen?"

Oskar and Gregor answered at the same time.

"We will meet you there."

An hour's climb later, the men stood outside the castle's ticket office. The shack appeared more decrepit, if possible, than during their first visit. Its roof tiles bleached by the sun, and the wood in the front of the house dry from the summer heat. The occupant of the past three decades, Nikolai Asilimov, showed himself outside this time. Unshaven and hungover, the keeper of access to Poenari slogged from his front door, just past the morning shadows. He wore a black wool sweater and blue work pants, and waved them on with an exhausted flick of his right hand. Nikolai shuffled back to the shack's confines, another trip outside planned for no time soon.

Oskar and Gregor arrived ten minutes later.

The five approached the footbridge. Oskar stopped before crossing. He swept his arm in a half circle away from the remains of Poenari Castle. His hand stopped at Nikolai Asilimov's shack.

"The bottom floor of the castle will be the last stop for the elevators during construction. It is how we will get materials and men to help reconstruct Poenari Castle," explained Oskar. "Initially, we'll have a platform which replaces the footbridge. It will allow earth moving equipment to move across this entire plateau if need be. When the park opens we remove the platform. Though practical for transportation, it will be razed and replaced with a pedestrian suspension bridge along the lines of the Tower Bridge of London, built prior to Bram Stoker's writing and release of *Dracula*."

He shaded his eyes and directed their attention back to the shack.

"And, yes, that warm and hospitable shack will be gone," said Oskar. "Much as we all like it."

He grunted as he laughed before continuing.

"After construction is complete, we'll convert the multiple construction elevators to a series of people movers. Nicer interiors themed along the lines of the castle. Maybe some photos of the park under construction. I anticipate being able to put three hundred visitors an hour through the castle."

"I don't think three hundred per hour is enough," said Garrett, who started across the footbridge, the front and back of which met the ground flush. The middle sagged from years of harsh weather and lack of maintenance. He heard a crack, like a branch snapping beneath his feet. None of the other members of the party moved, save for RJ, who brushed by everyone and headed for Garrett.

Garrett continued across, ignoring the sound and the danger it might have signified.

"Given the investment in the property, I'd put the number clo—"

Garrett jammed his right foot into a crack, stopping his progress. It caused him to pitch backward. He steadied himself. "Wow, I pulled an Elizabeth right there."

"Don't run, Garrett. Not a good idea," warned RJ.

Lying in the middle of the bridge, hidden due to the sagging construction, lay the biggest dog Garrett had ever seen. It lifted its head from boxing-glove sized paws.

The dog's coat, the color of copper. White markings on its chest, muzzle, and front paws. Black flecks streaked the entire body, particularly on his two-foot long, dust-brush shaped, and almost white, tail.

Its head, shaped like a retriever's, had that breed's droopy ears, and blocklike nose, jaw, and sloping dome. But what struck Garrett most about the canine was not the size, though it significantly outweighed any mastiff he'd ever encountered.

It was the dog's light brown eyes, almost golden in color, that drew Garrett closer. Another crack from the footbridge. The catlike eyes gave the dog character. A long, lolling pink tongue, also flecked with black, slid out of its mouth with a yawn. The opening in its maw exposed gleaming white, flawless teeth.

Another crack from below. The dog's hair rose on its back. It gained its feet when RJ charged toward Garrett. Its mouth opened again, but only enough to bare canines a shark would have coveted.

RJ stood in front of Garrett.

The dog craned his neck toward RJ and a low rumble came from the back of its throat. Max reached into his pocket and pulled out a Beretta 9mm. The bodyguard flew past Gregor and Oskar. He stood at Garrett's left side, RJ in front of both. The dog withdrew his forward stance by rocking back into a sit. He stared at Garrett. His eyes traveled to Max.

No one moved. RJ and Max gripped the handles of their guns.

The dog's hair remained raised, and it returned to all fours.

The wind, mild for most of the morning, shifted to gusts and blew across the footbridge, which swayed. The wood beneath their feet dropped an inch. Max grabbed Garrett and the rope hand rail. RJ widened his stance. The dog growled and reared back.

One of the boards beneath Garrett's feet broke off and dropped into the dry gully below. Max tightened his hold on both Garrett and the hand rail. He pulled Garrett back to an unbroken slat. It too cracked, but held.

"Hold on, Max," said Gregor. "He has a collar. I don't think this dog is one of the legendary Romanian strays."

Gregor passed by Garrett, RJ, and Max, and approached the dog. He walked to the canine, holding out his hand, palm-side down. The dog's head reached Gregor's breastbone. It ran a tongue along both jowls and exhaled the remnants of a growl. It sniffed Gregor's hand, and turned its attention back to Garrett, RJ, and Max.

The dog lifted his right paw and pointed it at Max, who approached and accepted it. Max ran his other hand over top of the dog's head. Everyone exhaled, including the dog.

"Let's find out what your name is, and where you belong," said Max. He smiled for the first time since the group came upon the dog, and reached for the collar. "Wherever you come from, I'll bet it is a ways from here. Maybe you like climbing hills?" Max looked back at the footpath.

The collar, a simple, frayed, nautical rope, had an aluminum nameplate tied to it with sash cord. It read, "Kodiak - Poenari Castle."

Max read the nameplate aloud. Gregor laughed.

"Mr. Astor," Gregor said, "it looks like a dog comes with the castle."

"Wait a minute. I can't have a dog around here." He looked down at the aluminum nameplate. "Kodiak? Who names a dog after a bear?"

"Given his size?" asked Gregor. "It's a great name, Mr. Astor. He has to weigh close to one-hundred plus kilograms, er, your two-hundred-fifty pounds, and he's not fat."

"Doesn't look like he's going anywhere." Max offered, laughing now as Kodiak leaned against him, the dog's head at the tall man's ribcage. "Besides, Romanian dogs are a sturdy bunch. You've seen all the strays around, consequence of the Ceausescu regime. This one strikes me as a survivor."

Garrett stared at Kodiak, who returned the look.

"Mr. Astor." Max's voice broke. "Do you want me to get rid of him?"

Kodiak growled. He seemed to understand Max's words.

"Now that would be a good fight." Garrett laughed. "No. There will be many workers around for the next couple of years. What's one more big body to take up room?"

Max released his hand from the Beretta. RJ pushed Louise back into its holster.

"Find something for him to do, Max," said Garrett. "If he's going to eat as much as I think, he better be productive."

"How about adding another bodyguard?" asked RJ.

"How many do you think I need?"

An uncomfortable silence followed the question.

"This is Wallachia, boss, and you won't be winning any popularity contests with what you're proposing to do with this site. I don't think we can have too many," Max offered.

"I agree," said RJ. "While a dog might not be the answer, we're going to need a serious discussion about security, especially while you're on site."

"Of course," agreed Garrett. "But that's for another day. Let's see what Oskar has come up with while we walk the castle grounds. Then discuss security. Afterward, we'll head back to the hotel and draw up a construction schedule based on a spring opening."

He noticed a few slack-jawed faces.

"Spring in a couple of years." Garrett chuckled. "Come on. Who do you think I am? Caligula?"

Max gestured to the dog.

"Well, Kodiak, let's go."

The dog didn't move.

A dog owner for decades, Oskar smiled.

"Come on, Kode-yak. Time to take a walk," said Oskar. "Max, start walking. Go with Max, Kode-yak."

The dog stretched, and fell into a trot next to the bodyguard.

"Kode-yak?" asked Max.

"Two syllables, Mr. Capitanou," said Oskar from behind Max and Kodiak. "Dogs react to a two-syllable name more readily than anything else. Especially a name with hard consonants. It's probably what his original owner called him."

The dog never broke stride as he matched Max's cadence perfectly. They crossed the bridge, side by side, and headed to the castle. The bodyguard smiled at his new companion.

"He's your dog, Mr. Capitanou," said Gregor, noticing Max's smile. "He's chosen you . . . or perhaps you've chosen him. Or both. That's how it works with dogs."

The Construction — March 1

Six months after the discovery of Kodiak, a full construction crew began Phase I at the site of DracuLAND. The first project established a route which connected the parking lot to the castle via two heavy duty freight elevators, based on the specs provided by engineers from the Abu Dhabi high rises. Men and materials moved from the time of delivery to the lot to the castle in minutes.

A tunnel large enough to move heavy machinery from the parking lot blasted through the foothill underneath the castle, opened to the valley floor behind it. The freight elevators were placed halfway through the length of the bore. Forklifts moved pallets of construction materials from the lot into the elevators.

The bore of the tunnel was also wide enough to accommodate the construction trailers that were driven from the parking lot through the tunnel to the valley at the back of the foothill. They would be used for contractors' offices and as temporary quarters. The area buzzed with activity within a month.

Astor Holdings poured money into the project to overcome obstacles and delays, most of which occurred courtesy of the Romanian government. The company's team of attorneys and the Astors' checkbook breached every bureaucratic wall.

When the spring warmth descended upon Romania, the castle displayed its former glory. The 60-foot-high front wall, effective in repelling the Ottomans for decades, loomed tall and intimidating over the trees of the foothill, its size magnified from the perspective of anyone in the parking lot. The turret-style guard towers on the castle's four corners pushed higher into the sky. Wallachian flags fluttered once more.

Only the roof remained incomplete. A temporary construction-grade, blue plastic tarp topped the castle, soon to be replaced by a replica of the original stone and wooden crossbeam style roof. The floors, main door, and windows needed only finishing masonry, carpentry, and glazier work. Elizabeth insisted the castle be in the first phase on the construction schedule.

Elizabeth dashed past Garrett's admin and stomped into his office. She found him in his chair with his back to the door, on the phone. Actually, on his preferred headset. Garrett used them even on a landline. She cupped her hands around her mouth.

"Garrett!" she shouted. "I am not going away! Turn the eff around and talk to me!"

"I'm sorry, Stan," he said. "I'm going to have to call you back. Elizabeth is here."

He paused.

"Yes, I know."

Garrett laughed and hung up.

"What did you say to Stan, or rather what did he say to you?" She crossed her arms over her chest, but only for a moment. She unfolded them and slammed her hands on his desk. One hand missed.

Her chin smacked the top of the desk.

"Well?" she asked, rubbing her chin.

"He said that you have a lot of personality."

"What am I, a dog?" Elizabeth pushed herself away from Garrett's desk using both hands.

"Stan did not say that," said Garrett. "Speaking of dogs ... uh, never mind. Sis, what is it?"

"I heard you're going to Romania again."

"So?"

"So, you're there every week," she said. "Let me remind you that Astor Holdings has other ventures than this theme park."

"Hey, this was your stupid idea," said Garrett, brushing aside her comments. "But now that I've been there a few times, I'm warming to it."

Elizabeth walked to the sofa and sat. Garrett's admin, on cue, brought out a tray with a teapot and a couple of mugs. There were also several types of pastries.

"Thank you, Connie," said Garrett. "I'm not ignoring our other projects. This is unlike you. There you were, all hot and bothered by purchasing some 600-year-old castle, and now you don't want to go anywhere near the place?"

"God these are good."

Elizabeth had stuffed a couple of petit fours in her mouth.

"Trader Joe's," said Garrett. "Nothing but the best for my sister. And slug down some more of that British Blend Tetley. Don't think you're wired enough."

"Fanks," said Elizabeth, still chewing. She poured some tea. Swallowed two petit fours. And threw down a mouthful of tea.

"What gives?" asked Garrett. "Are you concerned that both RJ and Max are in Romania, and we're here? I've requested temporary replacements. They'll be—"

"You win," she said, putting down her teacup. It tipped over and Elizabeth took a few moments imitating a circus performer before it settled into the plate's notch. Her actions knocked the remaining petit fours onto the carpet, but she snatched one up, burying it in her mouth.

Garrett waited for the day's matinee performance to end.

"Win what?" he asked, curiosity piqued.

"I want out of DracuLAND."

"I see." Garrett shifted in his chair and brought both fingers to a TMJ-tormented jaw.

Elizabeth swallowed and started sobbing. Garrett sprang from behind his desk. He pulled her hands from her face and pressed a handkerchief into them. Garrett hugged his sister.

"Elizabeth, what is going on?"

"I can't explain it," she said, wiping her eyes. "Nothing feels right about this anymore. Not since you and Max were almost smashed into Romanian meatloaf during the climb on the first survey."

"Romanians make meatloaf?"

"You know what I mean, jerkweed."

"If I tell you everything is going to be all right, will that help?"

"Not even a little," she replied, and took a deep breath. Elizabeth stood, then walked to the door. "I needed that, Garrett, and it, uh, that does help, but we have to get out of this deal."

After the door clicked shut, Garrett returned to his desk, and picked up his business cellphone.

"Gregor Anghelescu, please. Yes, I'll hold."

Two minutes passed.

"Gregor? Garrett. A slight snag. Nothing I can't deal with here, but press ahead. I'll be joining you soon, but I may not have Elizabeth with me."

Garrett drummed a pen on his desk.

"No, Gregor. Elizabeth is not going to be a problem."

Max and RJ, Kodiak at their heels, walked the castle's main floor. The glaziers worked the stained-glass windows. Masons detailed the floor, an homage to symmetry, using slabs of stone tiles, cutting two-foot by four-foot rectangles.

"I think we should do an overnight, Max," said RJ. "It will be good to get a different sense of the castle. Especially if one of the offerings is going to be 'Spend a Night in DracuLAND.'"

They stopped in the middle of the floor. Kodiak sat, his enormous tail swiped back and forth across the tiles. Max scratched the dog's head behind his ears, a favorite spot of Kodiak's judging by the acceleration in tail swipes.

"What do you think he is?" asked RJ.

"He's a mutt, RJ," replied Max. "Like every dog in Romania."

"Biggest darned mutt I've ever seen."

"Yes, he is."

"Didn't show, chief."

"What's that?" asked Costea Jones, DracuLAND's Romanian/British general contractor. He sat at the edge of his desk, a dented metal relic from past jobs, and something of sentimental value and good luck. It followed him from site to site for more than twenty years.

Costea scraped spackle off a pry bar with his hands, more scar tissue than skin after decades of construction work.

"A couple of the day laborers didn't report to the crew foreman this morning. Second time it's happened this week," said Dorin Cerberin, DracuLAND's assistant general contractor. He leaned against the doorway of Costea's construction trailer, hands in the front pockets of his work pants, an orange safety jacket tucked under his arm.

Costea reached behind. He freed a clipboard off the wall, and eyeballed the job roster. Two absences from a couple days ago, and now this. While not out of the ordinary in construction, it seemed unusual for these workers, longtime reliable laborers for Costea.

"You called their cellphones?"

Dorin nodded. "Both went straight into voicemail."

"Are they married, and if so, did you try their homes?"

"Both single, and they've joined the generation of no landlines."

"How does this affect us for today?"

"They were working on leveling the valley floor. I can replace them," offered Dorin. "I could pull a few more men from the castle reconstruction. Poenari is essentially finished, except for the roof."

"A few *more?* How many have you taken so far?"

"Three to cover us earlier in the week, but I brought in additional masons to replace them."

"*Replace?* Why didn't I know about this?"

Dorin stood straighter, shifting his weight from his left foot to his right and then back again.

"I'm sorry, Costea. I handled it and I did not want to bother you with what I considered my responsibility. We managed to cover the time without any problems. I will not make that same mistake in the future. I promise."

Costea gave his direct report a tight, but genuine smile.

"Not a problem . . . until now. From this point forward, I want to know about any absences or labor replacements. I trust you, Dorin. You know that. But with this latest incident of these two specific workers, both handpicked . . ."

"Understood."

Dorin exited the trailer. Costea returned to the latest set of plans from Oskar, and plotted the daily and long-term work schedules. He added another day to the leveling project, despite Garrett's ability to find *every* delay.

He completed the schedule for the coming month, but now the timetable resembled a Tetris game. When he'd finished, Costea looked out the window of his construction trailer, which opened to the expanse of the valley floor. He sighed.

The Body — March 1

Later that day, Vasile Etemescu, a laborer investigating issues with underground water sources, drove his truck by the western edge of the valley. The vehicle kicked up dust on the dry, rocky surface. He had rolled up the windows when he departed from the construction trailers, but the rising temperatures of the day forced him to lower them.

Poenari Forest, a dense collection of ancient growth trees and untended brush, grew larger in his windshield.

Vasile parked his vehicle at the edge of the forest. He photographed the terrain, and noted access points that might expedite the work of backhoes. His assignment, though, was to identify below-the-surface streams, which cause runoff and erosion. And delays.

He returned the camera to the front seat of the truck and lifted a pickaxe from the back.

Vasile drove the pickaxe through the rock level of the valley floor. After half an hour, he put the tool down. He walked into the shade and stripped off his sweatshirt. The sun passed the midday point on its way to the horizon, but the heat continued.

He pulled a damp rag from his pants pocket and wiped his neck. He'd left his water bottle in the truck and returned to get it.

A chattering sound from the forest. Movement in the trees.

Vasile spun around and backed toward his truck one slow step at a time. A rustle this time, then another chattering noise. His throat dry. He swallowed.

"Who's there?" he yelled, his voice cracking.

More chattering but further away, and the sound of a heavy object being dragged through the untended overgrowth on the forest floor.

"Janos? That you?" he yelled, a reference to the coworker who knew where Vasile would be working.

Again chattering, but two different intonations. More dragging. Vasile motionless. Despite the heat, a chill swept through his body. He held his breath.

The dragging faded. Vasile exhaled, and lowered his head to his knees. Nausea ran a circuit through his stomach and he dry heaved.

Vasile collected himself and stood, wiping cold sweat from his forehead. His wobbly legs took him back to the truck and he drank half of the quart bottle of water in one gulp. Vasile leaned against the side of the vehicle and took deep breaths before returning to the site where he'd taken photographs.

His hands shook. Vasile retrieved the pickaxe from where he left it and continued breaking up chunks of the ground.

Vasile swung the pickaxe into the dry rock. The spiked head sunk with so little resistance the front blade disappeared. His stomach turned over, and he dropped the tool. It remained stuck in whatever he hit. Vasile crossed himself from head to ground and from left shoulder to right.

He'd run across animal carcasses before on construction sites, this one no different. The lack of insects evidenced a fresh kill. He pulled on the axe. As he did, whatever he struck rose from the ground with his blade as it had lodged in its ribcage. And then it slid off the axe and thumped to the ground.

Human. Headless.

He dropped the axe and ran toward the construction trailers before he remembered his truck, parked next to the forest—close to the body.

"I'll get … the truck … with …" Vasile panted. "Need some help."

He sprinted to the truck and climbed in. He dropped his keys a few times before jamming them into the ignition. The truck turned over and sprayed dust and dirt on the job site as it spun in a circle. Vasile stomped on the gas pedal and closed on the trailers as he crested the valley floor.

Vasile slammed on the brakes when he arrived at the first trailer. He tumbled out of the driver's seat and hit the ground. A couple of workers flew out of the trailer and raced over to him.

He croaked through a dry throat. Nothing came out. He pointed into the truck and one of the workers fetched the water bottle. Vasile choked some down. More workers stopped their tasks and dashed over.

"I … my … pickaxe," he stammered, panting, "stuck in the rock. I found," he took a deep breath, "a body!"

One of the men, named Sandu, briefed by Dorin to report anything odd, phoned Dorin to let him know what *might* have happened. He finished the call.

"Vasile," he said, and helped his coworker stand. "If I drive, can you return to where this happened?"

"Yes. Yes. Of course." Vasile coughed out the words. Sandu led him to the truck.

As they drove, Vasile related the afternoon's events.

"A typical day," he started. "Nothing out of the ordinary at all, but then I heard noises in the forest."

"Noises?" asked Sandu, who kept his eyes on the valley floor as he drove.

"Yes, it sounded like people talking, but very, very quickly, and I did not recognize the language," Vasile said. "And then I heard something dragging along the ground, and more talking. I called out, but got no reply."

"Did you go into the forest?" asked Sandu.

"No, I heard the talking and dragging getting further away and then it just disappeared. I returned to my tasks."

"You should have called it in," said Sandu. "Some workers are missing."

Vasile snapped his head in the direction of Sandu.

"*What?*"

"Yes, and from the valley floor job sites," said Sandu. "A few earlier this week and two men from yesterday. So what did you do next?"

"I, uh, tried to finish taking photos of the area, but my hands shook too much. I started to break some ground to establish markers. That's when I struck the … body."

"We are close," said Sandu leaning forward and ignoring Vasile's last statement.

Sandu peered over the wheel. Their truck approached the dig site as the sun dipped behind the foothills. He turned on his headlights, as the western foothills threw shadows over the ground.

Sandu slammed on the brakes.

"Is this a joke?" he asked.

The pickaxe no longer lay in the ground as Vasile left it, now jammed into a mound of dirt, handle down. Bathed in the light of the truck's headlamps, the tool reflected the aspect of a gravesite cross.

Dusk, the harbinger of night, intruded onto the site.

Vasile remained inside the truck. Sandu exited and grabbed a flashlight from the toolbox.

Sandu stomped toward the makeshift cross. He pulled it out, a remarkable feat given that the shaft of the cross-like pickaxe had been buried several inches deep into the mound. He turned toward the truck. When he saw Vasile remained inside, he walked back.

He threw open the door and grabbed his coworker, no small man, by the arm. Sandu dragged him out of the pickup.

"I ask, is this your idea of a joke, *Tovarăse?*" Sandu still used the old Soviet term for comrade when he addressed coworkers.

Vasile coughed.

"No, sir! I stuck the blade of that axe into the flesh of some poor unfortunate soul. I, uh, let go, dropping it to the ground and left here not twenty minutes ago! Someone has removed the body and left us this sign from the devil himself!"

"Vasile! Do not do this to me! As I've explained a few workers went missing this past week!"

"Yes. Yes. Of course. I hurried to find someone. I am so sorry. I should have called and waited."

Sandu relaxed his grip on Vasile. He returned to the mound and knelt on one knee to more closely examine the area. He noticed drag marks on the ground, not deep and not for more than a few feet. Then they disappeared.

"It's all right, Vasile," said Sandu, placing a hand on the man's shoulder. He walked the area to note the details for the report to Dorin.

"Vasile, we will return *only* after I am finished," said Sandu.

He pointed at the truck.

"I *think* I believe you, *Tovarăse*, but we must walk this site more. I want to figure out where that body could have gone, and in such a short period of time." He paused.

"What can I do, Sandu?"

"Look for evidence of anyone . . . or anything," said Sandu and he turned his flashlight to "flood." He reached around to the back of his pants and pulled out a sidearm.

The chattering returned. Far off in the forest. Sandu stiffened as the sounds moved closer and then further away. Then closer.

"Let us make this fast.".

An hour later, Sandu and Vasile returned to the main trailer. Sandu called Costea and Oskar after speaking to Dorin. He put the cellphone on speaker so Vasile could relate his part of the incident.

"Are you sure it wasn't an animal, Vasile?" asked Oskar.

"Yes, sir, I'm sure. I've been around worksites and seen enough dead things to recognize it as human. I stuck that axe into a corpse."

Silence on the phone save for Oskar's breathing.

"Any decomposition? Could you tell?" he asked Vasile.

"No, sir. A fresh, uh, kill. I don't think the body could have been there long. So close to the surface that . . ."

"Vasile, I've heard enough. There's not much more we can do until we find that body."

Oskar ended the call and sat. He tossed the phone back and forth in his hands before returning it to its cradle.

"Do not want to call Garrett, at least not yet," he said to Costea.

"You'd better call security if you're not going to contact the police," said Costea. "I think RJ is on tonight."

Oskar picked up the handset again and punched in RJ's number. He glanced out the trailer's window. A dark moonless night. The power surged, then shut off. For an instant the trailer and the surrounding work area fell into blackness. Both he and Costea exhaled when the lights came back.

"Oskar? To what do I owe the honor of a call at such a fine hour of the evening?" asked RJ.

"RJ, uh, how are you? Can you come out to the main trailer?"

"Well, I'm actually at the castle picking out new drapes for my room, but I could tear myself away." RJ threw in a guffaw or two. "Anything . . . wrong?"

"Would be helpful if you could get here as soon as possible," he said and he related Vasile's story.

"On my way."

RJ slipped a pair of night vision goggles around his neck, and rode the elevator down to the valley floor. He jumped into one of the golf carts used for transportation around the site. The fleet of 20 cars was outfitted with heavy duty tires and shocks to withstand the bumpy terrain, the body work and engines also modified to accommodate Garrett's need for speed. He turned on the headlights.

The black sky, which melted into the colorless forest in the distance, filled RJ's vision as he drove out onto the valley floor. The air changed, going from chilly to still to stifling. A cross-wind rattled the golf cart as he passed over the uneven terrain. RJ sucked in a breath. He shoved the air back out his nose. Another inhale through his mouth. He pushed the accelerator to the floor.

All the construction trailers by the foothill were dark save for the one where Oskar and Costea worked.

RJ thought he saw a wind gust push a ripple through the lit window of the main trailer. He patted Louise and switched on the high beams.

"Let's be ready, soldier," said RJ to himself. "The Middle East is like this at night—no definition in the terrain. And this place is darker than a Palestinian tunnel." He laughed out loud with his characteristic pirate guffaw.

The wind picked up—or something buzzed the cart. An audible whoosh of heavy air, then gone. RJ saw a change in the night sky. It had grown darker. The cart's headlights dimmed for a moment before the high beams came back.

RJ patted Louise, secure in its holster, again. He reached behind his neck and pulled out a titanium nightstick which he had carried in a quiver next to his spine.

He placed the nightstick on the passenger seat. He felt another whoosh, this time closer, and put on the night vision goggles. He switched off the headlights, and focused on Oskar's trailer.

"Hmm. The lights have dimmed there, too," RJ mumbled.

None of the exterior construction lamps were on. The general contractors' trailer looked small and isolated against the vast expanse of the valley floor which stretched out before RJ, then vanished into blackness when it merged with the sky.

On the periphery of the night-vision glasses, he saw it just before it flew over the top of the cart, a bird-like creature with a wingspan several feet across. It drew back its wings and dove.

RJ smashed his nightstick on … *something*. An earsplitting shriek of injury. The creature collided with the roll bar on top.

And lifted the cart.

RJ, one hand on the wheel, stood as tall as he could inside the cart and struck the creature's muscular legs as its talons gripped the roll bar. Another shriek. It dropped the cart. The high beams flickered off on impact. RJ lost his balance and toppled out to engage the attacker on foot as the vehicle sped away. The shrieking continued, but grew fainter, and eventually receded into the night.

He ran in the direction of the main trailer. The infinite blackness of the valley floor ahead.

About 100 yards on, RJ found the golf cart, flipped over, wheels spinning in the air. He switched off the engine, and shoved the cart over to its proper position.

RJ pulled a flashlight from the glove box and set it on "flood." It bathed the cart in white light. The industrial-grade plastic cross support beam, which ran from the back to the windshield, had been ripped from its supports. The roll bar remained, but the anodized coating scraped off. RJ jumped in, started the engine, and sped away.

RJ walked into the trailer. Power restored, lights were working in the construction trailer and around the site. Oskar greeted him.

"Took you a while longer than I thought. Everything OK?"

RJ grunted and removed his field jacket. Oskar and Costea both glanced at Louise, perched comfortably in its dark green shoulder holster. In his right hand, RJ gripped the nightstick, then slid it into its quiver.

"You going to need those?" asked Oskar, eyeing Louise, and the nightstick.

"If you took a ride in the golf cart back to the castle with me," said RJ, "you might want a gun of your own. I ran into *something* during my trip to meet you. The golf cart sustained heavy damage during the encounter. I'd ask if you'd like to see it, but I suggest remaining inside for the night."

"Actually, I was thinking about heading home," said Costea, not taking his eyes off RJ, whose military posture hadn't relaxed since entering the trailer. "Haven't seen the family for a few days."

RJ stood next to the desk nearest the trailer door. He pulled his goggles over his head and set them down on the metallic desktop. He picked up a landline handset and pointed it at Costea.

"Call them and explain that you're going to be working late this evening. Now, what more can you tell me about why I'm here?"

RJ dropped into a chair.

"Nothing that's going to improve your outlook."

Oskar and Costea filled RJ in on Vasile's encounter.

"Vasile thinks something moved the body while he was running to the trailer, or when he and Sandu rode back to investigate? Or both?" asked RJ. "What I mean is, how much time did it, uh, *have* to move the body?"

"Vasile estimated his trip back and forth from where he discovered the body took thirty minutes at most," responded Oskar. "As I mentioned, when his coworker returned with him, the body had disappeared with no trace save for a few drag marks embedded in the hardpack." He hesitated. "They weren't sure what left them."

"They weren't sure? I have a good idea what," offered RJ, swiveling his head in the direction of the parked golf cart. "The assumption is that something lifted the body out of the valley, *or* someone elaborately covered their, ahem, tracks?"

"Yes," said Oskar.

"That might not be as farfetched as it sounds," mused RJ. "I've changed my mind about leaving the construction trailer, but be on guard. Let's take a look at the golf cart. I'll show you what I mean. Grab a flashlight, Oskar."

RJ pulled out the nightstick. He opened the door, and hand-signaled Costea and Oskar to follow him. The golf cart still sat upside down in front of the trailer. RJ shined a flashlight on the roll bar.

Oskar and Costea examined it. Long, raking scratch marks ran along the silvery coating with sections of it peeled away. Oskar's breathing caught.

"I do not think a crash would have done this," said Oskar running a shaking hand along the roll bar.

"No."

"What do we tell Garrett?" asked Oskar.

"I think we tell him about the cart," said RJ. "I'll explain Vasile's encounter as best I can. The more immediate concern is the missing workers, and whether that vanished body could have been one of them. I'm not ready to tell Garrett about *that* yet, but I will have to soon. Have you contacted the police?"

"Uh, no, but so you understand, Romanian law is similar to American," volunteered Oskar. "Twenty-four hours before the police will consider looking into a missing person. Might call them in the morning, if none of the workers show by then."

RJ's head snapped around as he, Oskar, and Costea heard a faint, high-pitched screech. RJ switched off the flashlight and hustled the men back inside. Oskar killed the outside lamps. He went one step further and shut off the inside lights, including the computer screens.

"Tell me some good Romanian folktales, Oskar," smiled RJ as he settled into the chair. "I think we're in for the evening."

"Cannot help you there, RJ," he replied. "Spent the first twenty years of my life in Bonn, Germany, before marrying a Romanian woman and becoming a citizen here."

RJ removed Louise from its holster and settled even further into the chair. He two-fingered his cellphone out of his shirt pocket and dialed Max's number. When his colleague answered, RJ filled him in on Vasile's encounter with the body, and his own with the golf cart.

"I suggest that we meet here tomorrow morning and head out to that job site," said RJ and hung up.

"Is there anything we can do tonight?" asked Costea.

"Get some sleep you two. I'll wake you if there's a problem," said RJ, returning his gaze to the window that looked out onto the valley floor.

Garrett Astor—March 1 and 2

"That's what we eat, Sis."

Elizabeth turned away from the tablet, its screen filled with a spreadsheet.

"How the hell did we get in so deep on this?" she asked, her tone aggressive.

"You joking? We've been at it for eight months. The construction elevators are in. The castle is almost finished, and the back is being leveled. Good God, Elizabeth, *now* you're having a change of heart?"

"Did you speak with the government?"

"About what? The bureaucrats have us where they want us. If we walk away from an unfinished project, they've got lots of leverage. We *own* the castle. We *own* the land around it. We *own* the back valley, the front parking lot, the—."

"Oh, so we're just giving up?"

"Elizabeth, you have the numbers."

"Yes, and I WANT OUT OF THE DEAL!" Elizabeth barked. Then she closed her eyes and in a Zenlike motion, inhaled. Calmly, she stated, "Don't care what it costs. We are done with DracuLAND."

She slammed the door on her way out.

"No, we aren't," said Garrett to the closed door. "And it ain't just the money."

Morning arrived at the construction trailer park. RJ, Costea, and Oskar pulled themselves out of their sleep and walked outside.

Oskar and Costea stopped. No golf cart. Gone. Vanished. As with the body, no evidence it had ever been there. Fortunately for RJ, he had taken them outside to look at it prior to retiring for the evening.

"How much does a golf cart weigh?" RJ asked Oskar.

"With the modifications? I'd estimate more than five hundred pounds."

"You may want to check with your supervisors and see if those two missing men reported to work today," suggested RJ. "I hope to God they have."

Oskar agreed and called Dorin. RJ walked to the area where the cart once sat. He took out his cell and called Max.

"Clear your schedule for the morning, partner. We've got two places to examine. Bring those two former MI-6 agents with you, the ones we hired last month for extra security. Check if they have their crime scene examination tools. If not, get your hands on a couple of complete kits."

Max repeated the instructions back to RJ.

"And, Max, use the armored SUV with the full weapons drawer."

Max clicked off. RJ's eyes took on a one-thousand-mile stare as he looked across the valley.

"What the hell is out there?" Distracted, he scratched the stubble on his right cheek. "Don't know, but I know who might."

Max arrived an hour later in a black SUV with two British former MI-6 agents, Alvin Chen and Doug Mackie.

RJ greeted them, introduced Costea and Oskar, and relayed Vasile's discovery of the body.

Max, Alvin, and Doug, dressed in field jackets and cargo pants with slots for hunting knives, walkie-talkies, and sidearms.

"I have something else to share with you, in addition to Vasile's encounter," RJ said as he looked them over. "And you're just going to have to take my word for what happened. I guarantee none of you have run across anything like this."

"Like what, Mr. Brancatelli?" asked Alvin, a Korean expat with an uncharacteristic five o'clock shadow. Alvin, almost as tall as Max, with broad shoulders, short-cropped hair, and a strong physique.

"Rugby, Mr. Chen? And call me RJ."

"Yes, through university."

"It shows."

"Are you avoiding the question, mate?" asked Doug, an expressionless face staring at RJ. Doug stood a foot shorter than Alvin, but he appeared as athletically built. Hair cut the same, but clean shaven.

"Why, yes I am. I think a visit to the site is in order," said RJ. "Shall we?"

"Anything you can tell us?" asked Doug.

"Yes, be prepared for a full day of forensics," said RJ. "But be on your guard. Last night also had its own strange incident. Listen up."

RJ ran through the attack on his golf cart the night before, and the vehicle's disappearance this morning.

"Who would want to steal a damaged golf cart, Mr. Brancatelli?" asked Alvin.

"You've heard of helicopter skiing?" joked RJ. "My guess is that we're dealing with a band of rogue helicopter golfers."

Alvin, like Doug, sat stone faced. Max, who had adjusted to RJ's sense of humor, decided a laugh might be a good way to smooth things over between the men.

"You'll get used to it," sighed Max, placing a hand on Alvin's shoulder. "Shall we go?"

The SUV bumped along the valley floor, a turbulent ride made worse by RJ's lead foot. Over Alvin's objections, RJ moved one of the high-caliber sniper rifles into the area between the driver and front passenger seats.

"Not a good place for a high-powered rifle, RJ," snapped Alvin, who reached for the gun.

"Had you been with me last night, you'd do the same," sneered RJ, who steered with his left hand and grabbed the gun with his right. "We're all pros with extensive weapons training. Believe me, you'll want to be at the ready, even while inside an armored vehicle."

"What for?" asked Doug. "This is all very mysterious, Mr. Brancatelli."

"RJ," he insisted. "And I need you to bear with me *and* report everything you find at this first site. Everything. Anything. Are we good with that?"

"Yes," responded Alvin. "Still don't like the loaded rifle. It could go off if we go over a large rock."

"You'll thank me some day . . . like today."

The gun remained by RJ's side.

RJ parked the SUV and grabbed the rifle. He stepped out of the vehicle, and slung a backpack over his shoulder.

The drag marks and pickaxe remained, with the tool lying on the ground since Sandu's removal the day before.

Alvin and Doug walked in circles around the site, avoiding the drag marks.

Doug stopped after ten minutes, took out his binoculars and scanned the valley. It formed a cul-de-sac with the construction trailers at the east end. Poenari Forest surrounded the west, north, and south sides of the rocky terrain. In some places the trees had grown so close together, Poenari Forest appeared covered in patches of black.

"Forget a cart or human being. You Yanks could hide an entire golf course in these hillsides," said Doug to RJ. He lowered the binoculars. Alvin finished his reconnaissance, and turned his attention to the pickaxe where RJ, white latex gloves on, examined the tool. RJ kneeled, his left eye an inch from the handle. He ran his index finger along the wood. He took photographs and loaded them onto a laptop.

RJ motioned for everyone to gather around as he directed the screen away from the already bright sun.

The first photo displayed a close-up section of the top of the handle, focusing on three evenly spaced indentations on the wood. Next to that photo, one of the underside of the handle. The underside had a single indentation.

All four indentations appeared to have been made by animal claws or talons, and judging by the scale, a large creature.

"That is one big eagle. I didn't know they were indigenous to Eastern Europe," said Doug. The Brit's expression changed to one of curiosity. His brown eyes more closely examined the photos.

"Eagle?" asked RJ, his left eye characteristically half closed. "Eagles don't have claws that articulate like this, Doug.

This is not just any bird, Mr. Mackie. I do, however, think that whatever it is, it flies and is extremely powerful."

"Why do you think that?" asked Alvin.

"Gosh, other than the fact that it lifted a five-hundred-pound vehicle, and a human body out of the valley? I'm just not sure, Alvin."

A nonplussed stare by the Brits.

A few minutes later, Max returned from making his own sweep of the area. He too, found no evidence of the body. RJ showed him the detailed shots of the pickaxe.

"We should send these photos to DracuLAND's vet," suggested Max.

"How well do you know him?"

"He's a good vet, RJ," said Max.

"I'm sure he's an excellent veterinarian, Max, but let's send these photos off to a zoologist I know." RJ looked at the three of them, one at a time. "And let's keep this between us. Don't want this to get out and cause mild hysteria, or any hysteria."

"There are two, maybe three, men missing, Mr. Brancatelli," said Alvin. "Perhaps a bit of an overreaction is in order."

"RJ. Please call me RJ," he asked again. "I agree, Alvin. I do. Whatever *it* is—and maybe there is more than one—removed a body in the late afternoon and attacked me last night. I don't think this animal, or whatever it is, spends much time out in the daylight." RJ looked at the forest. "Or without the cover of the wooded areas."

Doug burst out in laughter.

"What are you saying, RJ?" Doug asked. "We're in Romania, on the site of Dracula's Castle, so we're what? Searching for vampires?"

RJ emailed the photos and made his way to the skeptical Doug.

"No, Mr. Mackie. What I am saying is we have a bigger problem than vampires. And *we* are not the hunters. We're the prey. Some fun, eh?"

Further "Desertions" — March 2

They returned to the SUV after collecting more photographs of the area and bagging a few soil samples around the drag marks. Alvin questioned RJ during the ride back to the construction trailers.

"Mr., uh, RJ, you have no idea what this is? Any more information you can share?"

"Something appears to be hunting us, Alvin."

"But really—"

RJ abruptly stopped the vehicle and turned to face Alvin. He removed his sunglasses.

"I don't know what this is, and why it—or they—are hunting us, since that's what they're *doing*," said RJ. He pointed the sunglasses at the occupants of the backseat. "I have been to a lot of places, seen a lot of strange things and been surprised by what I have encountered, though I have yet to encounter what *this* may be. I know someone who might be able to identify it. I need verification, and that should be coming."

"*This*? What *this* may be?" shouted Alvin, his tone derisive. "What the hell—?"

RJ turned and stared straight ahead.

Alvin opened his mouth to continue. RJ's cellphone chimed, indicating a message.

"Stand by, Alvin. Now that the internet reception is improved out here, I might be able to tell you what *this* is."

He opened the email from his zoologist contact in South Africa.

It contained one word.

NEKREDUM

RJ closed the cellphone and turned to Alvin.

"OK," said RJ. "We sit down in Oskar's trailer and I urge each one of you to hear me out, unless you want to end up with a pickaxe through your chest."

RJ pressed on the accelerator.

"Ain't a good look."

The passengers exited the SUV at the main trailer. Costea waited outside, eager to tell them the news. Another incident had occurred at the castle during the late-night hours while he, RJ, and Oskar spent the evening in the trailer.

"How many?" asked RJ.

"Oh, uh, no worker 'desertions,'" Costea explained. "There was a tremendous amount of damage done to Poenari Castle. The grounds were not touched. No workers were hurt. But Kodiak was involved in the, uh, invasion, and appears to have suffered some injuries."

"Kodiak?" asked Max, alarmed. He charged toward Costea, who backed away. "Is he OK?"

"He will be fine, and perhaps is already telling everyone to 'see the other guy.'" Costea placed a hand on Max's shoulder. "Kodiak is at the main floor of the castle, and he's resumed guard duty. Remarkable."

"I think we should get back to the SUV," said Max, an urgency in his voice as he hustled out the door. "I need to go to the castle." He turned back to Oskar and Costea. "I'll meet you there."

"Wait," said Doug. "We need to get debriefed by RJ."

"Sorry," said Max. "We'll do it at Poenari. This is related."

He slammed the driver's side door and started the engine. The tires spun and Max accelerated toward the construction elevators.

RJ tapped Doug on the back.

"Let's go," said RJ, breaking into a run. "Ten more minutes ain't going to make any difference, and Max won't be satisfied until he sees Kodiak."

Max sprinted to the main floor of the castle where Kodiak greeted him by shoving his nose into the man's midsection. Max buried his hands into the dog's fur behind his ears and rubbed him until Kodiak panted.

Max's smile switched off when he noticed Kodiak's injuries. The dog had a gash on his side, somewhat crusted over. Cuts marked the area around his eyes and muzzle. Patches of hair on his hind legs were torn out.

RJ arrived minutes later, and gave Kodiak a look.

"Nothing *looks* life-threatening, but he should be taken to the vet," said RJ. "He's limping, but can't tell if he has any tissue damage or broken bone. Might have some internal injuries. Only a veterinarian is going to be able to tell."

"We've tried to take him to the on-site doctor," replied one of the masons, who stood behind RJ. His left hand held a pair of safety goggles. "But he won't leave the castle."

Something glinted off Kodiak that caught RJ's eye. He grabbed a pair of tweezers and a magnifying glass from the forensic kit and approached the dog, who growled.

"Easy, Kode-yak," said Max to the dog. "RJ just wants to help. Hang on, RJ. Let me sit next to him."

"Nooooooo problem," said RJ. "I'll wait."

Max at his side, Kodiak relaxed. RJ re-examined the wound with the magnifying glass. Something protruded, which caused the three-inch-long cut to weep blood, hours after the attack. RJ removed the object. Kodiak growled. Max scratched the dog's head.

RJ held a piece of curved translucent fiber up to the light. He looked closer at the injury.

Kodiak's wound was closing around the open area. The dog sat on his hind legs and wagged his tail.

"Kode-yak, I *would* hate to see the other guy," quipped RJ. After dropping the shard into an evidence baggie from the kit he turned his attention to the damage done to the castle. New stone torn from the walls, the stained-glass windows smashed, and the heavy oaken main door ripped from its hinges.

Alvin, RJ, and Oskar walked out the front "opening" and spotted the door about a half-mile away down the wooded access path to the castle. It lay on top of the tree canopy, next to the trail.

"Looks like it was carried away and then dropped."

"Or thrown," added RJ as he peered through Alvin's binoculars. "It didn't just land on those trees. It sheared off the tops of several of them before coming to rest."

"You are correct, Mr. Brancatelli," confirmed Oskar. "That door was indeed thrown a great distance."

"Oh? How do you know this?" RJ's signature left eyebrow raised.

"I'll explain soon. In the meantime, finish the inspection. I would like to see if you find anything else."

RJ and Max walked Poenari Castle's floor. The tapestries suffered the worst damage, shredded into thousands of long strips and strewn about. Near the doorjamb, a wooden joist protruded from the stone wall. RJ removed a knife from one of the forensic kits and dug out another piece of curved translucent fiber. He passed a magnifying glass over it. Flecks of green and blue greeted his eyes.

He photographed it, as well as the one he'd pulled from Kodiak, and forwarded the photos to the same zoologist. This time he put "Urgent" in the subject line.

"Have you called Gregor?" Max asked Oskar, while RJ completed his work.

"For what reason?"

"He should be informed that someone is vandalizing this property. Perhaps he knows who that someone could be, a competitor who also looked at purchasing Poenari? A group opposed to the building of a theme park on such a hallowed place? I'm certain, knowing my compatriots, that his government office has received threats."

"I don't need to contact Gregor," said Oskar, "since we have a witness." Oscar smirked.

RJ, Alvin, and Doug stopped what they were doing.

"This witness. Unharmed?" asked RJ.

Oskar nodded.

"Enough with the Sphinx act, Oskar," snapped RJ. "Who is it?"

"The former caretaker, Nikolai. Garrett kept him on and gave him a job checking that all the security gates are closed and locked around the various construction sites when the workday is finished."

"Sounds like a good job for a drunk," said Alvin, familiar with Nikolai. "After-hours security guard."

"Let's get him over here," suggested Doug, but Oskar waved him off.

"The poor man won't leave the inside of his shack. He nailed his front door shut. We can go over and talk to him, but he swears he's not going anywhere unless he can be safely escorted around the premises."

"We can do that," said RJ.

His phone chimed, indicating a message.

NEKREDUM. YES. YOU NEED TO FIND THEM.

Another chime.

YOU DON'T WANT THEM TO FIND YOU FIRST.

Nikolai and the Late-night Visitors — March 2

Nikolai Asilimov hammered a couple of 2 x 4s behind the front door, then sat with a half-empty bottle of *Tuica*.

He dropped the bottle when Oskar pounded on the door. It bounced and rolled across a carpet that hadn't been cleaned since Stalin rose to power.

"Nikolai," said Oskar. "We have *both* bodyguards here. They will walk you back to the castle."

"Can't I answer their questions here?" asked Nikolai, his head against the barricade. "I don't see why I have to go to the castle."

"Let's go, Nikolai."

He pried off the boards. The doorknob turned. Nikolai drifted out of shadow and into the weak sunlight of the morning.

Nikolai looked like the survivor of a car accident. His face bruised and bloody. The drab green work shirt and pants from last night torn at the arms and knees, and ready for a trash can. His shoulders slumped and his head down, Nikolai fell in line between RJ and Max. The group walked back to the castle.

Nikolai stared at the castle floor.

"Nikolai," said RJ to the reluctant man.

"Uh, OK," said Nikolai.

"I finished my rounds before nightfall, and locked the exterior gate of the construction fence at the footbridge. I turned to watch the sun set over the valley. Never seen a sunset like it.

"Black clouds, like the bony fingers of a skeleton, cut the valley sky. Only a weak, red light pushed through the darkness. The castle towers stretched into that light.

"I turned from the locked gate and headed home. A strong gust roared up from the gorge and pushed me to my knees. That's when I heard Kodiak growling, loud and long over the noise of this brutal wind from the valley.

"Another gust knocked me down. I dragged myself to the posts holding up the mannequins of dead Ottoman soldiers. I grabbed a base and held on. Kodiak's barking cut into the wind, which increased in intensity, then dropped to a breeze. The air carried the bitter smell of metal, of iron. I lifted my head, and saw the, uh, I don't know what, object of Kodiak's growls.

"Two flying creatures with wide wingspans hovered over the castle. A lone work light from the roof cut through the blackness. I could see their blue and green bodies when they passed through the yellowish illumination."

He gulped, his face reddened, as he shouted, fist in the air, "Spawn of Lucifer, they were! The breath flew from me, and that lonely sound turned their hideous heads in my direction. They talked like cicadas.

"Then, silence. The wind gone. No sound. The creatures hovered. Their wings pushed the odor of death and decay before them. Spawn of Lucifer, I say!"

RJ listened, but Mackie and Chen looked at each other and rolled their eyes.

"I-I slipped off the post, then crawled down the hillside until I could no longer see them. But I heard them. That chattering like, uh, cockroaches."

"Cicadas," said Doug Mackie.

"Shut up, Agent Mackie," snapped RJ.

"They crashed through the roof of the castle," Nikolai finished.

RJ looked over at Kodiak.

"Maybe I could fill in the blanks here as to what happened inside," said RJ. "I know something about the creatures."

"What?" asked Doug, incredulous. "You don't believe this, do you?"

"Doug," said RJ. "Listen. This is speculation on my part, but based upon a reliable source."

RJ paced the floor as he spoke.

"These creatures, Nekredum as they're known, crashed through the roof and flew to the floor where they encountered Kodiak. While one tore this room apart, the other engaged the dog."

"What? Nekredum? You're joking, right?" asked Doug. "What is Nekredum?"

"I'm not. Do you understand the horrifying strength of these creatures? Look at what one did to the stone. Look at it! They ripped it out of the walls. They tore a one-ton door *off* its hinges and *threw* it a half mile. Pay attention, or we're all dead. And our deaths are just the start."

"Come on, RJ. You're as crazy as this drunk."

"Careful, Doug."

"Or what, mate?"

"There is more," said Nikolai, halting the confrontation.

"Go ahead," said RJ, relaxing his posture.

"I dared not move," he continued. "I only wanted to see those creatures leave the castle and fly far, far away. I pressed myself hard into the ground and waited. I'd never encountered anything like it. Sounds worse than animals fighting over a carcass. A smell of death drifted down from the castle."

RJ motioned for Nikolai to continue.

"The noise stopped." He swallowed hard. "I couldn't find the courage to help the dog, and prayed he would be fine. Then I saw the two creatures rise up over the castle. One was slumped into the arms of the other. Kodiak injured it, most likely, and badly. I had to get to the castle."

"You should have helped Kodiak sooner!" shouted Max.

"Max, please," said RJ. "If Nikolai had done that, he'd be dead now and we'd know none of this."

"Don't care," said Max, who remained by Kodiak's side. "Nikolai?"

"I, uh, I waited until the creatures flew away," said Nikolai, one eye on Max. "Ran to the castle and found Kodiak lying in the doorway."

"Look at the bright side," said RJ. "At least we aren't hunting vampires."

Max grunted.

"Oh, come on," said Doug. "Like I said, you don't actually believe this, do you?"

RJ walked to Kodiak, who stood at the ready. Max called his name to distract him. Kodiak turned his head.

RJ pulled out his phone and photographed what was an open wound, now dry and healing. He whispered something to the dog, who got to his feet and walked back to the group.

"What are you doing?" asked Max as RJ delivered Kodiak to him. "We need to figure out what to do about this, and what we're going to tell Garrett."

"This is *your* dog, Max," said RJ. "You have to stay with him until he's a hundred percent."

"I have security rounds to make," said Max.

"Looks like you're going to have a partner," said RJ. "Look, Max, I've known the Astors much longer than anyone here. If it's all right with you. I'd like to call the shots."

Max rubbed a five o'clock shadow.

"Yes, one of us should be in charge," said Max. "But Kodiak—"

"I know it's not standard operating procedure, whatever caused this destruction will be back."

"How do you know that?" Doug asked.

"Revenge . . . and there must be some other reason it's come to the castle in the first place," said RJ. "I don't know enough yet, but they're capable of traveling. Why stop and tear the castle apart?"

"OK," said Doug. "What might that be, do you think?"

"Haven't a clue, but the zoologist who's been looking at the evidence from the missing body and Kodiak's wound and the fiber I found in it, will. Give me some time."

The group, save for Max and Kodiak, departed for the main trailer.

Nekredum — March 2

RJ washed his hands in the trailer's restroom when his cellphone buzzed. He looked down and saw, "Dr. Margaret" on the screen, wiped his hands on his pants, and hit the answer icon.

"Your timing is, as always, excellent," said RJ.

"Oh, so you're in the bathroom again."

RJ smiled. "What have you got for me, Dr. M?"

"You tell me," said Margaret, a natural redhead whose classic good looks dominated even a cellphone screen.

"You were right, again, Dr. Barnes. The Nekredum are here in Poenari."

"Thought so, Mr. Brancatelli. How do you do it?"

"Just lucky, I guess. What the hell are the Nekredum doing here?"

"Lucky? Not a term I'd use right now." Before RJ could offer a rejoinder, she added, "Now, I have to insist you *do not tell anyone* I am your source of information. Understand?"

"M, I have apologized for opening my big mouth on the last assignment. We got the big guy, though, didn't we? I mean we saved the Prime Minister's life and all that."

Margaret exhaled *and* screamed at the same time. RJ put the phone on the sink, and looked for a paper towel to finish drying his hands. He couldn't stifle a laugh as he picked up the phone after Margaret finished.

She pulled her hair back and secured it with a clip.

"If you want information on the Nekredum and what they're doing in Poenari, you won't mention my name. Got it?"

"Got it. I suppose this means you won't be joining me?" he joked.

"Really, RJ?"

RJ moved out of the bathroom and took a seat behind a desk in the trailer. He held his phone close to his ear with his right hand. His left thumb massaged an eyebrow.

"Let's go over some old territory first. That will help," said Margaret. "While it's not exactly scientific, the closest match I could make is to photos, artists' renderings, and sculptures." She paused. "Nekredum is some sort of Sanskrit and/or Latin derivative of fallen angels. Yep, Lucifer's minions on Earth."

"Damn." RJ cleared his throat. "Where does that leave us?"

"I can only give you my *theoretical* point of view on this. Even secularists know the story of Lucifer, the angel who fell from grace and from heaven. God cast him down to hell for his attempt to, well, play God."

"I am a practicing Catholic, you know," said RJ to Margaret, who continued.

"What many secularists do not know is that Lucifer was not the only fallen angel. God cast down many from heaven and hurled them toward the depths of hell. Lucifer and a few of his closest minions passed through the boundaries of mortal man and found themselves captive in the biblical underworld. Other disgraced angels merely crashed to Earth."

"You're covering old territory. I know all this." RJ yawned loud enough for Margaret to hear.

Margaret drew in a breath.

"Bear with me, RJ," she said. "We have a larger problem than just exterminating an unknown number of Nekredum and saving a proposed theme park. Yes, I know of the Astors' ambitions to build Romania's version of Disneyland."

"OK," said RJ.

"Listen carefully. Charlemagne first encountered the Nekredum. He defeated them at the Battle of the Basilica in 802 AD. It's laughed at in historical circles as myth. However, the Holy Roman Emperor saved the papacy, and the world, from the Second Coming of the Messiah, which also presages Armageddon. Lucifer is the lynchpin to the appearance of Jesus on Earth in modern times. Lucifer and the Messiah will battle on Earth for the soul and the survival of Man.

"Had the Nekredum proved victorious in 802 AD, Lucifer would have ascended to the Holy Roman Emperor's throne at St. Peter's and thrown the world into darkness. So, RJ, the Nekredum have a dual purpose which drives them. The downfall of the Age of Man, and the subsequent ascension of Lucifer from hell."

"Did not know of their encounter with Charlemagne." RJ swiveled and turned away from the desk. "OK, but how did they get *here?*"

"Charlemagne tasked his son, Pippin, with finding a place to secure them. Dacia, the ancient name for Romania, presented as the logical choice since the Romans had conquered it and turned it into an outpost. The Nekredum were imprisoned in Poenari.

"It is legend, folklore, or myth, that the grandfather of Vlad the Impaler confronted and defeated them in 1430 AD after they somehow escaped Pippin's prison."

"To initiate a Second Coming?" asked RJ. "But how would they have done that in Dacia in 1430 AD?"

"The leader of the Nekredum, Animarus is the name I've come across in my research, negotiated with Vlad Dracul, the grandfather, to help defeat the Turks. In exchange, Vlad would allow Lucifer to occupy Constantinople, the new seat of religious power in the world."

"And what would the Draculs get, other than driving the Turks from what was then Dacia?"

"Eternal freedom from the Turks . . . but only to be ruled by Lucifer. Vlad, or Lord Dracul, an Orthodox Christian, would *never* allow the Nekredum to pass out of Dacia and into the world of Man. Lord Dracul, according to my research, sealed the Nekredum up again, but did not kill them. I don't know how or why."

RJ exhaled and squeezed his phone like a stress ball.

"Sealed them up? For more than five hundred years?"

"Yes."

"Then how did they get out?"

"I assume construction of the theme park has been using a significant amount of explosives to, uh, open up some areas? If so, the Hive has been reopened, and freed the Nekredum and their helpmates."

RJ slumped in the chair. It let out a rusty sound of metal on metal. He closed his eyes and rubbed the bridge of his nose.

"RJ?"

"How do we stop them?"

"You must kill Animarus, *and* find the Hive of the Nekredum. The only way to eradicate them forever, *after* he is killed, is to flood it with holy water. When the waters recede, the area must be covered in Dead Sea salt."

"M-Margaret—" RJ stammered. "How does killing the leader stop the Nekredum?"

"He is their lifeforce on Earth and Lucifer's conduit," she said. "He imbues them all, Nekredum and their helpmates, with the ability to exist here on Earth in the Age of Man."

"Uh, helpmates?"

"Yes. The Nekredum have allies somewhere in the Poenari Forest. I don't know *what* they are."

"Great."

"However," she continued, "only a person from the bloodline of the Draculs can kill the leader, the one with the blue and green head. His followers and spawn have gray heads. And—"

"How do we find a descendant of the Draculs?" interrupted RJ.

"According to my research you *cannot* find a descendent of the Draculs. The last one died in 1720."

RJ exhaled.

"Finally, here's a bonus," Margaret said. "The spike of the Family of Dracul, called Mors Aeterna, must be driven through the heart of Animarus by a Dracul, to ensure that neither he nor any Nekredum will ever rise again. Mors Aeterna is *why* Animarus searches Poenari. In his possession, it will allow the Nekredum to leave Poenari and end the Age of Man. Vlad's grandfather cursed the Nekredum and *bound* them to Mors Aeterna. It is what keeps them within the confines of Poenari."

"Spike?"

"Yes," said Margaret. "Royal families in other parts of the world passed swords from generation to generation, a signifier of military superiority. The Draculs used the spike to kill their enemies. They drove them through an opponent's midsection, then hoisted the person up into the air to die over a period of hours, even days. You've seen the paintings and wood carvings of such? Vlad was especially skilled."

She paused.

"Mors Aeterna is the Dracul's equivalent of the family sword."

"Is there no other way? What about the dog? He badly wounded one of them according to Nikolai."

"Kodiak? Yes," Margaret continued, her voice dropping. "You've seen the famous painting of Vlad the Impaler eating dinner while several Turks die, impaled on spikes, in front of him, yes? The dog lying at his feet is known as the Sentinel of Poenari. Kodiak has been such for more than six hundred years. He is a powerful ally, but even he cannot kill the leader of the Nekredum. The best you can hope for, RJ, is a neutral outcome—which is the mistake Charlemagne made, and the choice Lord Dracul submitted to, in order to rid themselves of the problem *in their lifetimes*."

"Wait a second," said RJ. "Kodiak is almost six hundred years old? Ridiculous."

"Yes."

"Just a moment. Are you saying Kodiak is immortal? I'd accuse you of messing with me, but that's not your style.

"Vlad the Impaler couldn't bear to lose the dog and blessed him with long life. He cannot die, but I believe, like Animarus, he can be killed. There is a difference. According to my research, he has a mortal enemy, one of the helpmates. Again, I don't know what they are."

RJ opened his mouth. Nothing came out.

"I can't accept a neutral outcome," said RJ. "Find me a descendant."

"What?"

"You heard me."

"RJ."

"I'm not giving up, Margaret."

"All right," she said. "But be careful looking for Mors Aeterna. If Animarus finds it, he can escape the confines of Poenari. He will be able to bring Lucifer out of hell with it. If you find it, you must secure it in some sort of holy sanctuary. Even then the Nekredum might be able to get to it."

"Wonderful. Any more good news?"

"Yes. The apocalypse has begun, RJ," Margaret said, and hung up.

RJ stared at the cellphone. He opened a memo app and typed in the names of the security detail. Alvin, Doug, and Max. Plus himself and Kodiak. Not a lot to battle Lucifer's army.

Back in New York City — March 2 and 3

Toward the late afternoon Oskar called Elizabeth and Garrett. They listened to the lead designer detail the turbulent events of the last few days. He started with the loss of several workers. When he got to the part about the cross and drag marks, the attack on RJ's golf cart, and the destruction of the renovated main floor of the castle, Elizabeth interrupted.

"You're asking me to believe Nikolai? Honestly, Oskar, what is going on over there? Max has a climbing accident and tells us about his vision. Now, a couple million dollars in materials and labor has been trashed and I'm supposed to buy into the ramblings of some drunk?"

"Ms. Astor, I can only —"

"OK, I'll play this Romanian mythology game. What if it's true? Which it's not. What do we do about it?"

"We should halt construction until we find out what's happened to the missing men. Also, I think the authorities should be called in to take a look at the damage. There might be a local gang or activist group involved."

"Forget it, Oskar," said Elizabeth. "We'll get the company jet and be there by tomorrow morning, your time. I know RJ and Max have given that castle a thorough examination, but have them look at it again. As soon as we get in, I want to meet at the castle and discuss these issues with everyone, including you. I'll email my travel arrangements to Max and RJ. Have them pick us up at the airport."

"Yes, ma'am."

Elizabeth hung up. She called her admin to make arrangements.

"Thought you wanted out?" chided Garrett.

Elizabeth shot her brother The Look.

"We have to get to DracuLAND, but I want this return trip to be our last," she replied. "I'm initiating legal action to void the contracts with the Romanian government."

"You sure?"

"God, I don't know anymore, Garrett."

"Then let's get to the airport."

"Let's."

He spun his chair around to look out the window. A fast-moving storm approached New York. Heavy gray clouds filled the sky over the city.

Garrett and Elizabeth arrived in Bucharest 12 hours later. RJ and Max waited outside customs. Garrett's cellphone read 6:00 a.m. local time when he and Elizabeth climbed inside the Mercedes town car for the drive to Curtea de Argeş.

"RJ. Max." Elizabeth said, her voice rising. "What in hell is going on at DracuLAND?"

"The choice of the word 'hell' is a good one, chief," said RJ.

"What the —? What's that supposed to mean?"

RJ turned to face Garrett. Elizabeth avoided his stare, and looked out the window. She pressed her head forward, but rammed her nose into the glass since she hadn't bothered to lower the glass.

"That hurt," she said, returning to confront him. "Go ahead, RJ. This better be good."

"Allow me to get this information out before you interrupt," said RJ.

"I can't promise that," said Elizabeth. "Nothing I heard from Garrett on the flight over made any sense. I'm in no mood for more of the same."

"All right, Elizabeth. Then we have nothing to talk about."

"Don't forget who you work for, RJ."

"I never do."

"That's not what I'm hearing," said Elizabeth, still rubbing her nose.

"Elizabeth, for God's sake," said Garrett, reaching over to touch his sister's arm. "Relax."

RJ turned away. The car entered the newly constructed superhighway and headed northwest. He called ahead to check that the site staff had prepared the castle for the Astors' arrival—no small order given the damage.

Since the attack by the Nekredum, construction crews removed the debris, and scrubbed the room clean of all blood, both Kodiak's red and the Nekredum's black.

"It's a long drive," said Max after RJ finished the call.

"All right, chief, what would you like to hear?" asked RJ.

"Not what Oskar told us," said Elizabeth.

RJ tapped his fingers on the glove compartment.

"Here's what I think we should do," he said. "Let's enjoy the scenery of southern Romania for the duration of the ride. When we get back to DracuLAND, we'll set up on the main floor of the castle and I'll show evidence of what is going on at Poenari. If I can get my zoologist friend on the phone or on a video feed, I'll have her join us."

"Agreed," said Elizabeth. "But no flying creatures."

"Their ability to fly isn't our biggest concern, but let's enjoy the drive."

They rode on in silence.

"The survey crew!"

Oskar, working in his trailer, slapped himself on the forehead.

Two days before the attack on Poenari Castle, he'd sent a three-person crew—outfitted with camping gear, digital cameras, tripods, and survey scopes—to map the footpaths in the area. The trails ranged from simple, flat, one-mile walks along the perimeter of the park, to overnight hikes several miles long.

He picked up the desk phone and punched in their number.

RJ, Max, Elizabeth, and Garrett arrived at Poenari. A light mist spread over the foothills, thin enough to allow a clear view of the wooded area which fronted the castle. RJ beckoned Elizabeth away from her own examination of the damaged stone of the main floor and led her, Garrett, and Max to a viewing point along the walkway.

RJ pointed to the door that sat on top of two oak trees a quarter of a mile down the hillside.

Elizabeth stood at the edge of the walkway, staring at the wrecked foliage that had slowed the damaged and cracked wooden door on its aerial path.

"Hey, Klutzy! Get away from that ledge. You have a hard enough time keeping your feet on the sidewalk."

"Ah, back off, Garrett."

"Let's go before we're collecting your remains with those of the door."

They returned to Poenari Castle's main floor.

Kodiak, who'd been guarding the front door, stood on all fours, his tail swooshing back and forth with such ferocity that it knocked over a stepladder left behind by the cleanup crew.

He became even more excited when Max, who'd lagged behind, came in from the ramparts. Max again ran his right hand through the hair on the top of the dog's head and scratched behind Kodiak's ears. The dog thumped his back right leg against the stone floor. Their routine.

Costea greeted Elizabeth and Garrett. He described the damage while sharing photographs. He also showed the construction pictures taken the day before.

"The castle was vandalized. Yes," said Garrett. "But does it really mean some huge mythical, uh, monsters did it? And why?"

"RJ believes they are looking for something," volunteered Costea.

"Oh, and what would that be?" Elizabeth fixed her gaze on RJ.

"It's all part of the same story, boss," said RJ. "If you're interested in hearing it, I'll lay it out."

"What are our options?"

"You don't have to hear me out," he said patiently. "All you have to do is wait a while. They'll be back, and if we're, uh, *lucky*," here RJ used air quotes, "you can see for yourself."

"Come on—"

"Garrett, this is serious," interrupted Elizabeth. "No matter who or what did this, the damage to the castle is astonishing. I don't care if it's people in jetpacks. They vandalized DracuLAND's signature piece."

"I can see that, Elizabeth," said Garrett.

"Good. So can I. Might do you some good to actually listen to someone for a change."

"Oh, look who's talking. You do know that's my line?" Garrett jibed.

"Not today," said Elizabeth.

Garrett snorted and shoved his hands into the pockets of his suit pants. He walked the main floor and glanced at the photos.

"You're on, RJ," she said. "Make it good."

"Nekredum?" questioned Garrett when RJ finished.

"Yes."

"Lucifer's fallen angels," said Garrett, his inflection flat.

"Actually, God's fallen angels, should you want to be accurate."

"*Accurate!?*"

"Garrett," said Elizabeth, trying to calm her brother.

"I can't buy this nonsense," said Garrett, who looked directly at RJ. "You'd better come up with something that sounds a lot more logical than God's fallen angels, RJ. The amount of damage and setbacks is in the millions, and I don't want a repeat. I want the vandals brought to justice."

"Yes, sir," said RJ. "May I suggest we take up residence in the castle? As stated before, I am certain whoever did this will be back."

"To the castle?" asked Garrett.

"Yes, sir. I understand Elizabeth wanted to stay here before the climbing accident. Now would be a good time."

"All right, RJ," said Garrett, nodding in the direction of Elizabeth. "But we're not calling in the authorities just yet, *and* my sister does not join us on this overnight."

Before RJ could reply, Elizabeth jumped in.

"Oh no you don't, buster," she said, and walked straight up to Garrett and poked him in his chest with her right forefinger. "You and I are in this *together*, whether you're buying into this or not. Got it? You dragged me out here—just shut up—despite my misgivings. You're stuck with me."

"Have it your way, Sis," said Garrett. "But this isn't a dormitory. You're in a separate room from the boys."

"Fine," said Elizabeth. "Let's get started."

"Whoa," said RJ. "Hang on. Misgivings?"

Elizabeth glanced at Garrett, who took a deep breath, and blew it out. She shook her head and turned to the group.

"We're thinking of pulling out of the deal," she said.

"Astor Holdings has a different deal going on right now, ma'am," said RJ. "I don't think we're in a position to do anything but pay attention to what is happening at Poenari Castle."

114

The Survey Crew and the WolfThane — March 3

On March first, Oskar's survey crew reached the edge of the wooded area where the foothills — those that served as the western border of the park — rose again from the valley floor. The crew worked the area closest to the proposed theme park, and were satisfied after they mapped out the short, easy trails that lay nearest the castle.

They turned their collective attention to more difficult hikes and walked into Poenari Forest.

By the time the site staff finished preparing the makeshift bedrooms for Elizabeth, RJ, and the others, the survey crew had vanished.

Oskar slammed down his cellphone when again he received no answer from anyone on the survey team. He shoved his desk chair across the trailer floor. It crashed into a bookshelf, dislodging several volumes. Benjamin Saperstein, one of the assistant designers, entered the trailer. He looked at the books on the floor, and hustled to his desk.

"Damn it!" shouted Oskar. "Where the hell is the survey team?"

The tall Israeli adjusted his black-framed glasses and grabbed a satellite phone. The team would be well past the walkie-talkie grid. Benjamin punched in their security code and waited.

And waited.

"No answer."

"I know there's no answer!" shouted Oskar. "Who in hell do you think I was trying to reach? I've called each of their cellphones." He caught himself. "But thank you for thinking of the sat phone."

"They've only been out for a couple of days. They could not have gone far. Do you want me to go after them? We've got all-terrain bikes."

Oskar watched the late afternoon sun dip toward the horizon.

"Yes, but not alone."

Ben pulled on a riding jacket and dialed a number on the landline.

"Nate David, please. Look for a tall, sketchy looking dude drawing pictures on the main floor of the castle," he said into the phone, and laughed. "Yes, I know. He always *looks* busy. He's not."

Oskar paced the trailer floor. Benjamin hummed.

"Benjamin," said Nate David. "How did I know it was you? The local admin hasn't quite caught onto your sense of humor."

"Get down here, and bring a bike. We're going to do a little night hunting."

Benjamin laughed again. The sound cut through the heavy air in the trailer.

"No, not local wildlife. Lost contact with the hiking trails survey crew. They aren't picking up their cell or satellite phones. See you in about ten minutes?" Oskar pushed up his index finger to grab Ben's attention. "Hang on a second, Nate."

"Ben, tell Nate to be careful coming over here," cautioned Oskar.

"We'll take care of this, boss," said Benjamin, noticing Oskar's posture and demeanor, arms crossed, one free hand rubbing two days' beard growth.

"Bring your sidearm. Yes. Bring the knife, too. Oskar's worried about vampires or something, I guess. Yes, I know. And he's not even Romanian!"

Benjamin hung up. Oskar's cheeks reddened from rubbing the bristle on his face.

"Boss, Nate and I will find them, I promise," assured Benjamin.

"Thank you." Oskar continued rubbing his beard, but doubt rose in his voice.

"I went into the West Bank myself when I served with the Israeli Defense Forces, and with Nate a few times. We knew nothing more than our assignment," he said, "and we're both still here."

Oskar's chin dropped to his chest. He looked like a parent whose teenage offspring hadn't returned home from a party, and the clock in the living room read 2:00 a.m. with a midnight curfew.

Nate pulled up outside the trailer, shut off the bike, and hustled inside. He shook hands with Oskar, noting an uncharacteristically limp grip. Nate embraced Benjamin.

Twin sons from different mothers.

Neither man particularly imposing, Benjamin the taller of the two. Both swarthy and lean. Full heads of light brown hair and sporting those hip five o'clock shadows favored by millennials.

Nate asked, "Oskar, what is it?" He set his gear down on a desk.

"There's something about this job and this site that just isn't, uh, right." Oskar said. "You both know about the laborers who haven't shown up for work the past few days, and not yet been found?" He swallowed hard. His voice weak, he continued. "And an attack occurred at Poenari Castle a couple of nights ago."

"An attack?" asked Ben, who looked up from packing his gear. "What do you mean an attack?'"

Oskar shuffled over to his desk and placed his hands on the top of it.

"Nikolai saw some of the destruction at the castle while it happened."

"The dude in the shack? Really? If it is so bad, why haven't we seen police?" asked Benjamin.

"Yes, why is that? I'm working just across from that shack and I haven't seen the authorities," said Nate.

"Because," replied Oskar. "I don't think they would believe Nikolai's story. I'm not sure *I* believe him. We are doing something about it, but I don't like the current approach either, because it involves *only* Mr. Astor's private security detail." He put his hands on his hips and exhaled. "And now our survey team . . ."

The early evening winds picked up and blew open the thin metal door to the trailer. The two former military men didn't react when it slammed into the wall. Oskar, though, stepped back and moved away from the noise. He shook his head, and whispered a prayer.

Benjamin took his IMI Tavor TAR-21 and KA-BAR hunting knife from the supply closet. He grabbed several clips and placed them in a satchel. He wheeled around when he heard Nate loading his own automatic weapon. He laughed out loud, as did Nate. Oskar failed to see any humor in the exchange. He sat in his chair and fidgeted with his hands.

"I see you obeyed the Israeli military's rules about returning your IDF-issued weapons," said Nate, as he secured the gun. "I did, too."

"So you still have your sidearm," replied Benjamin, "and I can guess what it is."

Nate smiled and flashed his Jericho 9mm, his favorite.

Benjamin pulled out his sidearm, also a Jericho 9mm, and checked the clip, while Nate unsheathed his KA-BAR commando knife and ran a gloved finger gently along the side of the jagged blade. Oskar backed up all the way into a corner of the trailer.

"You two ready for a war?" asked Oskar, trying to break the tension. "How'd you get that rifle through customs?"

"Hah! You don't want to know. Thought it might come in handy, but let's hope we don't have to use it."

"Uh, OK." Oskar said.

"It's all right, Oskar. As far as we know, you're on our side." Benjamin smiled. "Now, can you give us the survey team's proposed route? Is anything not passable? We can go on foot, but it'll be quicker if we use bikes."

Oskar pulled the site survey plan and showed them where the team planned to enter the northern side of the foothills. Nate and Benjamin could follow a footpath for the first mile or two, but after that passage might prove difficult.

Benjamin tossed Nate a helmet. Before he could protest, he noticed the night-vision goggle attachment.

"You want to run silent?" asked Nate.

"What do you think? Be more effective if we don't announce our presence, depending on what's out there. We can always switch to the gas-powered engine. Maybe that would help, if the survey crew could hear us? Don't know. The bikes can run for about forty miles with a single electrical charge, and then another twenty miles from the solar charger in case we're still looking come morning."

They glanced at Oskar.

"Anything else we should know?" they asked simultaneously.

"Yes, got a message from RJ. I'm needed at the castle," growled Oskar. The resolve in his voice evaporated. He slumped into his office chair. "Just please find them."

The WolfThane, the Nekredum's helpmates, sat in a stand of trees that marked the boundary between the valley floor and the forest. In the darkness, a 300-pound gray wolf lifted its nose in the night air, its yellow eyes spotting movement approaching this heavily wooded section of Poenari Forest.

A rumble escaped the wolf's throat. The muffled noise from Nate's and Benjamin's bikes, running on the electric battery, filled the animal's sensitive ears with a roar.

The gray wolf skulked from the edge of the forest and headed into the dense foliage, its snout to the ground. Another wolf, a mottled white, black, gray, and brown, ran from the trees and joined him. The two fell in line and ran a mile into the woods.

They came to a grove of oak grown close together. The two WolfThane halted and sat on their haunches in front of a twisted latticework of old vines and new green branches.

They howled, low in their register, a sound of grating dirt and broken bone. Movement came from the center of the latticework. A shadow passed in front of the gray wolf and moved onto the mottled one. Both dropped to their bellies and placed their heads on their paws.

The yellow eyes of the two prostrate WolfThane fixed on a 400-pound wolf of blood-red color. Their eyes followed its pacing until it turned back toward the latticework, the entrance to their Lair. A growl, raspier and deeper than theirs, echoed from its throat. Then rustling and cracking branches at the entrance. A fourth wolf, silver-white and lean, no more than 250 pounds, joined them.

It took its place alongside the gray and the mottled WolfThane.

Their ears picked up at the sound of Benjamin's and Nate's bikes. The blood-red wolf snorted and the three took off in a dead sprint in the direction of the noise. The silver-white, the fastest, led.

In the darkness, Benjamin and Nate arrived at the survey team's last campsite and found it deserted—tents collapsed, supply packs and gear strewn around the entire area. Drag marks along the ground ended at the edge of the cleared underbrush.

Ben and Nate unholstered their handguns and released the safeties. They hopped off their bikes silently, and crouched. Nate's head snapped around.

Breathing behind me.

A scuffling sound. He pointed to his eyes with his first two fingers and then behind them, where the noise originated.

Nate entered the brush, his left hand on the gun. His right hand hovered above the commando knife. The shallow breathing and scuffling continued.

A primordial roar and a silver-white wolf leapt out of the brush and slammed Nate to the ground. The animal clamped down on Nate's left forearm and sank its teeth into the sleeve of the heavy jacket. Its fangs ripped through the fabric, straight into the flesh and bone. Nate dropped the handgun, and howled.

Benjamin sprinted toward the noise. He broke through the brush.

Nate's uninjured arm grabbed his knife and plunged it into the shoulder of the wolf. It snarled, but released its hold, and limped into the underbrush.

Nate, his jaw clenched to stem a scream, pulled himself to a kneel. His eyes slammed shut. Blood spurted from the wound. Benjamin holstered his handgun and grabbed a piece of torn tent canvas from the trashed campsite, and fashioned a tourniquet just above his elbow.

In unison, they breathed rapid, shallow breaths. Then Nate's slowed. They heard a howl. *Not far.* Nate and Benjamin scanned the campsite.

"No cover," panted Nate, grunting. "If there are more than a couple of them . . ."

"Can you ride?" asked Benjamin. "Use the gas-powered engine. Faster."

"I can now," replied Nate, his breath still catching. He grabbed the handgun from the ground.

The bikes sat in the open campsite.

Ben calculated the time it would take to get to their bikes.

He slapped Nate on the top of the head and they sprinted the distance to their bikes as two more WolfThane broke from the underbrush.

Nate leapt onto his bike, as did Benjamin. They tore off in the direction of the construction trailers, now a couple of miles away.

The mottled wolf howled. It and the gray wolf sprinted away from the campsite, leaving the wounded silver-white wolf behind. It yelped and then delivered a howl of its own, a long and grisly sound with a rasp of sinew and blood.

High beams illuminated the footpath. Benjamin took the rear position. They rode single file through the forest, Nate wobbling from the loss of blood. The WolfThane in pursuit.

Benjamin glanced at his speedometer. Already 45mph, their speed should have separated them from the WolfThane, but if anything, the two had gained on the men. Benjamin spotted their shapes in his rearview mirrors.

They closed on his bike.

He took his eye off the mirrors. The gray wolf veered off the path into the side underbrush and then reappeared between the two bikes.

"How did—"

The gray wolf leaped onto Benjamin's bike. Its 300-pound bulk put the bike into a skid, but Benjamin kept his balance. His right hand pulled his gun from its holster, and he struck the gray wolf with the butt end of the pistol, catching it on the forehead as its jaws tried to clamp down on his arm. A shrill howl as it bounced off the bike and fell back into the brush.

"That ain't the end of that," mumbled Benjamin to himself. He pressed the accelerator. The bike roared in response. Nate heard it and increased his speed.

A half-mile survey marker nailed to a tree revealed itself in the wash of moonlight. Nate slowed to read it.

"Not a good idea!" Benjamin screamed.

The mottled wolf flew out from the side of the road and landed between the bikes.

Nate couldn't see the wolf, which veered off the path and back into the brush.

He's trying to cut Nate off! thought Benjamin, just before he saw the flash of fur.

The gray wolf, recovered from the blow to its head, slammed into the back wheel of Benjamin's bike causing it to skid once more. This time the bike hit the brush on the side of the path and flipped onto its side.

The gray wolf shook off the collision and got to all fours.

Benjamin yanked shrubbery out of the spokes of the wheels with one hand, then pushed the bike up to its side with his right leg. He fired the Jericho 9mm with his left hand. The gray wolf caught a round in its front leg. It still managed to lunge at the bike.

Benjamin disappeared down the path with the bike in full throttle, the gray wolf not far behind.

Nate turned off the high beams and dropped the night-vision goggles over his eyes.

"Better late than—" he muttered as the night-vision capability engaged. The path widened. He did not see the WolfThane. Not yet.

More howling from behind. Nate wheeled around amidst a cloud of dirt and dust. He accelerated, kicking up more debris and turned back toward Benjamin.

Benjamin intercepted him, and Nate's bike fishtailed and the two headed for the valley floor and the safety of the trailers, less than a quarter-mile ahead. The path widened and they rode in tandem.

The mottled wolf and its gray companion sprinted after their prey, no more than twenty yards away. The bike taillights shined in the dark. The WolfThane closed.

The mottled wolf accelerated and aimed for the rear wheel of Nate's bike. It sprang forward and sank its fangs into his ammunition satchel. The wolf tried to bite into the man's flesh, but kept jamming its muzzle into the metallic clips of ammunition.

Benjamin pressed the bike to its maximum. He saw that the mottled wolf had planted itself onto the back of Nate's bike, its back paws gaining purchase on the rear fender, taking aim at Nate's legs.

Benjamin fired, but the shot went wide as his bike gained its own passenger.

The gray wolf.

Benjamin lost sight of Nate.

The gray wolf lunged toward Benjamin's left arm.

Nate screamed as the mottled wolf sank its teeth into his ankle. His thick work boots yielded. His vision faded. The trail doubled in front of him. The trees thinned and the brush shortened, the valley just yards away. A signpost marked the trailhead. He bit his tongue to clear his head.

He nicked a tree trunk, which caused the bike to carom and slam into the hardpacked surface of the valley floor. The rig flipped over a few times. Nate released himself from the seat as the bike — and the mottled wolf — crashed to the ground.

Nate gained his feet and turned to find the wolf. Using his night-vision goggles he scanned the valley floor.

Then he spotted it.

The mottled wolf tore along the valley floor and made straight for the forest while Nate fired at the animal. It disappeared into the forest.

Then reappeared. Sitting like a domesticated dog at the trailhead, it looked straight at Nate and emitted a deep, ugly, prehistoric growl.

Nate fired.

Benjamin's bike, without rider or wolf, flew out from the trees.

The mottled wolf melted into the woods. Nate limped toward Benjamin's bike, wheeling his own rig alongside.

The bike lay on the valley floor, the rear wheel spinning. Nate switched it off, and shouldered Benjamin's rifle, when he heard gunshots, and a tremendous tearing of fabric.

"Ben!" Nate steadied himself, and pointed his bike toward the trailhead. Nate jumped on, his left arm now hanging numb at his side.

"I will find you. I promise," he hacked out as he engaged the engine.

A bloody Benjamin Saperstein stumbled out of the forest and into the valley. The gray wolf stopped at the trailhead. It held a blood-soaked boot in its mouth. The wolf dropped the boot, bared its fangs, and howled. It reared back and launched itself onto the valley floor.

Nate emptied a full clip from the rifle in the direction of the gray wolf, his aim compromised by the loss of blood.

The wolf caught several rounds, which slammed it onto its back. It fled into the forest. Nate dropped his bike to attend to Benjamin, bent over in exhaustion, his leg covered in blood.

"That wolf … knocked me off the bike," he panted. "We fought … in the underbrush. I stabbed it … several times and I kicked it so hard in the head … I heard bones break, I swear."

Benjamin swallowed.

"But that animal … clamped its jaw down … and locked it on my foot. … wouldn't let go!"

Ben caught his breath as Nate bound up the ankle wound.

"I pulled out my knife and cut the laces straight up the middle. The wolf pulled so hard it fell backward, which gave me time to draw the 9mm," he said. "I fired several rounds in its direction. I know I hit it. It bought me time to run."

Nate finished the dressing. The air in the valley settled. No movement from the forest, and no sounds from the WolfThane.

"They've both just quit. Have you ever seen such behavior in wolves?" asked Benjamin, as he pulled his sock over the dressing.

"Not quitting until an opponent, or the wolf, is dead? No."

"Benjamin, what in God's name is going on here?"

"I've no answers for you, my friend. Let's get out of here. Those wolves will be back. Oskar is not going to like what we have to tell him."

The men rode off under the vigilant eyes of the three WolfThane that remained just inside the trailhead. The silver-white one had limped the entire way from the campsite to the end of the path to be with its pack. They were joined by the blood-red leader. All sat hidden by the perimeter trees and heavy brush. The WolfThane trained their yellow eyes on the disappearing rear lights.

The gray wolf reared back to attack again, but the blood-red wolf growled. The four WolfThane watched as the lights grew dim and vanished.

The Second Battle for Poenari — March 3

The air around the castle, silent and still most of the night, and far enough from Nate and Benjamin's fight with the WolfThane to remain so, now filled with the sound of beating wings and a dog's bark.

The sound of the Nekredum's flight reached down to the lower level of Poenari Castle, where everyone slept. Garrett's eyes popped wide with fright. He threw back the covers and bolted from his cot. Max, Costea, and RJ roused to the sounds. The four ran from their room toward the elevators, Max in the lead.

Alvin and Doug were out of their cots too.

"Secure the rest of the castle." RJ mouthed.

When they balked, RJ whispered, "We *need* to leave someone behind as backup. In a worst-case scenario . . ."

Max grabbed Garrett by the arm. He pulled him back from the open elevator.

"Not staying behind, Max," said Garrett, yanking his arm away. "I have to see this."

The two entered the elevator but held the door for RJ who pushed Costea back onto the "dormitory" floor.

"Costea," said Max, pointing down. "You must stay here."

"I have to help!" he protested silently.

RJ set his lips in a straight line, closed his right eye, and glared at Costea with his left.

"You can help by staying down here," said RJ. "The main floor is not the place for you. We'll be back. The three of you, stay on the walkies."

RJ again shoved Costea. The man stumbled and backed away as the doors closed. Costea watched his friends disappear.

Inside, breathing the only sound. The elevator stopped.

"Hug the wall," instructed RJ in a muted voice. "Do not expose yourselves to the center of the room."

Kodiak, ever vigilant, stood on the main floor, his body forward. When the three arrived, the dog joined them, and the four crept along the perimeter. Max reached for a flashlight, but RJ pressed his hand against Max's wrist to stop him.

Something arrived at Poenari Castle, but did not walk the stone floor.

A shape flew past RJ. Its wings emitted a foul odor. RJ drew his nightstick. His left arm brought it down on the Nekredum's right wing, which slowed its flight.

He smashed the nightstick down on the appendage again. The Nekredum spiraled down and crashed onto the floor, landing on its side. RJ stumbled, but kept his balance.

It screeched. A stained-glass window shattered causing Garrett and the others to cover their ears. It stood up and shook itself in a bird-like fashion to straighten its broken right wing. The Nekredum stared at the appendage, fowl flesh hanging where RJ struck it, a bone protruding. Black blood oozed from the wound. It screeched again, this time directly at RJ. It advanced into a shaft of light which pierced through one of the castle's crenellations.

Max eyed the creature. Seven-feet tall with a gray-green torso resting on a pair of muscular legs. Long, curved talons on three-toed feet pressed against the stone. Four-taloned claws finished a pair of equally muscular arms. An asymmetrical head topped a long and crooked neck.

Max moved to the creature's damaged side. The Nekredum ground its teeth and snapped its jaws at Max. It flew away using its left wing only, like an annoying moth swatted away from a candle.

In the foul air of the main floor of the castle, it joined two other Nekredum at the top of the unfinished ceiling.

The chattering, as described by Nikolai, commenced. It sounded like the biblical plague of locusts, increasing in volume until it filled the stone chamber. Kodiak growled and coiled back on his haunches.

Max shouted in Romanian toward the ceiling. The largest of the three Nekredum, the one so dark blue and green it appeared black in the darkness save for the white streaks on its body, cocked its head, the left side blue, the right, green.

Animarus.

Max reached into a sheath at his side and drew out a titanium nightstick, courtesy of RJ.

Garrett's eyes swept the dim room. He looked for something, *anything*, to help Max and RJ. He spotted a framing hammer in the corner near the construction tools. Just as he wrapped his hand around the grip, Elizabeth dashed into the room.

"Elizabeth, no!" shouted Garrett.

The uninjured Nekredum, this one a muddy green with red streaks, swooped down from above and snatched the hammer from Garrett's grasp. It hurled it across the room where it shattered some of the stone wall. The Nekredum grabbed Garrett and lifted him into the air, but before it could get too far above the floor, Max charged and hacked at the creature's torso with his nightstick. It dropped Garrett and in the same motion swatted the weapon out of Max's hand.

Max ducked another parry by the creature's wing and raced to retrieve his nightstick. Garrett thudded to the floor, unconscious. Elizabeth ran over to check on him.

The three Nekredum resumed their chattering. Kodiak snarled as one attacked the canine, who grabbed it by a wing and threw it across the floor.

Animarus screeched and headed for the dog. RJ intercepted it before it could reach Kodiak. The Nekredum hovered above them and backed RJ toward one of the walls by slashing at RJ's nightstick with its wings.

Kodiak howled. The Nekredum attacked once more. The dog snarled and snapped at the Nekredum, who would move forward a step or two, then retreat.

RJ smashed his nightstick against the left wing of Animarus, but had little effect as the creature moved forward to corner the bodyguard. The air, whipped up by the wings of the creatures, stank of rotting flesh. RJ stopped backing up. From above Animarus came incessant chattering from the third Nekredum.

RJ charged. Animarus retreated, but in the direction of Elizabeth and Garrett. The leader of the Nekredum grabbed Elizabeth.

Kodiak's opponent also left the floor and flew to the opening in the castle roof.

Animarus drifted down, but remained above the floor. And now RJ spotted Elizabeth under its left wing. She smashed Animarus repeatedly in the face to no effect.

Animarus chattered and held Elizabeth out in front of itself like a child's doll, as if to drop her. Her punches continued. It ignored her blows. Then, the three Nekredum flew away, the one with the injured wing assisted by the other two.

They screeched as they left the castle. The sound echoed then diminished in the cold, dank air over Poenari.

Garrett groaned and rolled onto his left side which had caught the blow of the Nekredum. A spasm of pain blasted his temples, forcing him to a sitting position.

He rubbed his head and lunged for the hammer. The Nekredum gone, and his sister with them. RJ slumped against the wall, but when he saw the conscious Garrett, he stood.

"Elizabeth has been taken, Garrett."

Garrett shot to his feet, too fast. Blood drained from his head and he collapsed. He pounded the ground with his fists, but recovered again and, in one movement, charged at RJ. Max grabbed Garrett under his right arm and RJ did the same to his left.

"You had better be messing with me, Mr. Urban Myth!" screamed Garrett. "That's my sister!"

"Garrett—" Max tightened his grip on Garrett's arm.

"Shut up, Max! I blame you as well!" Garrett roared and screamed into the night air. He struggled, went limp, and sobbed. Max and RJ lowered him to the floor, where he continued to wail.

Kodiak padded over to Garrett. The dog laid down next to him and put his head on Garrett's shoulder.

The quiet broke when the elevator doors opened.

Doug and Alvin walked in supporting the bruised and battered bodies of Nate David and Benjamin Saperstein.

The Draculs — March 3 and 4

RJ unclipped the walkie-talkie from his belt. He inhaled and gagged, which sent him into a coughing fit. The stench of the Nekredum filled the room.

"Costea!" he shouted into the device. "Get up to the main floor immediately. Bring a medical field kit and my laptop."

Minutes later the elevator doors opened. Costea stepped out. He hustled to Max, but stopped when he saw Benjamin and Nate, a pair of walking contused flesh, open wounds, and clothing soaked in blood.

"G-g-good G-god." Costea's voice shuddered.

RJ took the laptop, and positioned it on a folding table used by the construction crew.

Dr. Margaret Barnes, her eyes almost slits from sleepiness, opened her mouth wide . . . and yawned.

"Jesus, RJ." Her voice drowsy. "It's REM time. What could you--"

"—Margaret," he interrupted. "We've had another visit."

She cleared her throat and ran a hand through her hair. RJ described the encounter. He tapped his finger on the laptop screen.

"RJ?" she asked.

"They have Elizabeth."

She sucked air in through her teeth.

"Leverage?"

"That's my guess," said RJ.

"*Leverage?*" shouted Garrett. Costea shined a penlight into Garrett's eyes looking for signs of concussion. He pushed away Costea's hand. "Leverage for what?"

"Mors Aeterna," said Margaret from the laptop. "And thanks for keeping me a secret, RJ."

"Who the hell are *you!?*" Garrett screamed at the laptop.

"Garrett—" Costea placed his hand on Garrett's shoulder, but he knocked it away.

Garrett saw Nate and Benjamin stumble into view.

"Please tell me your altercation involved human beings," said Garrett, staring at them as Costea went to work on their wounds.

"Only if they were wearing wolf costumes," stated Benjamin. Nate sat on the floor and drifted off. Benjamin, plenty of training with battlefield wounds, hooked up an IV and fluid bag, and he held it above Nate's head. He slipped a needle into Nate's arm.

"Nate needs to be taken to the clinic, Costea," said RJ. "If not the hospital in town. Benjamin?"

"Just a puncture wound," replied Benjamin. "Take Nate first. Give me that first aid kit. I think I can take care of this. I want to stay here."

"Clinic is closer. I'll take Nate," said Costea. "If I can get some help."

"I'll go," volunteered Alvin. "Let's get him to the elevator. We can put him in the back of one of the golf carts when we get to the valley floor."

"Wait," said RJ. "Clinic is out near the construction elevators."

RJ closed an eye and stared at Alvin with his open one.

"Costea drives," said RJ, pointing a finger in Alvin's face. "You, Alvin, literally ride shotgun. Capisce?"

Alvin nodded and helped Costea carry Nate to the elevator.

Margaret, still on Zoom, took the opportunity to make herself a cup of tea. RJ returned to the laptop.

"Sorry, Margaret," said RJ, noticing for the first time that Margaret's long red hair had been cut boyishly short.

"No problem, RJ," she said. "It's only the middle of the night, as I'm sure it is for you. Speaking of which, it looks like you've had quite the evening." Margaret's eyes settled on Benjamin. "You've had a very close encounter with the Nekredum, young man. You're lucky to be alive."

"Margaret," said RJ. "Benjamin was not at the castle with us just now."

"Where were you? Outside the castle?" Margaret moved closer to the screen.

"Yes ma'am," said Benjamin, who sat on a piece of broken stone large enough to act as a seat, and remained as still as he could while RJ sutured one of his wounds. "In Poenari Forest."

Before she could ask, he volunteered the information. "By three large, uh, Arctic wolves."

Garrett opened his mouth to protest the latest assault on common sense, but nothing came out.

"RJ, it appears your young charge has found the helpmates to the Nekredum, and unfortunately you have a pack of what are called WolfThane in your backyard." She delivered the information with the calm repose of a repairman discussing an issue with an automobile. "He mentions three? I am sure there are more."

She directed her attention to Benjamin.

"Did you fight with them only in the forest?"

"Mostly," he replied.

"Mostly?"

"At one point, the one Nate fought got onto his bike and was dragged out onto the valley floor."

"Oh . . . "

"Margaret?" RJ lifted an eyebrow.

"I'm afraid the WolfThane can now leave the forest as they wish. Nate has inadvertently broken the barrier that restricted them to their Lair and the forest by engaging them in the valley. They are free to roam now."

"The WolfThane—"

"*WolfThane?*" Garrett snapped, regaining his previous energy and attitude. "What? No vampires? This is Dracula's Castle, is it not? Jesus Christ, this is insane! And they're from the Arctic? Are you—"

"Mr. Astor!" She paused and composed herself. In a measured voice, she said, "Yes, I know who you are. I am Dr. Margaret Barnes, a longtime colleague of RJ Brancatelli."

"So what?" snapped Garrett. "Fallen angels? *Arctic* wolves closer to the equator than the Arctic? I'm not—"

"Yes, you are." Margaret broke in. "You're smack in the middle of it. You broke ground in a part of the world that should be left alone. You've awakened the emissaries of Lucifer and disturbed the Lair of their helpmates, the WolfThane. You've got a big problem, bucko."

Garrett sat next to Benjamin on the broken stone. RJ joined them. Kodiak, with Max at his side, sat on his haunches and lowered himself to his belly. Max remained standing.

"All right Dr. Barnes," Garrett replied. "I apologize. I've seen these Nekredum with my own eyes. What can I do to get my sister back?"

Margaret cracked her knuckles, one at a time. She then placed her right thumb and forefinger on the bridge of her nose and shook her head. She cleared her throat. Loudly.

"OK," said Margaret. "If you've seen the Nekredum, is it a stretch to imagine large wolves outside their habitat assisting them?"

RJ picked up the laptop and carried it over to Garrett.

"I suppose not."

"The Nekredum have all the leverage since taking Elizabeth. They want one thing only: Mors Aeterna, the sacred spike of the Draculs. It is somewhere on the premises of Poenari."

"Mors Aeterna?" asked Garrett, his voice rising. "Mors Aeterna. What is Mors Aeterna? *How much more—*" Garrett screamed the last few words.

"Garrett."

"Mr. Astor," said Margaret. "You either want my information and help, or you don't."

"Don't push it, Margaret," cautioned RJ.

"We don't have a lot of time, RJ," Margaret continued. "This spike, fashioned by Vlad's grandfather. Forged and blessed in holy water and used to force the Nekredum into prison." She stopped and slugged back some tea.

"I believe your construction broke the walls of their Hive and freed them, though from what I have read about the goings on at Poenari, Animarus could have been roaming the area since the first use of explosives months ago."

"Go on," said Garrett.

"As I told RJ, the Draculs, practitioners of black magic, cursed the Nekredum, and bound them to Poenari through Mors Aeterna. They cannot leave the castle's property line. Mors Aeterna is a Dracul talisman, but if the Nekredum physically possess it, they will have the ability to break the spell."

"Wait one moment," said Garrett. "Why would they want such a thing? For lack of a better term, it is kryptonite for them."

"Yes, it would be, if it were yielded by a descendant of the Draculs, but without one, the Nekredum can control it. Mors Aeterna is a powerful weapon. It will free them from their bonds to Poenari." She paused. "And unleash them on the world."

"What?" asked Garrett. "All *three* of them? So what? Kodiak handled one of them, easily I might add. I'm sure killing all three won't take much."

Margaret shifted in her chair.

"Oh no, Mr. Astor. It isn't that simple. You have only been introduced to their leader and two of his guards. Like the WolfThane, there are many, many more. Perhaps hibernating, but since you've opened their prison, that hibernation will end soon. There will be thousands of those winged Spawn of Lucifer. And you have but one Kodiak."

Margaret's countenance dimmed.

"Listen to me carefully. If the Nekredum gain Mors Aeterna and their army comes out of hibernation, they will return to their former strength. Lucifer himself will be summoned by Animarus, and initiate the Second Coming. Armageddon."

"This is ridiculous," snorted Garrett.

"Really? Looking around at our modern world, I have to say that now is the perfect time for the Prince of Darkness to emerge. He failed in the eighth century because Christianity was so powerful. He failed again in the fourteenth century, because the Orthodox Draculs fought his minions and drove them into what would have been eternal confinement . . . if not for you."

She swallowed her tea.

"And not just you. I understand this whole DracuLAND concept came from your sister? Is that true?"

No answer from Garrett.

"Christianity is weak now. Its global leadership and mission is not what it has been, and that descent has been going on incrementally for decades. You *and* Elizabeth, in your zeal and ambition and despite warnings, have freed the Nekredum and their helpmates, the WolfThane."

"I'm sorry, Dr. Barnes, but there's a flaw in your logic," said Garrett, now rising up from his stone seat.

"Really?" she chided. "And what would that be, Mr. Astor?"

"If I'm following this, Mors Aeterna holds sway over these so-called forces of evil through a Dracul. There are no more descendants of the Draculs. The last one died in the 1700s. The curse should be broken."

"Yes," said Margaret. "That is correct. The curse should be broken, and the Nekredum should be wreaking havoc on the world by now, but they are not."

RJ touched the side of his face. A wound continued to bleed. He pushed himself to get in front of Garrett.

"So, there is a Dracul?" asked RJ.

"Yes," said Margaret. "There must be, or Garrett would be correct."

"Where?"

"It's a thin thread, RJ."

"Margaret, you could have gotten to this sooner."

"Yes, and you could have kept your promise to not bring me into this."

"Apologies all around, but don't mess with us."

"I'm not," she said, fatigue entering her voice. "It's a long shot, RJ. And someone is going to have to get on a plane to London, if I'm correct."

"Cut to it, Margaret."

"All right, genealogy points to a private investigator in London named Evan English. Does anyone get the joke?"

"An anagram of Van Helsing," said Garrett. "Sort of."

"Yes. A several-generations offspring of a bastard child of Vlad the Impaler. Still qualifies as a descendent."

RJ closed an eye and moved closer to the screen.

"Any other questions?" asked Margaret. "And I'm still verifying English's existence and lineage."

"Yes," said Garrett. "What happens if Evan English is not a Dracul?"

"Then the Nekredum and the WolfThane will kill everyone in Poenari. The Nekredum will find Mors Aeterna and summon Lucifer. Oh, and end the Age of Man."

"I think you should tell them everything, Margaret," said RJ, his tone dropping to a somber register. "Uh, ending the Age of Man aside."

"Given they have Elizabeth," said Margaret, equally composed, "is that such a good idea at this point?"

"Yes," said RJ.

Margaret inhaled.

"Out with it, Dr. Barnes."

"As you wish, Mr. Astor," she said. Margaret, her tone grave, addressed all of them. "The Nekredum increase their numbers by spawning. I am sure there is an army close to completion in their Hive."

"Is that all?" asked Garrett. "If so, then denying them Mors Aeterna is still the key."

"No, that is not all. They take human hosts to assist in the spawning," said Margaret, again taking her time. "And if any of you are captured, they will do just that."

"Then . . . Elizabeth . . ." Garrett couldn't finish.

"Yes, Mr. Astor. Elizabeth."

The WolfThane — March 3 and 4

Costea and Alvin loaded Nate into the golf cart's back bench seat. Costea pulled himself into the driver's side. Alvin, gun in his right hand, served as passenger and shotgun.

They drove to a construction trailer, now outfitted as an emergency room clinic. The power surged and machines blipped on. Alvin and Costea placed Nate in the care of the night shift.

An admitting nurse, a beautiful black-haired woman no older than 25, greeted them. She called for assistance. A gurney-pushing orderly arrived, and with the assistance of the admitting nurse, helped Nate onto the gurney. She took his vitals and gave the information to a doctor who appeared soon after.

"If Nate saw who admitted him, he'd come to," said Alvin, admiring the woman as she closed the hospital curtain around Nate's gurney.

"F-O-G," said Costea.

"Fog?"

"Friend of Garrett's." replied Costea, motioning toward the hospital curtain. "He's only made a few hires, but they all are attractive women. He's been nicknamed 'Hef' by the staff. You remember Hugh Hefner?"

"Uh, yes," said Alvin. "Vaguely?"

"Hah!" Costea laughed. "Vaguely? Not a chance."

Alvin grunted as another power surge flickered the overheads. He released the safety on his sidearm.

"Let's get back to the castle," said Costea.

"Yes, I think that's a good idea."

Costea headed for the door, but Alvin's strong right arm thudded up against Costea's chest preventing him from going further.

"I'm first," he said, his face inches from Costea's. "Do not leave this building until I'm in the cart. Drive faster since we don't have to worry about Nate. Some*thing* is out there."

Costea swallowed.

"What's out there?"

"Given the last few hours," said Alvin. "You know what's out there. Move when I tell you to move. Got it?"

"Ye-es."

Alvin opened the door, jumped the stairs, and vaulted into the cart.

Outside it smelled as it did in the castle, the iron taste of blood in the air.

"Move!"

Costea threw himself out the door and into the cart. Alvin had already turned the key to engage the motor. Costea stomped on the pedal and they were off, the safety of the construction elevator less than a couple minutes away. Yet another power surge killed the lights for a second. They flickered back on, weak.

The blood-red wolf howled.

Four WolfThane tore past their leader and closed in on Alvin and Costea. The golf cart a minute from the elevators. The LED lights of its keypad glowed crimson.

Doug heard Kodiak's growling from across the main room of the castle. He grabbed his sidearm and night-vision goggles.

"Kode-yak!" shouted Doug. The dog shot past him on the way to the construction elevators.

Kodiak pressed the down button with his nose and the door opened. The dog ran inside so quickly that Doug had to lunge for the opening before the door shut. Doug's night-vision goggles fell out of his hands, landed in the hallway.

Can't take the time to retrieve them.

The elevator opened onto the valley floor.

The dog left a vapor trail. Doug sprinted after him, and drew his sidearm. He spotted the cart, an inky black shape moving against the horizon.

A growling and snarling in the distance grew loud.

The golf cart slammed into a wolf with an Akita-like white head and black body. It glanced off the side of the cart and crashed to the ground, but gained its footing and returned to a dead sprint along the passenger side of the vehicle.

The white-headed wolf threw itself once more at the cart.

The cart fishtailed and went up on two wheels where it spun in a circle before landing, facing the opposite direction from the elevators.

Costea grabbed the green metal tool kit from under his seat and swung it in the direction of the white-headed wolf. It clipped the tip of the wolf's nose, giving Costea enough time to shove his foot down on the accelerator and turn the cart in a wide circle back toward the elevators.

The white-headed wolf shook off the blow and ran after the cart. It leaped onto the back seat and sank its teeth into the right arm of Costea, who dropped the toolbox. The wolf and Costea fell out of the cart and landed on the ground.

Alvin reached with his left foot and slammed on the brakes. The cart fishtailed again and stopped. Costea lay on his side, his right arm at an odd angle, and right shoulder dislocated. He looked up to see a pair of yellow-green eyes advancing on him. Two other pairs waited behind. They were joined by the blood-red wolf, his eyes glowing red in the dark.

Costea pulled himself up to a sitting position with his left arm.

"Come on!" shouted Costea. "Come meet your fate!"

The white-headed wolf coiled to spring. Costea screamed as it leaped into the air. Kodiak flew from behind the golf cart, met the wolf in midair, and knocked it down at the height of its jump. He clamped down on the wolf's neck and flung it away from Costea. The white-headed wolf got to all fours, shook itself, and snapped at Kodiak. Fur flew as their bodies slammed together. A yelp followed by sinew ripping and the crack of bone.

Dog and wolf separated. The white-headed wolf had an open wound near its jawline, and limped as it backed up. Kodiak hadn't escaped unharmed. Several small cuts and gashes on his left shoulder bled. The two squared off.

The other WolfThane closed to attack Alvin. He trained his gun on the glowing yellow-green eyes. He squeezed the trigger, but the wolves vanished before he landed a shot.

Doug, within twenty yards of the cart, witnessed Kodiak's take down of the white-headed wolf.

He also noticed the WolfThane behind the white-headed one disappeared, except the blood-red wolf.

A guttural howl from the blood-red wolf as it stalked toward the battle.

The blood-red wolf joined the white-headed one. They stood in tandem in front of Kodiak, who, if anything, inched closer to them.

Kodiak howled and charged the WolfThane. He threw both to the side when he slammed his body first against the blood-red one and then against the white-headed wolf. The dog turned his attention to the base of the foothill behind the castle. Kodiak sprinted to the safety of the Carpathians, but the blood-red one charged and locked its jaw on Kodiak's back leg.

Kodiak spun and threw the wolf across the ground. It landed in a heap, got up, and charged again. The two bumped chests. Kodiak clamped down on his opponent's neck.

The blood-red wolf broke the grip. Kodiak slammed into it before the wolf could regain its feet, and knocked it down once more. The dog ran to the forest.

The blood-red and white-headed WolfThane followed.

Doug arrived and spotted Costea lying on the ground several feet from the cart. He knelt to examine him but then heard the growling and snarling of the WolfThane. Alvin ran up and joined his compatriot. The growling had grown louder.

Doug pointed east.

"Nine o'clock," he said. "At least one."

Doug turned in the direction of the growling and held the sidearm straight in front of him. Sweat dripped into his eyes. Alvin bumped into him with his back.

"Three o'clock," said Alvin. "Trying to outflank us."

"Costea, can you run?"

"Absolutely, can you call for help?"

"Called from the elevator. Max and RJ are on their way," said Doug. "They'll be locked and loaded to cover us as we make our way back. Now, get up and face the direction of the elevators."

"They'll be ready," Doug whispered. "Two seconds after Costea starts, we shoot and run."

The elevator doors, no more than twenty yards away, opened.

"Move!"

Costea sprinted toward the elevator.

"One! Two!" Alvin and Doug emptied their clips in the directions of their adversaries.

And ran.

The elevator landed. Behind a barricade of folding tables, RJ and Max trained long-range rifles out into the black confines of the valley floor.

"No lights," said RJ. "Keep your eyes trained low to the ground. My guess, given the howls, we're about to meet our first wolf. They'll be on all fours."

Max wiped his eyes, and stretched his neck.

The darkness filled with the sounds of the WolfThane. Painful but angry. Shots fired from the guns of Alvin and Doug. From the pitch black ran bloody Costea. He slid into the elevator and crashed against the barricade.

"Close the bloody elevator door now!" screamed Doug. "Don't let them in behind us!" He and Alvin vaulted the rising lower door. Doug smacked his head on the top door as it lowered. Alvin, with Doug splayed over him, tumbled into the elevator.

Alvin, his back against the table, trained his weapon on the narrowing door.

Before the doors could shut completely, the head of the silver wolf appeared at the narrowing opening. Several shots fired by Alvin found their mark, but the wolf, its face a blood-soaked mask, only retreated when the doors slammed shut.

"Kodiak?!" screamed Max.

"Ran into the forest at the base of the hill," said Costea. "WolfThane in pursuit."

RJ picked up his radio mic and hailed Garrett.

"Garrett! Max and I have Alvin, Doug, and Costea. Meet us at the elevator. Check on Benjamin. See if there's anyone to tend to them."

"What are you going to do?" Garrett yelled into the mic.

"We're going after Kodiak. He headed into the foothills."

"What? What is Kodiak running from?"

"The Arctic WolfThane. The ones that don't exist."

The elevator doors opened on the main floor. Benjamin limped over, and with Alvin's help, dragged out Doug.

"Let's get to the parking lot," said Max. "Kodiak would probably go there in order to expose his adversary in the open."

"Adversaries," said RJ.

Kodiak sprinted into the wooded area behind Poenari Castle, on the north side just past the sheer drop. He ran up and over a sliver of foothill and onto the part of the Carpathians in front of the castle. He shot down toward the parking lot, crossing over the switchbacks, his breath now coming in short bursts. Wounded and exhausted, he halted and listened for his pursuers.

Stillness descended. Kodiak ran to a bright source of light in the middle of the lot. The only sound from the dog's footfalls.

Every corner of the parking lot under marker lamps, and unlike the back valley, the power remained on in the front.

Kodiak stood on all fours, his stare fixed on the trees at the base of the foothill.

The blood-red and the white-headed WolfThane flew down the hillside toward the parking lot, Kodiak's scent drawing them. It hung on the air, the dog's smell mixed with blood, canine and lupine. The WolfThane ignored their wounds. Blood marked their trail as they ran.

The white-headed wolf's breaths came out raspy. Blood had entered its lungs, one punctured when Kodiak broke its ribs. It lifted its snout into the night air and drew in the scent. The dog had stopped. The wolf's yellow-green eyes peered out from the trees and onto the flat area in front of the foothill. The bright light hurt its eyes. It walked from the cover of the forest and padded into the lot.

Kodiak charged head first into the contused side of the white-headed wolf, breaking several more ribs. The wolf howled and spat blood from its mouth. It collapsed onto its side and slowly crawled back to the hillside.

The blood-red wolf moved out of the forest. It halted at the edge and scanned the lot.

It saw Kodiak sitting in a pool of light. As the blood-red wolf advanced, two others, the gray and the mottled, stalked out of the forest. They were joined by the silver wolf The four of them slowed to a predatory walk as they closed in on the dog, who vacated the pool of light under the marker.

Kodiak gave ground, a bloody trail oozing from his wounds. The deep bites over his eyes also bled. A gash in his left hindquarters pulsed blood, which spread across the blacktop in front of him as he retreated.

The blood-red wolf moved to the front of the pack. Kodiak backed away to where the highway exit ramp entered the parking lot. His breathing shallow. He heard his own noisy, ragged gasps for air. The dog's right front paw, numb.

The four WolfThane, no more than ten yards from Kodiak, spread out into a phalanx, with the blood-red one in the front. The three smaller WolfThane stopped, and the blood-red one separated itself further from the pack.

Kodiak leaned back, ready to strike.

As did the blood-red wolf.

The blood-red wolf emitted a low, guttural sound of carnage and death. Kodiak responded with a growl of equal fury. The ground vibrated with sounds not heard in centuries.

The two advanced toward each other.

Kodiak charged. The dog slammed into the wolf's chest, throwing it back several yards.

The wolf snorted and jumped. Kodiak reared back and sprang. They collided in mid-air and both came down, their mouths clamped on the other's neck. Two colors of blood, one red and one black, spattered across the parking lot, discoloring the painted white stripes.

Kodiak yanked the wolf's head to the right and to the left several times to break its neck, but the attempts failed when it pulled its head under the dog's jaw and whipped it back up again, loosening Kodiak's grip enough for it to get free. Both reared up on their hind legs and charged again.

Kodiak, his strength ebbing, struck an enormous blow under the wolf's jaw. He heard a tear of sinew, but not the break of bone. The wolf lifted its head and, from its nose, blew a spray of black fluid and tissue into the air. The wolf shook its great head and snapped at Kodiak to show its jaw had not broken.

Kodiak retreated, his breathing more uneven and coming in longer intervals.

The three other WolfThane, sensing the kill, approached their leader. A few of them howled at Kodiak, who managed to return their cries with a deep and piercing growl. They all, save the blood-red wolf, halted their advance.

The two opponents again faced each other straight on. Kodiak prepared for the battle of his life.

The blood-red wolf sprang.

The Brutal Confrontation: The Blood-red Wolf and Kodiak — March 4

Nikolai Asilimov's vehicle squealed onto the lot. His headlights washed the battlefield, illuminating the confrontation.

He had returned to Poenari after a night out in Curtea de Argeş. Nikolai, too drunk to be driving, spotted the entrance to the lot at the last moment, and cut his wheel to the left, spraying gravel onto the pack of WolfThane, which broke ranks.

The blood-red wolf hung in the air, halfway to finishing off the badly wounded Kodiak, when Nikolai entered the lot and lost control of the car. The wolf completed its leap. Kodiak, small below the wolf opened its jaws, and aimed at the dog's defenseless neck.

Kodiak sat back on his haunches, unable to respond. The blood-red wolf's three companions halted their retreat from the gravel spray and returned to pounce as their leader connected with the dog's neck.

Nikolai had cut the wheel so sharply the car skidded more than 360 degrees on the blacktop. He saw the blurred shapes of Kodiak and a wolf. The two disappeared out of view as the car spun, but reappeared and again vanished. He felt a tremendous thud on the side of the car. His brake lights bathed Kodiak in red. Headlights illuminated the silhouettes of the three smaller WolfThane running along the perimeter of the parking lot. The car skidded to a stop. Nikolai's body slammed into the steering wheel and he smacked his head against the pad that activated the horn. The horn blared and Nikolai's head slipped off the pad and he fell over into the passenger seat.

Nikolai ended the battle between the WolfThane and Kodiak. In the dishwater gray of the new morning, the WolfThane dragged something with them as they trotted into the trees at the base of the foothill.

Max and RJ hurtled down to the parking lot. They scoured the area for activity. In the distance RJ spotted the WolfThane as they disappeared into the foothills.

"We're too late," said RJ.

"Maybe not," said Max. "Look over there."

RJ saw what Max pointed to, Nikolai's car in the far corner.

"There's Nikolai's car . . . and something else," said RJ. Max shouted. He and RJ sprinted off in the direction of the vehicle.

The glare of sunshine woke him. The warm Romanian sun heated the interior of the car. Nikolai, groggy, recalled pulling off the road too fast and hitting something. A series of blurry images ran through his head, then vanished.

Nikolai shook his head to clear it. DracuLAND work crews were vigilant about keeping the lot clear of deliveries, so he could not have hit any supplies. He took in a breath and exhaled.

He pulled himself out of his seat, and shoved open the door. His head spun. He reached for and felt a bump on his forehead. Nikolai stumbled from the car and walked toward the construction elevators, thinking only of his mattress.

The bottom of his right shoe landed on some gum. He knelt to remove the offending material, and noticed a red discoloration on one of the white stripes on the lot. Nikolai followed a stream of blood to the prone body of a golden mass of fur.

"Kode-yak!" he shouted, as he came upon the dog.

He crouched over Kodiak.

"What the—? Oh, no. I couldn't have hit him. No. No. No," Nikolai said, repeating the word "no" several more times. Behind him he heard the sound of running. More than one person, the staccato sound of their feet reverberated through the parking lot.

Max pushed Nikolai aside. He sprinted ahead of RJ, directly to Kodiak. He dropped to his knees and reached out his hands toward the motionless dog. A breeze rustled Kodiak's fur.

Max rocked as he knelt, holding the dog's head in his hands. His suit pants tore from the obsessive back-and-forth on his knees. Max cried in front of the others, unashamed.

"Oh, Kode-yak. I'm so, so sorry," Nikolai said mournfully. Max buried his head in the dog's right side, abruptly stopped, and raised his head in the direction of Nikolai.

"This is your fault, you drunken slob!" Max shouted at Nikolai. He got to his feet, and grabbed Nikolai's throat.

"Max!" yelled RJ, and broke the grip, but Max didn't back off. He swung at RJ, who ducked the punch and kicked Max's legs out from under him. Max hit the pavement next to Kodiak and laid his head down on the dog's chest.

And he felt, and heard, the dog's weak, but consistent, heartbeat. He fumbled for his cellphone, and hit the code for the construction site's infirmary.

Several rings. Max paced in a short circle, digging his shoes into the blacktop, and mumbling, "Come on. Come on. Come on."

"Yes, who is this?" asked the attendant.

"Max Capitanou."

"Mr. Capitanou! What is it, sir?" asked the attendant, sensing the urgency.

"We have an emergency!" yelled Max into the phone. "What is our vet's name? Actually, I don't care what it is. Get him here right away. I'm in the parking lot of the castle."

"Dr. Lapescu," said the attendant. "Is it one of the stray dogs?"

"Shut up and listen," snapped Max. "Tell Dr. Lapescu to meet us here and stabilize the dog, Kodiak. Then call the hospital in Curtea de Argeş, and tell them to prepare for an emergency."

"For the dog?"

"Yes, for the dog! Don't care what it costs."

"Of course. Hold on a moment." She put down the phone and called for the doctor, relaying the information. She picked up the handset again and said, "OK, done. Been a busy night. They brought Nate in a little while ago. I think he's going to be all right, but he's heavily sedated. Can you give me an idea of what's going on? Dr. Lapescu will want to know so that he can be prepared."

"You just need to know it's Kodiak and he's badly hurt. Get our emergency vehicle and personnel out here to the parking lot. We need to get Kodiak medical attention now!"

Benjamin and Doug rushed from the elevator to get a better look at the dog.

"Is he alive?" asked Benjamin, ignoring his ankle pain.

Doug, sutures covering both forearms and his face a patchwork of purple and green, after his collision with the elevator doors and folding table barricades, stepped toward Max, who again held Kodiak.

"Barely," said Max, his voice cracking.

A vehicle entered the lot, and Max turned to see the construction site's Medical Emergency Services van speeding toward them. Dr. Lapescu, an anorexic-looking man of forty jumped from the passenger seat. He and two EMTs worked to stabilize Kodiak. They rolled the dog onto a stretcher. Max didn't make it easy, holding Kodiak's head in his arms.

"I'm riding with the dog," said Max, and he boarded the back of the MES van. Doug, despite his condition, grabbed Max by the wrist.

"I'll go," said Doug, through swollen lips. "This is my fault. I screwed up getting down to help Alvin and Costea. I lost my night vision goggles in front of the elevator. They might have helped. I was shooting blind. You need to stay here and meet with Garrett, sooner rather than later."

"All right." agreed Max. "But you—"

"As soon as I know *anything*," said Doug, and he held up his cellphone.

"Max, I think it's a good idea that Doug goes to the hospital with Kodiak. He can be looked at by a doctor who can get him into better shape than we can here."

Max and the others headed off to the castle as the van drove off with Kodiak and Doug. Max looked down at the blood on the parking lot, and turned toward RJ and Benjamin.

"We've already lost Nate and Costea for now. Doug needs more serious care than he's gotten so far," he said. "If Kodiak is so injured—or even worse—that he can't help us, we're in serious trouble, RJ."

"We passed serious trouble yesterday, Max."

Doubting Garrett — March 5

In the castle's lower level, Garrett sat behind the folding table he used as his office desk. Up all night, he rubbed his eyebrows and temples to ward off fatigue. Garrett had not been at the parking lot to observe the aftermath of Kodiak's encounter with the WolfThane.

"Tell me about the dog," he said. Max, Benjamin, Oskar, and RJ had gathered in Garrett's office to run through the evening.

"We won't know for a while," RJ responded. "Doug is at the hospital. He'll call when he hears something."

"Garrett," said Max. "I've been giving it a lot of thought." He rubbed his hands together as if hesitant to vocalize it. "I think we have to bring in the authorities."

"We've gone over this, Max. The authorities will shut down site construction if I let them on site," said Garrett, and he pointed his index finger at Max and then waved it. "No. Not going to happen."

RJ coughed.

"What is it?" snapped Garrett.

"Garrett, we don't have the manpower or firepower to handle the Nekredum and now the WolfThane." He shot out of his chair and crossed the floor to Garrett's desk. "Stop looking for a rational explanation, or for this to go away!"

"RJ—"

"We have the Nekredum martialing their forces and once done, they will be on us in a few days. Their helpmates, the WolfThane, have suffered injury, but not been killed. They'll be back before Kodiak is healthy."

"We cannot call the authorities. End of debate."

"If we don't do something, Garrett, we're all going to be dead in a few days! That means the Nekredum will be free to find Mors Aeterna, and you know what *that* means."

Garrett sat, and pressed his lips together.

"Get Dr. Barnes on Zoom," he said between tight lips.

"What?" snapped RJ. He leaned across Garrett's desk and into his face.

"I have to see if there are any other options before we call the authorities," said Garrett, who refused to back away from RJ.

"We're going to need the *military*, Garrett." RJ growled.

"I'm not going to ask politely again, RJ."

Garrett glared at RJ as he picked up the laptop and opened the Zoom app. Margaret's face, once again sans makeup, appeared on the screen.

"I don't believe I have anything new, RJ," she said and reached forward to shut off her computer.

"Margaret, this is Garrett Astor. Please don't hang up."

"Make it worth my while, Mr. Astor."

Garrett, caught off balance by Margaret's comment, hesitated.

"Hurry up, Mr. Astor," she said.

"I need to know if there's any way to rid DracuLAND of what you call Nekredum and WolfThane, without killing the leader of the Nekredum."

"No," she deadpanned.

"No?" he shouted. "No? That's it? I thought you were some expert in this field of . . . just what in hell is your field, *doctor* Barnes?" Garrett gestured air quotes, the universal sign for I don't really believe you.

"Mythocology," she replied.

"Is that an actual science?" Before Margaret could answer, Garrett went on. "Where do you get a degree in mythocology? Night school? Hah! That's funny, isn't it? Night school! You can study with the rest of the undead."

"Mr. Astor, if you want my help, you're going about it in an odd way."

Garrett paced back and forth behind his desk, leaving and reentering Margaret's field of vision.

"Did you attend with Bela and Boris?" chided Garrett. "Wait. No that's too easy. How about Freddie and Jason? More modern day?"

"Mr. Astor!" She sounded indignant when she reached for the keyboard again.

"No. No, hold on, you're more of a classical person. I'm going to guess you were there with Caligula, Blackbeard, and Jack the Ripper. Or, maybe the occasional fictional good guy showed up to guest lecture, like, well, Van Helsing! Yes, Van Helsing! Now, wouldn't that have been an interesting semester and so appropriate for DracuLAND!"

Margaret pulled her hand back from the keyboard's power button. She looked to her right where another computer sat, and typed a few phrases into a search window.

"*Well*, Dr. Barnes?" asked Garrett. Red colored his cheeks, not from embarrassment, but from exertion.

"Garrett, I think that's enough," said Max, who checked his phone as often as a teenage girl, anxious for updates on Kodiak. "You've made your point."

Margaret turned back to the computer with the Zoom feed. She folded her hands in front of her and cracked the knuckles of her right hand.

"Quite a performance, Mr. Astor," she said, and addressed RJ. "How soon can you get to London, RJ?"

"Yes, you mentioned Evan English," said RJ. "It's just not the time for me to be away, hell for any of us to be away from Poenari."

"You need to find that Evan English I mentioned and bring him back to Poenari, and you need to do it in the next three days. I've verified his lineage as a Dracul as much as I can."

"RJ?" asked Garrett.

"Margaret," said RJ. "Is this really the only option?"

"Yes, RJ. If you remain at Poenari, in a few days you will be facing thousands of Nekredum, not three." She took a breath. "And if you can find and bring back this *possible* descendent of the Draculs, there is a slim chance you can save Elizabeth."

"How slim?" asked Garrett, his voice breaking on the question.

"Slim."

The First Meeting with Evan English — March 5

RJ trotted down the stairs of Astor Holdings' private jet, just landed at London City Airport. He jumped into a cab and handed the driver the address of 23A High Street, last known office of one Evan English, Private Investigator. They took off for Wandsworth. As they got closer to that part of town, streetlights became less efficient, if they worked at all. Soon only the cab's headlamps provided illumination on the pothole-damaged streets.

The driver twitched in his seat.

"Around here, mate?" he asked.

"You tell me," RJ responded.

"As close as I can figger," volunteered the driver.

"Anywhere then."

RJ paid and exited the car. He searched the street for a doorway or curb marker for 23A. He walked up and down the uneven sidewalk, the European numbering system providing no help. RJ spotted a doorway labeled 19.

Nineteen? I must be close.

The next doorway read 162. He searched the winding street as he approached the top of a hill. RJ patted his nightstick. He reached into his shoulder holster and felt the reassuring grip of Louise.

The apartments and retail shops turned bleaker and more careworn as he trudged on. A flickering streetlamp burned out as he passed under it. RJ tightened his grip around the gun.

RJ heard a scraping noise . . . behind him.

Then a moan, raspy and weary. RJ spun around on his left heel. Nothing.

A thud as something hit the pavement.

In his pants pocket RJ felt for a key ring, knowing he had looped in a Maglite. He pulled it out, switched it on, and turned in a circle as the spotlight swept the cobblestones. The beam landed on a coat sprawled out on the curb. The lumpy garment covered something.

The shape rose, and with a great effort, managed to pull itself into a hunched-over seated position on the sidewalk.

The shape made a sudden movement with one of its appendages and threw something across the sidewalk. It smashed against a crumbling brick wall and bits and pieces of glass caromed into the air.

"Daaammmmmnnnn," slurred a voice. "That bottle still held a swallow or two."

The coat, propped up like a tent, sat and faced RJ. Rheumy eyes blinked from the darkness. RJ pulled Louise from the holster and pointed it, along with the flashlight, in the shape's direction.

"What the heck?" came a voice. "Mister, put that flashlight away. You might blind somebody."

"You're already blind drunk."

RJ lowered the flashlight. It illuminated the gun in his hand.

"Hang on," the shape continued, and struggled to its feet. The coat dropped to its shoulders and revealed a man, who tottered. "Ma'am, put that gun away. You might shoot me. Oh! Sorry, sir. Apologies for the ma'am stuff. It is dark."

RJ continued to point the gun at the unsteady person now standing in front of him.

"Tell me where 23A is, and I'll put the gun away."

"23A?"

"Yes. Do you live around here? You obviously drink around here."

The man lifted his right arm and waved a hand in RJ's direction. He laughed a jagged and drunk laugh, which led to a coughing fit. He spat and cleared his throat.

"That's funny. I like that. You obviously drink around here. Hah! Are you always this funny?"

"No." The words had a sobering effect on the man.

"You're looking for private investigator Evan English, I take it?"

RJ lowered the gun, but raised it again when the man lurched forward. He thrust out his right hand.

"I'm Evan's partner, Aloysius Sloan. You may call me Al. Very pleased to meet you, Mister—"

He swayed, closed his eyes, belched, and fell forward onto his nose, oblivious to the crack of bone and subsequent pain that would greet him after he regained consciousness.

RJ dropped the gun into its holster. He leaned over and searched Aloysius Sloan's ragged topcoat, pulling out several weeks' worth of lottery tickets.

"Do they actually call them 'sweepstakes' tickets here?" RJ mumbled the question as he searched.

He put his hand in an inside pocket and came across a set of keys. He directed the flashlight toward the door of a building with a badly damaged façade. After sweeping a few nearby buildings the narrow beam picked up "23A" over a warped wooden door, more graffiti than veneer.

RJ worked through the keys until he discovered the correct one. With the aid of the Maglite's beam, he unlocked and opened the door.

RJ found a light switch and pushed it to the "on" position. A few feeble overheads flickered and buzzed. The fluorescents revealed a one-room office that, judging by the bricked-up window, used to be a storefront. A distressed wood desk sat against the far wall, the top of it a mess covered by papers, a rotary phone with its handset off its cradle, an empty "In" basket, and a collection of paper cups and Styrofoam take-out containers.

He found a clean cup and walked to the water cooler.

No water.

He spotted a bathroom to his right. RJ took a deep breath, ran in, and filled the cup. Rusty water.

RJ propped the front door open with a chunk of fallen brick from the wall, and stepped outside. He walked to the comatose Aloysius Sloan, still face down. RJ shoved him over onto his back and doused him.

Aloysius coughed spasmodically as he inhaled. He retched and brought the upper half of his body to a sitting position.

"Let's go, Mr. Sloan."

"Leave me alone." He spat more of the water and rolled back onto his face, which nudged his broken nose. He shot up to a kneeling position with his hands over his face and howled.

Aloysius Sloan was awake, and RJ had his attention.

"All right. I'm about ready to call a taxi and get out of this godforsaken neighborhood. Last chance. You don't know who I am, but I'm a possible paying customer. I don't think you've had one of those for a while . . . judging by your palatial office."

Sloan pushed himself from the pavement and gained his feet, unsteady again. He squinted in RJ's direction.

"As I said, funny," said Sloan. "Now bugger off."

RJ, though loath to do it to drunks, jacked Sloan up against one of the walls in need of a fresh coat of paint. He had him by the throat.

"Where's your partner, Sloan?" RJ demanded. "Where's Evan English? Don't screw with me. I'm out of time and somewhat short on patience, or is it the other way around?"

Sloan felt the crackle of sinew as RJ brought his hands up and adjusted the broken nose. Sloan slipped back into unconsciousness. RJ let him drop to the ground and dragged him inside. He deposited him on the ragged carpet.

RJ took a wooden desk chair which rolled on unsteady casters and pulled it up in front of the horizontal Sloan. He gathered up some of the desktop trash. Every thirty seconds RJ tossed a paper cup or crumpled paper on the unconscious man's forehead. Sloan roused, grunted, and pulled himself into a sitting position. He looked at RJ, who wadded up another projectile.

"I'm going to need a cup of tea," said Sloan, squeaking out a request. "Oh, and regarding the paying customer bit, I don't do runaways. Lousy hours. And just what is *your* name?"

"My name is RJ Brancatelli, Mr. Sloan. My boss is Elizabeth Astor, the New York City real estate developer. Remember that name. After I explain my case, tea isn't going to help."

They sat in an all-night café for an hour. After a few cups of black tea, Sloan had gotten as sober as a functional alcoholic can get.

"Evan said Istanbul," volunteered Sloan. "He left yesterday. Did mention he would not be gone long, though Evan's a little lax with time management."

Before RJ could interrupt, Sloan went on.

"But are you joking about this DracuLAND place?" he asked. "I would say one of my friends cooked up this elaborate scheme, but I lost the last one of those two years ago."

"Not a joke. There's too much evidence to support it, including these two eyes. And, mostly, I'm concerned for Elizabeth. She might be dead already."

"What's the evidence? A few construction workers walk off a job in a former Eastern Bloc country's theme park construction site? A dog gets set upon by animals in the Carpathians? That's nothing."

RJ reached into his pocket and pulled one of Margaret's research photos of the Nekredum from it. He placed the photo on the table and slid it to Sloan. He placed another photo in front of him, this time of the WolfThane. Sloan looked them both over and turned his attention to the street in front of the cafe.

"I'll assume you're not a Photoshop expert?" he asked.

RJ looked right at Sloan. The detective cleared his throat and sipped more tea. He returned the stare.

"Mr. Sloan, can we cut the crap? I just need to know where your partner is. I don't need to convince you of anything."

"I told you. Istanbul."

"It's a big city, Mr. Sloan."

"Aloysius or Al, if you wouldn't mind," said Sloan. "Especially since we're getting to be friends, and so quickly I might add."

RJ again locked his gaze onto Sloan.

"Mr. Sloan. I have to say, for a man who, I presume, has no clients or prospects, you don't seem to be in a position to turn down money. You know more than you're saying. I'm offering you some quick cash for information."

"I reserve the right to refuse service to anyone. Isn't that what you Americans say?" asked Sloan. "But let me see the cash."

"If you didn't look so wretched, *that* would be funny."

"Wretched? Whatever do you mean?"

RJ drained his coffee cup and stood. He put the two photos back into his pocket and pulled out an envelope. He leaned forward on the café table, both hands pressed into the veneer, the envelope crushed under his left hand.

"Don't be dense. You know what I mean."

Aloysius Sloan pushed his chair forward. He tucked his chin, rubbed his thick eyebrows, and moved his hands around his teacup. His eyes, red-rimmed, were fixed on RJ.

"How much?" whispered Sloan.

"I'll give you $5000 US dollars, but I have to know the exact location of your partner." RJ pressed his left hand down harder.

For the first time since they met, RJ felt off-balance, his aggressive posture gone. He stood in front of the man across the table. Sloan appeared to be a hapless drunk, and RJ's body language softened in defeat.

"Are you going to help me or not, Mr. Sloan?"

Sloan stared into his teacup. Without looking up, he spoke.

"I can tell you where Evan is and what he's up to, but let's just say, Mr. Brancatelli, that he's attempting to bury the very past about which you speak. You *may* find him to be a willing traveling partner to Romania. Let me emphasize *may*."

"You let me concern myself with Evan's willingness or lack thereof," said RJ. He picked up the envelope. "Just tell me where he is in Istanbul. I have three days at most to get him back to Poenari."

"All right, but you've been cautioned," said Sloan. "Evan will be at the Fatih Mosque tomorrow night. Located in the fundamentalist section of town."

"What time? And why there?" probed RJ, as he handed the cash to Sloan, but RJ kept his grip on the envelope.

"He'll be there in the evening, in the Türbe of Mehmet the Second. He's breaking in to steal the head of Vlad the Impaler."

RJ shook his head like a wet dog.

"You and your mythocologist are correct," replied Sloan. "Evan English is a descendant of the Draculs. He wants to get his ancestor's skull back from Mehmet the Second's tomb. Vlad Dracul has been, as Evan states, 'a prisoner of the Ottomans since 1477, which will not stand.'"

"Thank you, Mr. Sloan," said RJ as he released the cash from his hand. "You had better be right."

"Oh? Or what? You'll come track me down again?"

RJ stood and pressed both hands into the table as he leaned directly into Aloysius Sloan's now-sober face.

"If you are not correct, Mr. Sloan, I'll be the least of your problems."

RJ departed the café. He boarded the Astor corporate jet an hour later and headed to Istanbul.

Sloan waited until RJ cleared his field of vision from the front of the café before pulling out a flip phone. Sloan tapped in a number, and a voice as ragged as Sloan's answered.

"Yeah?"

"Heads up, partner," said Sloan. "You're going to have some company in Istanbul, and I'm sure he's not coming to help you find what you're looking for."

"That's a surprise," said the ragged voice. "Tell me about him."

The Türbe of Mehmet II — March 5 and 6

Max walked onto the main floor of Poenari Castle, the injured members of DracuLAND security gathered in front of him.

"I've contacted everyone I would trust with what has happened at Poenari," said Max. "Which is not a long list. No one can get here for several days. We're on our own."

Alvin coughed and cleared his throat.

"Everyone understand their times for their watch assignments?" Max asked.

"Once more, Max."

"Alvin, with Nate now returned from the emergency clinic, has the first shift. After that, a rotation of Oskar and me. And then Costea and Benjamin."

"I don't think Costea is in any shape to watch over Poenari," said Benjamin.

"None of us are," Max agreed. "But this is what we have. If there's an issue, Doug can come back from the hospital. Let's go."

Max called Doug looking for an update.

"The dog is stable," Doug said. "That's all I can tell you. I'll stay at hospital unless you need me back at Poenari. The doctors assured me if there's any change, they'll notify me."

"Stay with Kodiak." Max rubbed his thumb along a folding table.

"I'm going to n-n-need s-s-several hours," said RJ to Jake, the Astors' pilot. Both stood on a tarmac spur at Ataturk

Airport, which serviced corporate flights. They'd flown in from London after midnight, beating dawn by an hour.

Cold also landed on Istanbul. RJ did not have a heavy jacket for the chill, his stuttering giving away his lack of warm clothing.

"Mr. Astor said to give you whatever you need," replied Jake, a former Marine replete with buzz cut and wearing an Astor Holdings uniform that never wrinkled. "Let's start with this."

He handed RJ a leather jacket, pilot's issue from Astor Holdings. Corporate colors of garnet and evergreen.

"How about something in a nice stylish black?" joked RJ.

"Sir?"

"Sorry. Thanks for the coat," said RJ. "I need something else, if you have it. I used up all the cash bribing Sloan."

"Not a problem, sir." Jake hustled up the steps into the jet. He returned a minute later.

"Another $5000?" asked Jake, handing RJ an envelope with the Astor Holdings branding.

A taxi drove RJ to downtown Istanbul and deposited him under the elegant portico of the Four Seasons Hotel, which he entered.

He spotted a handsome young Turk holding a sign that read "Brancatelli." RJ's hand went to Louise and released the safety when the man approached him. He held his position on the lobby floor and surveilled the lobby. The crowded area of the front desk to his right, the concierge station to his left. The Turk dropped the sign and reached into the same side of his suit jacket as RJ. The Turk's dusky hand closed around and pulled out a Russian Tokarev.

The tourists in the lobby backed away from the *High Noon* confrontation. A security guard, stuffed into his tight uniform, reached for a cellphone that sat on the planter of a potted jade tree. RJ glanced at him and the guard thought better of it.

RJ drew first.

"Bang!" he said, pointing his index finger at the Turk. "You're dead!"

Screams filled the lobby as the tourists retreated to safety behind furniture and potted plants. They relaxed when the joke played out with the Turk holding up his arms in surrender.

"You missed, RJ," said the Turk, laughing. "You getting old on me?"

The security guard recovered and stomped over to the Turk, to give him an earful about decorum. The next time he pulled this stunt the police would take him away.

"Yes. Yes," said the Turk, dismissing the guard and addressing him in a familiar form of the guard's name. "Apologies all around, but that was a good one, eh?"

The guard grunted and walked to his inert position.

"Tyrrel Amin," said RJ, shaking the young man's hand. "How are you, other than very slow off the draw?"

"I am fine, RJ. It is good to see you, though you do look awful," said Tyrrel. "You need to get some sleep." He patted RJ's shoulder. "We won't leave for the Fatih Mosque until late this evening. I haven't figured out how your target is planning to break in, but we have to assume he will be there. I do know, however, how *we* are breaking in."

"Oh, not that your diligence surprises me. How? I've looked into the security measures around the Türbe. They are impressive."

"Yes, on a normal day they *are* impressive, but there is a late-night reception planned in the mosque from nine o'clock until ten o'clock, and the infrared sensors will be disabled. The only measures we have to concern ourselves with are the security guards and they will be preoccupied. There will be, at most, one of them in front of the Türbe."

"So how do we get in?"

Tyrrel ran his right hand through his black hair. He removed his sunglasses and placed them in a protective case. His Western dress consisted of a black suit, gray tie, and blue shirt. He straightened the tie, which did not need straightening.

"From underneath. The mosque sits over a cistern, navigable by small boat."

"There's got to be a few feet of concrete to cut through, though," said RJ. "How do we do that in short order? If that's how we're getting in."

"Explosives," said Tyrrel, straightening the straight tie again.

"Don't you think that will attract some attention?"

"Ah, RJ, you know nothing about the reverence for the Ottoman's famous leader," said Tyrrel, having now moved onto straightening his collar. "The Türbe of Mehmet the Second is soundproof so there is no interference during his conversations with Allah."

"All right Mehmet the Second! Good move."

Tyrrel laughed. RJ reached into his jacket and pulled out the envelope with the cash. He handed it to Tyrrel, who faked counting it.

"Does that cover you?" RJ asked.

"You know it does. For you, I'd work for nothing."

"No you wouldn't."

No, I would not."

"Tyrrel, do you think Evan will find what he's searching for?"

"The skull of the Impaler?" questioned Tyrrel. "I did not—until I received Dr. Barnes' list of the burial contents in Mehmet the Second's sarcophagus. I'm still not convinced that it is buried there with the Sultan, but she makes an intriguing case for it. Like most mythocologists, I think it lays hidden in Sighisoara, the ancestral home of the Draculs."

"Really? Is there no way to find out?" asked RJ. "It might have saved me a trip. Sighisoara is a lot closer to Poenari than Istanbul."

"Yes, RJ," said Tyrrel, gesturing RJ toward the bank of elevators. "There is. We go to the Fatih Mosque, break into the Türbe, and take a look. I've checked you into the hotel already."

At the elevators, the operator, a young woman with classic Middle Eastern good looks, caramel-colored skin, dark eyes, and black hair, greeted them. She gave RJ a longer look than Tyrrel.

"Gentlemen, what floor?" she asked in a distinctive English accent. She eyeballed RJ again, and placed her left hand on her left hip and leaned into it. She half-closed her right eye in a slow-motion wink.

"Uh," stammered Tyrrel, inhaling her perfume.

"Sorry, ma'am," said RJ. "But we aren't quite ready."

"That's too bad," she said half winking again. "I'll be back. Don't go anywhere."

The elevator door closed.

"Anything else?" asked Tyrrel.

"What if we run into Evan before getting into the Türbe?"

"You *are* getting old, RJ," Tyrrel said with a laugh. "That's the idea, isn't it? Pay attention, geezer. We aren't here for the skull. We're here for Evan English."

"Jet lag," RJ shook his head.

"I think it was that elevator operator," said Tyrrel.

"I think you're right."

The elevator with beautiful operator returned. RJ and Tyrrel entered and stood back from the doors as they closed. The car didn't move. She finally turned around and flashed a coy smile.

"I think you might want to tell me what floor, since we have so many of them."

Tyrrel's voice broke as he gave the young woman the floor number. She smiled at him this time and pushed the button.

As soon as the doors opened, Tyrrel stumbled out of the elevator.

"Get some rest, RJ. Take a shower. Nap this afternoon. We have a long night ahead of us. The Fatih Mosque is nearby, but traffic in Istanbul can be quite daunting. I will retrieve you at 1930 hours."

"You're sure we can get into this place? Plan sounds optimistic, Tyrrel."

"I have done a dry run. Everything except, of course, use of the explosives."

"I will meet you in front of the hotel at 1930 hours," said RJ. "But explain *exactly* how we're breaking in. Perhaps you've missed something in your planning?"

"Not a chance."

The two chatted as they walked down the hallway, ornately decorated with classic iconography and gilded mirrors.

"The cisterns that run underneath the mosque have been used as the city's water distribution method since the fourteenth century."

"Certainly not for bathing."

"Funny. A smelly Middle Eastern person comment? I thought better of you."

"No, you didn't."

Tyrrel pressed on.

"One of the waterways passes underneath the Fatih Mosque Türbe. I have wired a section of the floor next to the sarcophagus."

"And?"

"The explosives blow a hole through the floor inside the Türbe. I toss a grappling hook, with rope ladder attached, through the opening. We climb up inside, catch Evan English at some point, who is *also attempting* to break into the Türbe of Mehmet the Second," said Tyrrel. "Grab him. Then you and I return to the insertion point, stuff him in a car, and head to the airport."

"What if he gets there first?"

"If he's breaking in during the reception, which is the only way to avoid detection, he'll get there at the same time we do. I don't intend to get inside the Türbe any later than the start of the reception."

"I hope you're right."
"Me too."

Seeking Vlad's Skull — March 6, Evening

Tyrrel picked RJ up at 1930 hours and drove to a side street in Fatih, the orthodox Islam section of Istanbul. The call to prayer finished, groups of Muslims walked out of a neighborhood mosque. Four women in head-to-toe black burkas walked past Amin's car, as the vehicle approached the insertion point to the underground waterways.

"Geez, how many mosques are in the neighborhood?"

"A lot. Fatih just happens to be the largest. Any other questions with an underlying slap at Islam?"

RJ laughed.

They parked in an alleyway perpendicular to the main boulevard, Fevzipasa. Tyrrel led RJ to a sewer opening on the cobblestone street. He lowered his backpack onto the ground and extracted a grappling hook. He attached it to the latticework and pulled the top of the grate open. He dropped a rope down until he heard a splash.

Tyrrel secured the rope to the inside of the sewer opening using a couple of heavy-duty carabiners attached to water pipes.

He placed the hook on his backpack, knotting a rope ladder to it.

"Let's go."

Tyrrel went first after RJ volunteered him.

"You need the exercise," said RJ. "Time to build up your man muscles. Besides I want to see if those carabiners will hold."

"RJ, if you need help getting down a rope, just tell me, I'm always happy to assist a senior citizen," joked Tyrrel. "I'll move the boat *after* I swim to it and place it underneath the rope, so your old self can stay dry. Put the grate back over the opening, but leave it loose, please. Easier for us to get back out."

Tyrrel shimmied down the rope and dropped into the water. He swam to the boat, a twenty-footer with oarlocks on both port and starboard slightly toward the stern. He maneuvered it underneath the rope, pulled himself inside, and waited for his companion.

RJ slid down the rope into the boat. Trickles of water echoed in the cistern.

Tyrrel switched on his flashlight and taped it to the bow. The beam flooded the waterway ahead. He picked up the oars. In the distance, he spotted the dim reflection of yellow light, a piece of luminescent tape he'd applied to the underside of the Türbe during his dry run. He rowed the boat toward it.

Tyrrel positioned the boat beneath the yellow reflector. He freed the flashlight, and pointed it upward. The beam revealed three wire cords painted with a streak of highlighter yellow, twisted together into a single snake, which dropped from the ceiling.

Tyrrel took the bare leads from the three wires and attached a small box with a toggle switch to them.

"Whoa," said RJ, grabbing Tyrrel's shoulder. "Let's take a time out here regarding the explosives. Are you sure they are *not* going to set off an alarm?"

"Yes, RJ," said Tyrrel, his eyes skyward, shaking his head. "I've set the charges downward, so the blast created is *below* the Türbe and will be dissipated in the cistern. And remember the Türbe is soundproofed? I mentioned that earlier."

"I hope you're right. But once we blow a hole in the floor of this Türbe, won't everything drop down onto us?"

"Just a very small piece of the floor. It's a precision blast. However, we should watch our heads," said Tyrrel.

"Oh, of course. Good advice," said RJ. "What could possibly go wrong?"

"RJ," said Tyrrel. "Again, all we have to do is toss the hook with the ladder through the opening and climb into the Türbe. We wait for Evan English, grab him, hit him with the rubber hose, and drop down into the boat. We row back to the insertion point. By the time the theft is discovered, you will be back in Romania, and I will be asleep at home."

"Oh, this cannot *possibly* fail," said RJ. He closed his eyes. "Please God, don't let me end up in a Turkish prison. You've seen the movie."

Tyrrel moved the boat a few feet away from the blast point. He toggled the switch, which blew the charge. A chunk of Türbe floor glanced off the side of the boat and splashed into the water. Tyrrel and RJ froze, waiting for something to happen. Alarms to ring. Guards to run. Anything. But only silence from above and in the cistern as ripples moved across the surface of the water.

RJ broke from his frozen position and tossed the grappling hook and rope ladder up into the Türbe. It caught and held.

"You first, Tyrrel. Again."

"How about a high five, RJ?"

"We're just getting started. I wouldn't be inviting hubris."

"So, no high five?"

"No."

"Darn. Always wanted a high five."

Tyrrel climbed. A few more pieces of flooring dropped into the water. He watched the ripples they made lap against the sides of the boat.

"Let's go, Tyrrel," admonished RJ.

Tyrrel got to the hole and scrambled through.

"I'm inside," came a whispered shout. RJ also heard some scraping noises.

"Everything OK?" hissed RJ.

"Yep. Just resecuring the hook. Don't want you to go for a swim," came Tyrrel's reply.

RJ climbed and pulled himself onto the floor of the Türbe. He got to his feet and didn't see Tyrrel.

Then he did.

"RJ Brancatelli," said a man in a Turkish military uniform, displaying an excellent grasp of the English language, complete with London boarding school accent. "How nice to meet you in person. And you've come with Tyrrel Amin, wunderkind of the archaeological world, at least the mystical part of it. I could not have asked for better assistants."

"I take it you're not the guard of the Türbe?" asked RJ, who found himself looking at a broad-shouldered, pale-skinned man of about 6'4". His black mustache seemed off. RJ recognized a fake. The man held a gun at Tyrrel's head.

"Bad disguise, *Evan*," said RJ. "I take it you weren't being generous in giving the regular guard the night off?"

"No," Evan answered, and smirked. "He's sleeping off a sedative. Slipped it in his evening meal. He's out in the mosque gardens. You should see them before you leave Istanbul. Quite lovely."

Evan glanced at his wristwatch wrapped around the sleeve of the uniform. He pressed the gun up against Tyrrel's temple. The young man showed no emotion, but tilted his head away from the barrel.

"Now, shall we get started?" asked Evan. "We've got no more than thirty minutes to blow the cover off this murdering sultan's coffin, and take back my ancestor's skull." He motioned toward Tyrrel's backpack.

"Got some more C4, kid?" asked Evan. "Actually, I know you do."

"Yes, but—"

"Then let's blow the cover off this coffin . . . *now!*"

Tyrrel dropped to the ground and opened the backpack.

"Careful with those sudden moves, sonny," said Evan. "And RJ, if you try anything I will shoot this young man until he's as dead as Mehmet the Second over there."

RJ held his position. His eyes scanned the room, something not lost on Evan.

"Oh, I'll just walk out of here," said Evan. "You two will have to exit the same way you entered. Alas, I don't have any spare uniforms."

Tyrrel walked to the sarcophagus under the watchful eyes of Evan. He stuck two chunks of plastique on top of the sarcophagus, placing them at the far ends of the cover, and wiped sweat off his forehead with the sleeve of his shirt. After sticking bare wires into the explosives, he dropped down onto the floor and connected them to another toggle detonator.

"I would suggest you two gentlemen find some cover," said Tyrrel, his arms over his head. "I can't vouch for where this cover is going to end up."

Evan lay right next to Tyrrel, the barrel of his gun still pointing at the young man's temple. RJ lay face down several feet away.

Tyrrel toggled the switch.

The top levitated, flew across the room, and collided with the front door of the Türbe, snapping its hinges. It held for a few seconds, then crashed to the ground. The soundproof barrier breached.

Outside, red lights flashed. A siren blared.

"Well, that wasn't planned. Guess I used enough explosives, eh, Butch?" taunted Tyrrel, and he turned to Evan. "The door could have been us. Now what?"

"Give me the grappling hook!" Evan ordered. "Our thirty minutes just got reduced."

Tyrrel handed him the hook, and Evan swung it with enthusiasm. He shattered the lacquered wood interior layer on Mehmet's sarcophagus.

RJ, the last one to stand, raced over to the exposed remains of the first Sultan of Constantinople. The lights and siren continued their assault on everyone's eyeballs and ears.

RJ yanked back a large cloth that covered Mehmet II. The body threw off a mild chemical scent. The three peered into the sarcophagus.

The sultan, brown and shriveled from embalming, was not dressed in the customary purple silk burial shroud. Gemstone-laden jewelry surrounded him, as did his personal encrusted and engraved scimitar. Gold and silver coins from the period lay scattered about the petrified corpse. The priceless decorations reflected the red lights of the alarm.

"Clock's ticking, you with the gun," said RJ.

"Where's Vlad's skull?" screamed Evan and pointed the gun between Tyrrel's eyes.

Tyrrel's ashen face glowed with sweat.

"I, uh-, I-, if it is in there, it's most likely tucked under his arm!" he shouted above the alarms.

"Kid, there's not even deodorant under those arms! *Where's the skull?"*

Sirens. Footsteps. Shouting.

"We're running out of time!" said RJ. "We've got about a minute before we're making the sequel to, you know, *that movie!"*

"It has to be in here!" shouted Evan. "I didn't come to Istanbul to go away empty handed. You're the expert! Now find the skull!"

"It ain't in here, Mr. English! Just the naked body of that jackal, Mehmet!" spat Tyrrel as Evan's gun barrel drew blood.

Tyrrel reached into the coffin and grabbed the remains.

"Naked?" asked Tyrrel more to himself than Evan or RJ. "Yes, naked!"

"What are you doing?" yelled RJ. "Let's get the heck out of this place!"

Tyrrel turned toward him, holding the carcass.

"Mehmet the Second is supposed to be dressed in formal burial gowns. This is not Mehmet the Second!"

"OK, some other dead guy. Who cares? Let's go!"

Evan did not take the gun off Tyrrel.

Tyrrel lifted the corpse in front of him, rattled it, and shouted, but he did not scream in frustration. He crowed with joy. Evan pressed the gun even more into the young man's head.

The skull fell off the body, and rolled across the floor. With his free hand, Evan reached down and picked it up. As he did, RJ pulled Louise from his shoulder holster. Evan stood, and though he still had his gun pointed at Tyrrel, found himself staring down the barrel of RJ's weapon.

"Yes, Mr. English, it is just another beheaded infidel . . . adorned with the head of Vlad the Impaler!" Tyrrel interrupted as a stunned Evan held the skull.

Tyrrel turned back to the coffin and pushed his hands under the coins, gems, and weapons. He pulled up a second body, this one wrapped properly in the appropriate indigo silk burial regalia.

"But why?"

"Keep your friends close . . . and your enemies closer. Ya know, that old trope. Where do you think the adage came from, Mr. English? I would imagine the body is that of another beheaded betrayer of Mehmet, and most likely one nearly as cunning, brave, and powerful as Vlad."

"But why combine—?"

"No time for a long explanation!" Tyrrel shouted as he rummaged through the contents of the sarcophagus. He handed RJ and Evan some jewelry and precious coins.

"Take these for bribes," he said. "Sultans beheaded many of their enemies. The Ottomans placed some of them in the sarcophagus with their departed leaders. That way they could keep an eye on them."

The sound of footsteps grew louder. Many pairs. Boot heels clicking on the marbled floor. No longer echoing, but clear and constant. The guards were crossing the stone plaza between the mosque and the Türbe.

Tyrrel eyed RJ, who held Louise in his hand.

"I will stall the police. Return to the cistern. Get out via the grate."

RJ hesitated.

"Tyrrel, why don't you and Evan exchange clothes? That should give you a better chance when the guards get here." "Not a bad idea," Tyrrel agreed. After the two exchanged clothing, Tyrrel looked at the standoff in front of him. "At this point, you two need each other to leave Istanbul. I'd suggest you work it out. You're not just going to stroll out of Fatih now, Mr. English."

Tyrrel handed RJ the backpack and motioned Evan toward the opening in the floor. RJ tucked the gun back into its holster, and followed Evan down the rope. Tyrrel turned and sprinted out the door of the Türbe to confront the police.

RJ and Evan dropped into the boat. Evan placed the skull in a plastic-lined sack, while RJ put the jewels and coins into Tyrrel's backpack. Inside he found a spare set of dry clothing. Each took an oar and pulled it through the water.

"Brave young man," said Evan as they rowed.

"Shut up, English," said RJ. "Tyrrel's short life will soon be over."

The commotion from the Fatih Mosque audible above them, they arrived at the sewer grate. RJ took the rope and shimmied up to the grate. He shoved it aside, peered out, didn't see anyone, then pulled himself onto street level. Evan followed. RJ helped him up.

"Now what?" asked Evan. The street silent save for the two of them.

"Tyrrel's car," said RJ. "Though the police will have it out on the wire very soon. I don't have fake ID. Do you?"

Evan shook his head

"As I said, now what?"

"Don't you find train travel romantic?" quipped RJ as Evan narrowed his eyes. "It's our best bet. Can't take the corporate jet. No way it will be cleared for takeoff. Hope the pilot is OK."

"Lead the way," said Evan. "I believe Tyrrel was correct. I'd have been spotted and detained."

"Just shut up."

RJ and Evan strolled away from the access grate toward Istanbul's main tram line.

"Let me know if you hear the tram," said RJ.

"A streetcar?" asked Evan. "Are you kidding? Do you think the police are chasing us on motorized wheelchairs?"

"I bet there's a Turkish equivalent of a BOLO out on us already. Every cab in Istanbul will be looking for sweaty Western tourists with swag. How far do you think we'll get?"

An approaching streetcar chugged up the hill.

"Your outfit will buy us some time," said RJ. "We'll ride as long as we can. I'd like to get as far as the train station in Old Town. That's where we can catch a ride out of Turkey."

RJ watched for the authorities until the tram arrived and they jumped aboard. Evan exhaled as it sped away.

RJ and Evan went to the first car of a two-car tram. A map across both sides of the windows laid out the stops. It highlighted tourist destinations for The Blue Mosque, Aja Sofia, and Topkapi Palace. They needed to take the tram ten stops to Sirkeci, which would put them at the entrance to the train station.

Two figures in black burkas entered the rear car. They slipped into the front car as it approached the third of the ten stops.

RJ spotted them at the fifth stop. Two burka-clad Muslims on a tram with a bunch of tourists. He locked eyes with one of them. A slender man in a city worker's uniform approached and passed in front of the Muslims.

RJ stepped forward and slammed the man into her. The domino effect pitched her partner off the tram and onto the street through the side opening. She regained her feet and gave chase as the tram moved away.

RJ's arm shot out and smashed the second woman on the forehead. With a very deep, masculine groan, "she" hit the floor of the tram. The other riders stepped away then advanced on RJ, who reached into his holster for Louise and pointed it at the building mob.

The emergency brake shrieked. Evan clutched the precious skull to his chest and grabbed RJ. They tumbled onto the hard pavement of the Caddesi, but Evan kept the sack away from the ground by absorbing the majority of the fall on his back.

"Let's go, RJ!" shouted Evan.

"But that was a guy! I didn't take out a Muslim *woman!*"

"They can't see that, you idiot!"

Both sprinted away from the tram and headed toward the Grand Bazaar.

"The bazaar?" asked RJ as they came upon the entrance. "Now you're Indiana Jones?"

Pedestrians clogged the front and blocked their way.

"Just keep going. There is a shortcut to the train station," panted Evan.

"What? How do you know?"

The two disappeared into the labyrinthine structure. The "woman" who fell into the street, caught up to the tram and spotted RJ and Evan running into the bazaar.

They slipped into one of the stalls in the bazaar and hid behind racks of gaudy clothing. An annoying store employee kept shoving goods their way. Evan pushed him away each time.

"We've been followed," said RJ. "One of them just passed this shop."

"Oh, and you're sure of that?" questioned Evan. "Got a few black burkas out there."

"The full beard gave it away, and what's with the disguise?" asked RJ.

"That is odd, but Istanbul is a city of surprises," answered Evan. "And I wouldn't call a burka a disguise. Not in Istanbul."

"Two *guys* in burkas?" said RJ. "That's a first for me, a crossdressing Muslim in traditional garb."

"Security from the Fatih Mosque," said Evan.

"What?"

"Guess they ran out of uniforms?"

"Are you joking?"

Evan waved him off and searched the crowded bazaar for an exit from its Escher-like layout. RJ tapped on his cellphone.

"Nice shortcut," said RJ. "Let's try this."

RJ held up his phone and showed Evan a map of the area.

"About a half-mile, with a few twists and turns."

"What about our pursuer?" asked Evan.

RJ winked at Evan.

"I'll take a wild guess and say that there is clothing for sale somewhere around here."

Ten minutes and several gold coins lighter, the two emerged wearing traditional native garb. Their clothes replaced with, as RJ referred to them, "longish nightshirts and beach pants," and on their heads, *keffiyah* secured with an *agal*. Evan reapplied his mustache, straight now with RJ's help.

They arrived at the main train station to find the Bosporus Express rail line had been under construction for the past year. It no longer ran directly from Istanbul to Bucharest.

"RJ," said Evan, a slight pique coloring his voice. "Now what?"

"Hold on, Evan. I'm looking."

The station buzzed—passengers walked to and from track entrances. Porters and hucksters carried luggage and items for sale. Despite the hour, stalls were open. Vendors hawked their wares.

RJ spotted a hard copy of a train schedule. He pulled it off a rack next to a ticket counter.

"Evan! Let's go! The Orient Express runs bus service to Edirne, the last Turkish city at the Bulgarian border."

"So what?" said Evan. "What's in Edirne?"

"A connecting train goes from Edirne through Bulgaria to Bucharest. I'll have Max arrange something when we get to Bucharest."

Evan tossed a newspaper back on top of the news agency's table, bringing a loud complaint from the proprietor, a handsome man with a resemblance to Clark Gable.

"Take it easy, Sharif," said Evan, who tossed the proprietor one of his gold coins, grabbed the newspaper, and joined RJ.

RJ bought two tickets while Evan searched the station for the authorities.

"God, I hate buses," said RJ. "Way too confined."

"Not crazy about traveling by bus either," said Evan, echoing RJ's sentiments. "Don't you think a rental car would give us more flexibility?"

"Sure would," replied RJ. "However, rental car agencies are very sophisticated in Istanbul. Everything they do is computerized. But did you see the cash register at the ticket office? Clerk didn't ask for a passport, and wasn't interested in anything except my credit card."

Evan spun around and grabbed someone by the collar. He reached into the guy's raggedy jacket pocket and pulled out a wallet. It belonged to RJ. Evan grinned and handed the wallet to RJ.

"Nice try, Fagin," Evan said to the pickpocket.

The thief lunged at Evan, who sidestepped him. The pickpocket cursed loudly. The confrontation drew attention from travelers in the station, some of whom closed in on the three. RJ kept his right hand free to get the nightstick. Louise remained in its holster.

A lone, scrawny security guard arrived. He looked like he'd just woken from a nap. His thin gray hair lay plastered flat on one side, his dull brown eyes shuttered by heavy lids.

He spoke decent English, and after some back and forth, the security guard sent the erstwhile thief on his way. The two thanked the guard, and walked to the outside of the station. RJ and Evan boarded the bus for Edirne.

More than two hours later, the same security guard's cellphone rang. It woke him from another nap, and after a few words of admonishment, he told his superiors that he had indeed seen two Westerners in the bus station that night, and, yes, he knew where they were headed.

Nikolai Asilimov — March 6

Nikolai Asimov passed out in his lounge chair. His shack, boarded up from the inside since the attack of a few days prior, cut off even more light from the outside world. Paper-thin rays of sunlight barely breached the space between the 2 x 4s. Nikolai, a shadow within the shadows.

He slept the sleep of an unrepentant drunk. But not a peaceful one. Winged creatures carried him from place to place, dropping him, but never allowing him to recover before descending like Harpies. They yanked out his hair with their claws, and screeched at him.

Finally, they pelted him with rocks as he lay face down on the ground. The noise filling his head, and waking him to a sound of rocks against his door.

Someone knocking.

"Yes? Who is there?"

"Police. Open the door."

"Police? Have I done something wrong?"

"Please open up, Mr. Asilimov!"

The pounding on the door started again.

"One minute, please. I am having trouble with one of the locks." He shouted over the knocking.

"Quickly, sir. I will break down the door, if I have to. Keep talking as you fix the problem. Do not walk away."

"Yes, Officer." Nikolai took a hammer and pulled the nails out of the 2 x 4s. The boards clattered to the ground.

He turned the deadbolt locks. The policeman pushed open the door and stepped inside. The officer entered so fast that he shoved Nikolai out of his way and back onto the lounge chair.

Nikolai landed with a grunt.

"Nikolai Asilimov?" A man with military bearing loomed over him. Nikolai was not small, but this policeman stood at least four inches taller than he. The officer presented his badge.

"Teomer Turrik," Nikolai read aloud.

"Yes," replied Turrik.

Nikolai reached into his pocket for his wallet. A rough hand grabbed him by the wrist.

"Just want to show you my identification, Officer," said Nikolai, pulling his hand away from the police officer's grip.

"Apologies, Asilimov," said Officer Turrik, who stepped back from the chair when Nikolai extricated himself.

Nikolai took hold of his wallet and pulled out an identification card. He also showed the officer his Ukrainian passport, secured in his pants' pocket.

"Ukraine? How long have you been in Romania?"

"My parents brought me here in 1990. I left the USSR at the age of five. My mother died that year, and my father got a job taking care of this castle. He died in 2004 and passed the job on to me. The Romanian government issued me the visa. It allows me to stay as long as I like."

Nikolai pointed to the worn card stapled inside his passport.

"Anything else you'd like to know?"

"Yes, Mr. Asilimov. What can you tell me about missing construction workers?"

"Nothing. I no longer work for Astor Holdings as of this week. They bought me out of this house and my job. I can leave anytime I want. I have nothing to do with the construction."

"Why are you still here?"

Nikolai rubbed his eyes.

"I'm finding it hard to leave," Nikolai confessed.

The officer took in the claustrophobia-inducing shack. Light leaked in from cracks in the walls, and the door jamb. The windows covered over by blinds and random 2 x 4s. The ceiling hung so low that a man of Turrik's size could develop bad posture if he lived here.

Clutter littered Nikolai's kitchen. Dishes, pots, and cutlery filled the sink. Turrik didn't want to know for how long. The living room, furnished only with the single lounge chair and a TV featured a futon-style mattress slung awkwardly on the floor near a three-legged table.

"Really, Mr. Asilimov? You are finding it hard to leave?"

"I know it doesn't look like much, but this house is all I've known since we left the Soviet Union. It is the last place I saw my father."

Turrik surveyed the dark and musty interior of the shack once more.

"I understand. But I'm here because some families in Curtea de Argeş have filed missing persons reports. Some of their men were working on this site and have not come home in the past few days."

"Honestly, Officer," said Nikolai. "What does this have to do with me? I don't work, as I said, for DracuLAND and I am sure I will leave soon. So why are you interrogating me?"

"You are on these premises twenty-four hours a day Mr. Asilimov, and you've seen *nothing?*" Turrik lifted both eyebrows.

Nikolai did not respond. Turrik motioned for him to go outside. Nikolai hesitated.

"We both need some air." More a demand than a request.

"And a few of those missing workers are part of an advance survey party," continued Turrik when he and Nikolai cleared the doorway.

"I phoned the site's general contractor, Oskar, this morning. He told me the site survey crew isn't due back until today. However, if they don't return by tomorrow—"

Turrik spotted someone walk out of the reconstructed castle.

Max Capitanou.

"That's the owner's bodyguard. I believe I'll have a word with him. Thank you, Mr. Asilimov. You have your wish. You cannot leave Poenari until this investigation is complete, and that may be a while. Good day."

Turrik put on his policeman's cap and walked across the bridge. Nikolai followed him until he reached the other side, then reentered his shack. Nikolai locked the door and hammered the 2 x 4s back in place.

Secure inside, Nikolai started a thorough cleaning, the first in weeks, perhaps months. First the kitchen, then he straightened up the living room. After an hour, Nikolai stepped back and admired his progress.

Nikolai found a flashlight and opened a trap door in the floor that released a tired rope ladder. He climbed into the storage basement, and went to his family's belongings in the center of the room. Dust and grime covered everything. He separated two boxes so old that the flaps broke off the sides when he grabbed them. He pulled his personal stuff out of one and from another badly disintegrating box, that of his father and mother.

Nikolai brought the items up the ladder and carefully placed the things out on the floor of the shack. He smiled when he came across a few faded photos, including one that showed the family of three in front of their apartment building in Ukraine. He could not have been more than four years old. His father, a slight man, posed in a long-sleeved shirt and blue coveralls, the uniform of the factory in which he toiled. His mother wore a plain cotton dress and the haggard look of a Soviet housewife.

He retrieved a garbage bag from the kitchen and filled it with the rescued items. He wiped away a lonesome tear.

"Mr. Capitanou?" Turrik approached Max, clearly on a cellphone call. Max held up a finger, and the policeman tucked his cap under his arm and assumed a military posture.

Max finished his call.

"How can I help you, Officer …"

"Turrik," he said. "I'm looking into a couple of missing persons reports. I've been unable to reach the property owner, Garrett Astor."

"I'm sorry. Mr. Astor is dealing with a family emergency, and has been unreachable, even by me," Max said.

"Did you inform him about the missing workers?"

"No. I have not."

Turrik exhaled audibly through his nose and stared straight at Max.

"I would think you would have informed the president of—"

"He's been informed, Officer," he said. "Just not by me."

"I see," said Turrik. "I don't take well to comments such as that, Mr. Capitanou."

"My apologies, Officer Turrik," said Max, pulling down one of his suit jacket sleeves. "I did not mean to mislead you."

Max turned on his heel to leave, but Turrik pressed the issue, and placed his right hand on Max's left shoulder. It stopped the bodyguard.

"All right, Mr. Capitanou. I could insist, but I am going to be respectful and give your boss one more day." He placed his cap back on his head. "But I want him back here from this family emergency. I need to continue my investigation into this matter. I hope you understand I will need to speak with him."

"Of course. I will get in touch with Garrett and explain the situation."

Turrik's eyebrows rose.

"What is going on here, Mr. Capitanou?" Turrik made a move toward the castle. Max blocked his way.

The police officer made another move as if to shove him out of the way, but Max did not move, and looked at Turrik's empty hands.

"No warrant?"

Turrik shook his head, and backed away a few steps, and cleared his throat.

"I will be back, Mr. Capitanou," said Turrik, moving again toward Max, who held his ground. The two men of equal size squared up to each other. "I want to speak with Costea

Jones and Oskar Naguschewsky, as well. You have twenty-four hours."

Max held up his right hand. Turrik took a step back.

"Get going, Officer Turrik. And when you come back, I want an official warrant with an itemized account of exactly what you want to investigate. Until I see that, you'll have access to nothing. Do we understand each other?"

"For now."

Turrik turned and walked back across the bridge and past the shack to the elevators. Once the doors closed behind him, Max pulled out his cellphone.

Across from the castle, Nikolai hammered another 2 x 4 as the sun crossed Poenari Castle and covered it in a golden-red hue, giving notice dusk would not be far behind.

Max watched the shadows lengthen while he listened to Nikolai's hammering. He punched in a number on his cellphone.

"Max?" Garrett asked.

"Had a visit by the local police today, Garrett. Missing persons reports have been filed by a few of the workers' families."

"Oh?"

Max took another breath. The air of early spring in Romania held some of winter's crispness in it. He blew it out and felt the coolness pass through him.

"It went about as well as could be expected, but he seems intent on looking into this matter. He has given us a day."

"Sounds like he's just doing his job."

"I know, and I think it will be fine for him to speak with Oskar and Costea, but even if that satisfies him for tomorrow, he's going to be back here the day after and with a warrant, wondering where you are. He wants to speak to you. What do I tell him?"

"Maybe I will be back from my family emergency by then."

"I'll leave that up to you, Garrett."

"Do what you need to do, Max," said Garrett, his voice rising. "In the meantime, what have we done about finding my sister?" Garrett did not wait for Max's answer. "As soon as RJ gets back here, *if* the Nekredum don't show by then, we're going to look for Elizabeth. I'm not spending too many more nights in this castle waiting for them to kill all of us, so they can look for some five-hundred-year-old piece of cutlery."

"All right, Garrett," said Max. He ground the palm of his left hand into the rail of the footbridge. "I want Elizabeth back as much as you, but even RJ's colleague, Margaret, doesn't know where the Nekredum Hive is. I'll call the police station and tell them we've decided to cooperate, which might delay their hunt for a warrant. I'll set up interviews with Oskar and Costea. I'll brief both of them beforehand. It might just be enough time for RJ to get back with Evan."

"Then what?"

"Then I'll go down to the station and meet with Officer Turrik before he heads up here."

"What good would that do?"

"I'll give him just enough information to get his investigation started, and maybe I can discourage him from meeting with you."

"That buys us at most two days. Then what?"

"The Nekredum will certainly be back by then if not before, because more than enough time will have elapsed for them to spawn, according to Margaret. The WolfThane will join them. Given their attack on Kodiak and his stalwart defense, they won't want to wait for the dog to be able to help us."

"And what if RJ, with or without this Evan English, isn't back by then? Bad enough we won't have Kodiak, but—"

"We'll do what we have to do, Garrett. Let us hope for the best."

"Yes. Let's."

Max hung up and sat on the grass. He watched the sun dip closer to the horizon. His eyes welled with tears.

He called Doug to get the latest on Kodiak.

Edirne, Turkey — March 6 and 7

"I hope they don't do a bag check when we switch to the train," Evan said. RJ dropped down into a window seat and Evan took the one next to him. The tired bus released its brakes and groaned away from Istanbul.

Evan shifted the backpack around on his lap. Every so often he would lift the cover flap and peer inside. When he did it for the fourth time, RJ reached across and took the bag from him.

"What's the matter? Got something to hide?" RJ asked Evan, who took the hint and sat back in the sprung seat.

Several hours into the trip, a tired official walked down the aisle checking tickets. A day's worth of stubble covered his face. His white shirt frayed at the collar and his blue pants hadn't seen a washing machine for a month.

"Not liking this," said RJ.

"What?"

"Don't think that's a ticket taker.".

"What?"

"I'll call the Eastern European Transportation Workers Union and check."

"The — ?"

"Switch seats with me."

The agent took tickets and punched them. His black book looked new, not a mark in it. RJ moved his hand to the nightstick.

Evan riffled his pockets for the tickets.

The official approached. As he got closer to RJ and Evan, he became less and less interested in looking at, tearing corners off, or punching paper tickets passengers handed him.

Just in front of RJ, he tore the cover off a passport handed to him by a passenger, a substantial woman dressed in a charwoman's outfit. She stood and cursed in Turkish.

The woman leaned into the aisle and continued shouting. The official screamed at her to sit down. His vest opened when he pointed at her seat, exposing the handle of a semi-automatic handgun which protruded from a shoulder holster. RJ fixed his stare on the official and the charwoman, her animated movements exposing the same type of weapon, bulging through her apron as she thrust her chest at the official.

RJ handed the skull-carrying backpack to Evan, and bolted out of his seat, yanking Evan with him. With his right hand, he pulled the nightstick out of its quiver, charged forward, and separated the official from the handgun just pulled from his holster.

Before the charwoman could raise her gun to fire, RJ knocked it from her grip. It skidded down the aisle toward the front.

The bus erupted. Passengers shouted. The driver turned his head to look back.

The bus left the highway and skidded toward a ditch at the side of the road. He jerked the wheel and the vehicle swerved, catapulting several riders from left to right. RJ gripped a seat for support. He saw an opening in the aisle and, and slipped the nightstick back in its quiver. He again yanked Evan The two ran to the back of the bus.

The official and charwoman recovered their handguns, but the driver slammed on the brakes, throwing everyone to the floor. The official, more agile than he looked, charged RJ and Evan. He grabbed at the backpack.

"This does not belong to you!" he shouted in English.

Evan reflexively punched the official in the face, who offered no resistance since he clenched the backpack with both hands. He relinquished it and collapsed to the floor.

At the front of the bus, the charwoman took a position behind a seatback and set her sight on Evan. He'd been holding the pack in front of him since took it back. She fired, but not before RJ delivered a slug through the seat and into her sternum.

The charwoman's body jerked as the bullet entered, but her shot hit the intended target. Almost. It entered the backpack Evan held in front and cracked the skull, then continued past Evan's right shoulder.

The charwoman slumped, dead in the seat. The official had not moved since Evan delivered his blow.

RJ turned to the back of the bus and fired Louise to blast the emergency door open.

"Let's move, English!"

The two men jumped out and hit the ground. They scrambled to their feet, sprinted from the bus, and toward the rugged hills of western Turkey. From behind they could hear shouting and screaming.

When they'd put a mile between them and the bus, RJ stopped and pulled out his satellite phone. He also fished out a device from a side pocket. He hooked it to the back of the phone and searched a map when it came up on his screen.

RJ kept his eyes on the phone. He heard sirens.

"The police are on their way," said Evan.

"Yes they are. The closest police station is three clicks south in Havsa, a 24/7 operation. The graveyard shift has one officer on patrol and one at the station."

"And?"

"Let's go, Evan. We're heading to the local police station."

"Police!" snapped Evan. "Are you insane?"

"Yes, I am," said RJ, and introduced Evan to the pirate guffaw.

Dawn loomed as the two men hustled along the access road.

Dmitri Selnikov, a Russian expat, poured himself a cup of coffee and sat down at the computer to get an update on the highway accident. Every officer working the early shift had been called in due to the incident. He remained behind at the Havsa police station.

Dimitri scanned the initial report. Westerners, most likely Americans, had stolen something of historic value from Istanbul's Fatih Mosque.

He took another sip of coffee, but spat it out, and found his neck in a chokehold. Dmitri dropped unconscious onto his keyboard. His coffee cup rolled off the side of the desk and hit the floor. The cup shattered, porcelain and liquid covering the bottom of the policeman's pants and shoes. RJ released Dimitri's neck and rummaged through a supply closet behind the policeman's desk. He tossed Evan a roll of duct tape and three pairs of handcuffs.

"He'll be out for about two or three hours. Make sure he can't go anywhere. I want this boy to have a hard time making a distress call before we're through Bulgaria."

RJ raised the shades covering the back windows of the station. The parking lot.

"Pick one, Evan. Make sure it's filled with gas and it's fast," ordered RJ.

Evan took a pair of the cuffs and worked one onto the right wrist of Dimitri.

"Hang on!" RJ barked.

"Now what?"

"This officer is about my size. Dimitri Selnikov and I are exchanging clothes," said RJ. "After you bind him up, find the station locker room and put on some street clothes. Then take care of getting us transportation."

"Just how far do you think we're going to get in a stolen police car?" Evan asked.

"Not one of their cruisers," RJ smirked.

"Then what?"

"If this is like most police stations, personal vehicle keys are left on some sort of check-in board. If not, just identify one that you like, and I'll get it started—after you bind up our rookie."

Evan found the pegboard of keys in one of the station's closets. He saw more than a few sets that looked promising.

"And Evan?" yelled RJ from the front.

"Yeah?"

"We need to re-arm. Gimme a few minutes to look around."

Evan pulled a new Mercedes around to the front of the police station. RJ came out with two assault rifles slung over his shoulders and a gym bag filled with ammunition. The handle of a K2 handgun protruded above his left hip. Six smoker-style grenades dangled in a small pouch near the left side of his ribcage.

"*Love* the purse," said Evan, popping the trunk.

"*Love* these former Eastern Bloc countries," said RJ. "They don't screw around when it comes to arming their police."

After depositing the weapons in the trunk, RJ moved to the driver's side window and tilted his head first at Evan and then in the direction of the passenger seat. Evan exited, walked around the car, and grunted as he dropped into the "shotgun" position.

RJ handed a hardcopy map to Evan. He pointed with his right index finger to where they will cross into Bulgaria.

"A map?" chided Evan. "Just how old *are* you?"

"Not taking any chances," said RJ. "Dug this out of one of the desks in the station. No GPS. No cellphones."

Evan slammed into his bucket seat when RJ stomped on the accelerator. The car peeled away from the police station. A cloud of dust trailed the vehicle. It thinned, revealing the first appearance of sunshine for the western side of Turkey.

RJ passed a leather wallet to Evan. He opened it and pulled out Dmitri Selnikov's police credentials. RJ had cut and glued his passport photo over Dmitri's.

"Great," said Evan. "What about me?"

RJ tossed him a pair of standard-issue handcuffs.

"You're my prisoner. I'm transporting you back to Bulgaria."

"How come *I'm* the prisoner? Why can't *I* be the policeman?" Evan whined like a six-year-old.

"*Çünkü Türkçe konuşmuyorsun.*"

Evan stared at RJ, who broke into his annoying pirate guffaw.

"Because you don't speak Turkish."

Evan, who had scored a black baseball cap at the police station, pulled it down over his eyes and drifted off. RJ, accustomed to going days without sleep, sat straighter and pushed the Mercedes above 100 miles per hour.

"We'll be at the Bulgarian border within the hour," said RJ.

The border guard didn't even glance at RJ's face after looking at the Turkish police ID. He ignored Evan, who snored and drooled. He handed the identification back, and trudged into the guardhouse. The security barrier lifted.

RJ took a cellphone out of his pocket, attached the encryption box, and dialed Max.

Evan, asleep despite RJ's enthusiastic driving, snorted a half breath and woke.

"I thought you said no cellphones," Evan grumbled.

"I put the encryption device on it. I have to call Max," said RJ, his eyes on the road.

"RJ! We've been trying to reach you!" Max shouted into the phone.

"I know. I didn't want to give anyone a chance to track me."

"Do you have Evan?"

"Yes, but it's complicated." RJ explained the purloining of the skull and the near-disasters on the tram and the bus. "We're going to need help getting through Romania, Max. I'll need to ditch the car we're in. Can you get us transport?"

"Yes. Hold on."

RJ placed the phone on speaker and laid it on the center console. Several minutes passed. RJ glanced at the phone more than once. Max's reassuring voice came back on.

"Yes. I'll have a car waiting for you in Giurgiu, Romania. Located just across the border from Ruse, Bulgaria. The Soviets used the town to swap assets during the Cold War. I'll send you the coordinates via code to the sat phone. Keys will be in the ignition."

"Thanks, Max. Can you do me another favor? Get Alvin and Doug to check out Interpol chatter. They must have some contacts from their Intelligence days. See if there's any mention of an American operative, cover name 'Staten Island.' If there is, call me back."

"Anything I should know?"

"Not yet. Just arrange the transportation."

"Will do. Try to call or text when you are safely in the transport. We're counting on you two."

"Sorry, Max. I've got to go." RJ hung up.

The road through the rugged Bulgarian countryside had deteriorated into an obstacle course of uneven blacktop, potholes, and missing shoulders. RJ concentrated on driving.

After an hour of video game driving, RJ peeked at the digital clock in the dashboard.

Still several hours to Romania.

Nikolai's Decision — March 7

Nikolai spasmed awake. He grunted his way out of the sprung cushions in his lounge chair, which also groaned as he extricated himself from its confines. He let out a yawn.

"Time to go," he said, his voice clear and loud in the musty morning air.

He opened the suitcase he'd packed earlier and lightened it by removing all but one change of clothes. He kept the picture of his parents, a few other photos in an envelope, and a couple of pieces of cut glass from their home in Ukraine. He closed the suitcase.

He opened his badly worn wallet and put its contents on the table. It amounted to fifty euros and a few Romanian leu. Nikolai had plenty more in the bank, a result of the buyout by Astor Holdings. He repacked his wallet and stuffed it into a side pocket.

Nikolai removed the 2 x 4s, and unlocked the door. The sun broke the horizon sending shards of yellow light across the footbridge and grounds in front of the castle.

"Don't think I wanna take the car," he said to himself. "Not after the other night."

He grabbed his bike, and rode the elevator down to the parking lot.

He slung his leg over the seat and pushed down on the pedals. Alcohol hadn't yet ruined his physique nor his conditioning. He flew through the lot, down the road, and into Curtea de Argeş. Nikolai passed the Orthodox Church and Monastery on his way to the Banca Transilvania, ensconced in a building on the main street of the city. A line of tour buses parked next to a series of concession stands, adjacent to a cemetery. Visitors congregated, waiting for admission.

Nikolai entered the bank and asked the security guard to watch his bicycle. The guard, a young man neatly attired in the bank's security guard uniform, tipped his hat and placed the bike next to his kiosk.

The building maintained the personality of its former life, a government building during occupation by the Soviet Union. Cold, cracked marble columns adorned the hollow interior. The poorly circulated air smelled like 1969. A clock, an hour and sixteen minutes slow, ticked. It caught on the hour hand for a few seconds, contributing more lost time.

Nikolai's footsteps echoed on the stone floor, scraped and gouged in places by heavy shoes and work boots. One lone teller peered from behind a barred window. The chill, stored in the stone walls and floors for decades, ran down his back.

Nikolai walked past the sole teller. At the end of the corridor two cubicles held a single banker each. Neither appeared eager to assist anyone. Nikolai chose the woman, whose wan skin registered as just slightly more robust than the gray of her coworker.

"Hello. I am Nikolai Asilimov."

"Jana," said the woman. "How can I help you?"

"I need to close an account," Nikolai replied.

He sat in a circa Cold War era metal and vinyl chair, across from her desk, and gave his account information. Jana verified the information and noticed the amount on her computer screen. She perked up, ran a hand through a rat's nest of bottle-brown hair, and checked her makeup in the reflective glass top on her desk.

"You do know, Mr. Asilimov, your father left you a safe deposit box?" She glanced up from the computer screen.

Nikolai leaned forward in his chair. His breath caught in his throat.

"N-no," he choked out. "What could my father have in a safe deposit box?"

"Um, he prepaid it for twenty-five years," she continued. "But I have no idea what might be in there, Mr. Asilimov. We aren't privy to such things. Bank policy."

Jana managed a weak smile, but kept her lips together, covering mediocre dental work.

"Would you like to see the contents?"

"Uh-uh, y-yes, sure." he stammered. "But I'll also need to have the bank account transferred to one in Ukraine, where I am moving. Some traveling money as well, please."

"Very good. I'll start the process to transfer your funds to a relational bank in Ukraine, just need the town or city. I'll draw some of the balance in cash for you. How much would you like?"

"Oh, uh, how about 500 leu, 3000 hryvnia, and 200 euros?"

"That's fine, Mr. Asilimov. Let me take you down to our deposit box vault."

Jana led him to a stairwell. They walked past the main vault, a leftover from the '50s, and into another room that contained additional relics of the past—wooden privacy desks divided by purple curtains, a ceiling supported by chipped and scored marble columns, few unbroken chairs.

The bank's safe deposit box system, also a Cold War antique, had not changed in decades. Nothing computerized. Everything done by pen and paper on hard copies. Manual signatures required for release. The keys were kept with a guard who sat at a desk in front of a faded wood veneer file cabinet.

"Asilimov, Andrei," said Jana to the heavily jowled guard.

The guard, who moved at the rate of mammalian evolution, reached into a cabinet drawer and withdrew a file. Nikolai's father's name, typed on a crack-and-peel label, faded but legible. The guard verified the accuracy of the information. It matched a hardcopy coded key sheet, which the guard lifted from the desk drawer to his right.

The guard procured the coded key from a rusted collection on a tarnished brass ring. He handed it to Nikolai to show the numbers matched.

Nikolai followed Jana into the safe deposit box vault.

Windowless and unheated, the walls not painted in decades. The cement floor cold through his shoes. Nikolai shuddered. He stamped his feet against the dampness. The guard took the key, marked A13, and located the locker that contained Andrei Asilimov's safe deposit box.

The guard unlocked the 3"x 5" door, pulled out the box, and placed it on a bare metal table in the room.

Nikolai picked up the box. It felt heavier than he would have expected for its size when lifted. He, Jana, and the guard walked out.

The guard escorted Nikolai and Jana to one of three private rooms. It measured seven feet by seven feet, the ceiling nine feet high. It contained another metal desk, desk chair, and trashcan.

Nikolai stared at the two bank employees.

"I will wait out here," said Jana taking the hint, "unless you feel you need to have someone in here with you."

Again, her pinched smile.

"I will be fine," said Nikolai.

On the desk lay a lonely pen chained to a desk lamp, secured by sheet metal screws. The walls bare. He switched on the lamp. The bulb blew out. His pupils dilated as Nikolai adjusted to the weak light. He went to the door and turned the lock.

He placed the box, 18" long by 5" wide, on the desk. Whether through age or wear, it had taken on an asymmetry.

Nikolai turned the box over, and shook it like a child left unsupervised with the gifts under a Christmas tree. Unlike a present however, it did not rattle. Whatever occupied the inside filled the space.

He set it down on the desk again. The box landed with a thud that startled him, and caused Jana and the guard in the outside room to look up from their conversation. The banker smoothed back her hair and knocked on the door.

"Everything all right, Mr. Asilimov?" she shouted.

"Fine," Nikolai assured the banker.

The box sat on the corner of the scratched desk. Perspiration broke out on his forehead. He wiped it with his shirt sleeve. Nikolai flipped up the front part of the box and inhaled the distinct smell of camphor. A shiny, black silk cloth lay in the box. He grabbed ahold of it in his sweaty hands and yanked.

This is heavy for a cloth.

It's a pouch!

Nikolai laid the pouch on the desk, and ran a hand inside the cloth cover. The odor of camphor increased, now mingled with musk.

Nikolai pulled out a leather sack. Several cords of the same leather tied it closed around something heavy. Nikolai loosened the stays and removed the object. He grasped a tapered piece of polished silver metal with Cyrillic letters etched on one side, indented with four finger-sized grooves.

Jewels no larger than a quarter inch in circumference adorned the opposite side, inset in a row along its length, about 15 inches. One stone appeared to be missing, but Nikolai realized a groove replaced it. He slid his thumb into it and raised the object. The metal gleamed with no hint of wear or age. He held it in front and brought it to his face, where it glinted from every angle even in the dull light of the room.

What is this? Have I held this before?

He closed his eyes. His father, holding the taper, flashed in front of him.

Nikolai slipped it back into the sack and tied the leather cords at the top.

He had brought a satchel with him and placed the sack inside. He closed and clicked the safe deposit box and walked out. He set the box down on a table in the waiting area, handed the key to the guard, and said goodbye.

"Would you like us to keep the safe deposit box account open, Mr. Asilimov?" Jana asked.

But he was already up the stairs, and on his way to Poenari Castle.

The Border between Bulgaria and Romania—March 7

Bulgaria. The roads pockmarked with missing blacktop and faded white and yellow dividing lines. The stolen high-performance vehicle shot through the country, ignoring the divots. RJ didn't let the needle drop below 120 miles per hour. Evan spent most of the ride gripping the headrest, too scared to ask for a bathroom break.

They emptied the trunk of the weapons from the police station and abandoned the car behind a clump of trees – which Evan used to his benefit – and when he was finished, they ran into the closest ditch.

"Keep your head down, Evan. You probably never saw military action, or you wouldn't need to worry about where to buy your next hat," RJ cracked.

"Ah, why don't you kiss my -"

RJ shoved Evan's head below the top of the roadside ditch.

"Don't know what you're worried about," said Evan. "There's no one around."

"And that's what concerns me. I don't want some bureaucrat or bored soldier showing up. It strikes me as a popular place to cross the border, and an even better place to shake people down. Or shoot them."

Evan raised his eyes above the ditch.

"What now? Where do you think the car is that Max arranged?"

"I know where it is. We just have to get there."

RJ put his right arm out straight and extended two fingers toward the sky, as though measuring a drink.

"Scotch, neat?" quipped Evan.

"About twenty minutes past sunrise. Let's go," said RJ. They climbed out of the ditch and headed for the nearest cluster of buildings, none of which appeared occupied. A series of one- story shops lined the sides of a single paved road that ran through the middle of Ruse, Romania.

"Welcome to Ruse," said RJ. He watched as Evan dawdled behind him. "I'd suggest a little more hustle, Mr. English. I want to be back on the road before anyone in this two-latke town wakes up."

"What's the hurry? We're out of Turkey and Bulgaria."

RJ walked straight up to Evan and slammed the heel of his right hand into Evan's chest.

"You don't get it, do you Mr. English? I just didn't pluck you out of Istanbul to save your ancestor's skull. I am taking you to Poenari Castle. As I explained, you are *needed* there."

"I, uh—" said Evan from a doubled-over position.

"Shut up, and listen," hissed RJ in Evan's face. "There are killing machines massing in Poenari, ready to slaughter anyone there in order to get something that will free them from the bonds of the castle. The only way to stop them is with you, a third-rate PI from London."

RJ stopped, but when Evan opened his mouth, he continued.

"If we fail, there won't be much left on God's green Earth besides them."

"Look at me, RJ."

Evan dropped to the ground. He landed with a thud and lay there.

"I'm not the man for this," said Evan, still lying in a heap.

"Evan, you are the *only* man for this."

They looked up at the sun ascending the rugged Eastern European foothills. As it cleared the Carpathians, a flash of sea-green filled the sky.

"Odd," said RJ. "That normally only occurs over water, and at sunset. Let's take that as a good omen, shall we?"

RJ double-timed it down and across the dusty road that divided the two sets of store fronts. Evan wiped his eyes and fell in behind him.

"You know RJ, we had a $75,000 car we left a ways back."

"Time for a switch. Max called me back. The make, model, and license plate of that car are out on the Interpol wire services. Keep running. We'll have a new car in a couple clicks."

Evan stopped.

"*A couple clicks?*"

RJ ran on.

"You do know Aloysius isn't the only alcoholic at the detective agency?"

RJ pulled a water bottle from his pack and handed it to Evan.

"Have a drink. It's on me."

They arrived at an abandoned roadside Elf gas station. RJ preceded Evan by a full minute. Parked on the side of the building sat a twenty-year-old Fiat Punto.

"This … cannot … be our ride," said Evan, panting and jerking his thumb in the direction of the Punto.

"Too conspicuous?" RJ laughed.

"Yes. I mean, how conspicuous can two Anglos look pushing an out-of-date automobile down Romania's only superhighway? Provided we get to the superhighway in this."

"Don't worry, Evan." RJ laughed, while clapping Evan on the shoulder, "we're going to fit right in with the rest of the Romanians."

They climbed into the unlocked car. As promised, the keys in the ignition. RJ started the car.

"Purrs like a kitten, eh, Evan?"

Recovery and the New Nekredum — March 7

The gray and mottled WolfThane lay on opposite sides of the sleeping blood-red wolf, all three wounded by their encounter with Kodiak. A garnet-colored one, not part of the fight with Kodiak, watched over them. It panted and walked to the white-headed wolf, which had not stirred since collapsing on the floor of the Lair.

Blood matted the white-headed wolf's black fur into a mangy carpet. Kodiak had contused both sides of its ribcage. The wolf's front right front leg hung from its shoulder.

The blood-red wolf inhaled, then snorted a breath that echoed around the Lair. It opened its eyes for the first time since the fight with Kodiak, and lifted its head.

The blood-red wolf eyed its fellow WolfThane. It fixed its gaze on the white-headed wolf. The blood-red wolf snarled until the white-headed wolf got to its feet. It began limping as fast as its dislocated shoulder would allow. It hurled itself against the Lair's wall, shoving the joint back into the socket. The white-headed wolf howled, rolled onto its side. Then it stood and shook itself, spraying crusted blood and fur.

Each member of the WolfThane pack got to its feet. The blood-red wolf sat in the middle of the group. It leaned back and loosed a primal howl. One by one the WolfThane joined. Their full-throated, ancient voices echoed throughout the walls of the Lair. The ground above shook with a lupine cry powerful enough to travel across the valley floor and intrude on the confines of the Hive of the Nekredum.

The garnet and mottled WolfThane thundered from the Lair and headed south.

Below ground and back in the confines of the most northern part of Poenari Forest, a thicket of vines, older than the Draculs, covered a gash in the earth. A few hundred yards down, the three Nekredum slumbered in coves. Cocooned further back in the cave, thousands of Spawn neared the completion of their metamorphosis into Nekredum.

In another 24 hours they would join Animarus.

The howling of the WolfThane awakened Animarus. He raised his blue and green head and pushed himself from the cove. He spread his wings. Animarus drifted to the bottom of the Hive, a stone cavern with blackened moss stalactites and stalagmites littering its ceiling and floor.

Lashed to a stalagmite, her stays cut into the slippery rock to hold her, Elizabeth Astor had given up struggling against the vines which secured her and dropped off to sleep. Animarus chattered and awoke the other two Nekredum.

All three gathered around Elizabeth.

Her slender body twitched like a dog having a nightmare. Elizabeth's eyes snapped open. Her vision adjusted in the dark and she saw her captors, shadowy reptilian figures. She sucked in a breath of the fetid air and retched.

"What do you want!?" she screamed at the shapes in front of her.

Familiar chattering. Animarus stepped forward on its powerful legs.

"CH-CH-DraCH-CH-cul," it chattered.

"Guess again, gargoyle!" she shouted back.

"CH-Pah!"

Animarus reached forward with the taloned claw of its right arm and clenched her face.

"CH-Dra-Cul!"

Elizabeth worked one leg free and snap-kicked Animarus between its legs.

Unaffected, Animarus released its grip and chattered something to the other Nekredum. It walked away from Elizabeth, flew into the confines of the adjacent chamber, and examined a number of Spawn cocoons. From the recesses of the cave its wings beat in a deliberate rhythm.

Animarus repeatedly traveled from the floor to the upper parts of the walls, his wings quickening to a hummingbird's pace. Each time he stopped in front of a cocoon and ran a talon along the webbing holding a member of his army. Animarus chattered to the Spawn, low and deep in his register.

An hour later, he returned and again grabbed Elizabeth by the face, digging one talon into her cheek and drawing blood.

"Dra-CHUL!"

Another kick from Elizabeth.

It released its grip and chattered to the other Nekredum. They flew back up to their coves and fell into a deep sleep.

The Lair emptied of sound. The blood-red wolf growled and charged at the gray wolf. It turned and slammed into the silver wolf and then the white-headed one.

The WolfThane had recovered and were battle ready.

Snagov — March 7 and 8

RJ twitched awake.

"Don't bother looking for your gun," said Evan.

RJ felt the barrel of Louise pressed against his temple. "What's that stupid name for it? Louise? Bad experience with a woman?"

RJ sat still.

"And I've got that nightstick of yours as well. Nice piece of gear. Did you make it yourself?"

"Yes, out of titanium, if you're curious," replied RJ, a thousand-mile stare aimed at Evan.

A couple of hours ago, the Punto had pulled off the highway onto a side road when both RJ and Evan agreed a few hours of sleep would be beneficial to get them to Poenari. Without it, whoever drove might fall asleep at the wheel.

"What gives, Evan?"

"We're making a deal, Mr. Brancatelli."

"Oh?" asked RJ, arching his thick right eyebrow. "And what exactly is that?"

Evan pressed the barrel of Louise even harder into RJ's temple.

"We're—"

RJ's right arm shot up. The gun discharged and blew a hole in the driver's side window. Evan, however, did not yield control and with the palm of his left hand punched RJ in the right cheek. The struggle continued as both men traded blows in the cramped confines of the Fiat's front seat.

Evan fired another shot through the already smashed window and regained the advantage, the gun once again pressed up against RJ's temple.

"I'd suggest a negotiated truce, RJ," said Evan. "Or the next bullet from this gun goes straight through your head."

RJ's right cheek swelled and he sank back into the driver's seat. Evan held his aggressive posture and leaned forward.

"Now, you're going to drive to Lake Snagov," demanded Evan. "We're going to retrieve the torso of Vlad Dracul and after that, we will go on to Poenari Castle. I will help you, but only if I can put my ancestor to rest in his ancestral home."

"We might not get there in time, if we stop in Snagov," argued RJ. "And who knows how long it will take to find the body of Vlad Dracul. Do you even know where it is?"

"Yes. I know exactly where it is."

RJ steered the balky car down the access road to Lake Snagov, following the hardcopy map. The surface of the road had turned from bad public works to really bad public works. The auto dipped into and out of potholes.

He parked past the last stucco houses that populated the right side of the road. Both exited the car and stretched after the long drive. A sign for Lake Snagov sat in front of them at a trail head. Bent and dying trees lined the beginning of the path to the lake.

"Next time we get a rental car, it has to be bigger than the potholes," Evan said to the brown owl that sat on an overhanging branch just above where they had parked. The owl jerked its head and flew straight at Evan. He put his arm up to ward off the attack, but at the last instant the owl shot past him.

"No sense of humor," said Evan as he spun around in case of a return. He saw the object which caused the owl's sudden movement. A rat scurried across the broken asphalt. In one seamless motion, the owl swooped down and snatched the rodent by the neck, shook it, and flew off to enjoy the results of the hunt.

"OK, Evan, who are we today? The owl or the rodent?" asked RJ, his cheek turning green and purple.

Evan grunted and motioned with Louise for RJ to walk down the side road toward Lake Snagov.

"Hold on, RJ." Evan opened the trunk of the Fiat and pulled out two of the police rifles, and the ammunition RJ had purloined.

"I'm trusting you, RJ," said Evan. "I think you're honorable. I also think you want both of us to be armed on the island."

"I think you're correct," said RJ.

"Excellent," said Evan. "And I would like you to give me your word that we will not leave this area until we retrieve my ancestor, no matter what."

RJ hesitated.

"RJ?"

"Yes. You have my word."

"Then let's go," said Evan, motioning with Louise. He turned the gun so the barrel pointed at the ground. "Take her back. I still have mine, and you know how to use this better than I."

RJ holstered Louise.

They traversed the trail. It opened and exposed Lake Snagov, a slow-moving but pretty body of green-blue water. The object of Evan English's quest, an island in the middle of the lake, separated from the shoreline on which they stood by a couple hundred feet of water. They could see a dock with a motorboat tied to it.

From RJ and Evan's vantage point, they saw a path leading away from that dock and into Snagov Island.

Just before the path disappeared into a wooded area of bent and dying trees, a chimney topped a pitched roof on a bungalow, which housed the island's resident monk.

"OK, Evan. What's our next move?" RJ pointed to the island.

"Snagov Island is where the torso of Vlad the Impaler is interred. The monk's hovel is what you see from here. He takes care of the belfry, and the chapel, where my ancestor lay at rest. This Orthodox Christian monk named, coincidentally, Vlad, has lived there for decades. We are going over there, getting the torso, and returning it. And the head to Poenari."

"Are we swimming?"

"We're going to use a little larceny, RJ. I know that's counter to your *fine* character, but if you'll cast your eyes up and down *this* shoreline, you'll see a handful of docks with a few, oh how shall I put this? Pleasure craft?"

RJ looked to his right and left, but saw nothing of the sort. The only dock on the shore lay in front of them, where, presumably, the monk picked up and discharged passengers using a motorboat now tied up at the island.

The dock at the shoreline had no boat to offer.

"Let's get going," said Evan. "I'd say our best bet is to the right . . . or left."

RJ headed off to the right.

"How do you think Tyrrel fared?" Evan asked, as they broke through another tangle of vines along the shoreline. They'd been hiking for half an hour and turned up no docks and no boats.

"Not sure how strong these currents are," said RJ, ignoring the question.

Evan muttered something about the similarities between his partner and the owl. RJ spun around. Evan pointed the gun right between RJ's eyes.

"Let's get it together, and make this a quick trip," said RJ in a low but clear voice, looking past the gun and straight into Evan's eyes. "You want some place to bury Vlad Dracul other than an island in the middle of Romania? Great. I'm all for it, but we need to get back to the castle before more time passes, and stopping here isn't helping."

"If anyone understands the nature of deadly forces, Mr. Brancatelli, it is a Dracul. You don't have to remind me what's at, uh, stake?" Evan laughed at his joke.

RJ inhaled sharply.

"Like I've said a few times. Let's go," said RJ.

They broke through more underbrush. Evan tripped but regained his feet. RJ disappeared into a clump of trees and Evan crashed through to find RJ making his way down a rotted wooden dock. At the end of it they saw a green rubber raft.

They dropped it into the water. RJ got in easily, but Evan's entrance was not as graceful. He attempted a feet-first approach which resulted in the raft being pushed so far from the dock that RJ had to row it back. Another try. Evan stumbled off the dock, bounced off the side of the raft, and landed in the middle, directly on top of one of the oars.

"Welcome aboard!" shouted RJ.

Evan removed the oar from underneath him. RJ pushed away from the dock.

The one dock on the island faced west, visible by the monk. The men risked waking the monk by coming in the "front door." But heavy old-growth trees encircled the rest of the island, which did not allow RJ and Evan access.

"If the monk causes any problems," said RJ, "I'm prepared to sedate him. The same for those dogs I hear barking."

Behind them, on shore, something slipped into the waters of Lake Snagov. Evan turned when he felt the disturbance.

"Ah, nothing. Fish," he mumbled to RJ.

RJ, though, went on high alert, and scanned the lake.

"I think we were followed, Evan. We need to step it up." He released the safety on Louise and the rifle between strokes.

"Didn't see anyone on the roads," said Evan, who shouldered his rifle.

"That means nothing," replied RJ. "Get to the front of the raft and pull us into the dock. Want to see if I can spot anything."

RJ shaded his eyes to more thoroughly search the water. Not a ripple.

The raft touched the wooden dock on the island. RJ heard the tap of the contact, and nothing else. The monk's outboard lay tied up on one side. Evan placed the raft opposite.

The dogs ceased barking. If the chapel had a bell, it did not chime. The birds sang no songs. A leaf from one of the trees above them floated to the ground.

A silhouette in the water slid past from behind. Evan saw it in his peripheral vision.

"There any way our crossdressing Fatih Muslims would come this far?" asked Evan

"Not a chance," said RJ. "Hurry!"

"Good idea," said Evan.

Another movement. They heard the splash of water. RJ climbed out of the raft with Evan at his heels. They hustled past the monk's hovel.

"It is not anything human," RJ said, sucking in his breath as they ran. "Does that help?"

"Anything else?"

"It means we have to keep running, because I have a pretty good idea what's behind us."

"I thought you said the Nekredum were bound to Poenari by the spike of the Draculs?"

"They are," said RJ. "This is something else. These are the Nekredum helpmates, WolfThane, with an allegiance to the Nekredum. Margaret said they are free to roam and not bound to Poenari."

"Great. Can they be killed?" Evan asked, as they cleared the house and approached two wooden structures. The one to their left had a steeple, the one to their right, a flat square building.

"Yes, but not easily."

"I think I've … heard that somewhere before," replied Evan, panting. "Chapel to the left."

"The steeple give it away?" RJ smirked.

The garnet and mottled WolfThane breached Snagov Island and tore past the monk's hovel.

"How in hell did they find us?"

"Not important. Let's go!" hissed RJ. "They're on the island!" He grabbed Evan by the wrist and they bolted toward the chapel. "Run straight inside!"

RJ released Evan's wrist and threw himself against the door, shattering the dry-rotted wood. Evan shot in two seconds later. They had made it to the chapel, but now the entranceway offered no security from the WolfThane. RJ pointed a rifle at the opening and Evan followed suit, training the site of his rifle at the breach.

"Aim for their throats. I have the one on the right."

Beads of sweat dripped into Evan's eye. He closed it and swallowed. No more than ten feet from the chapel, the WolfThane skidded to a stop. They howled in unison, turned tail, and retreated. The men lowered their weapons.

RJ looked around the chapel. He smiled and nodded.

"Sanctuary," he said, breaking the tension. "The WolfThane will not enter this holy area. We are safe as long as we remain inside the chapel."

"That's fine for now, but how do we get out? Is the monk going to come to our rescue?"

"Doubtful." RJ shook his head. "He's going to be dead in a few minutes."

"The good news is that until we locate and exhume the body of Vlad the Impaler, there's no need to formulate an escape plan," said Evan. "We aren't going anywhere until we find it. What do you say?"

"That ain't good news."

Evan slung his rifle around his back. For now, the two were trapped inside the chapel, which measured about 35 feet in both directions. It took Evan five seconds to find Vlad's burial site.

Positioned on an easel in the center of the square structure sat a painting of Vlad. No marker, but a rectangular outline on the floor with a worn tapestry partially covering it, marked the final resting place of Vlad the Impaler.

In the distance, the WolfThane howled like hyenas gathered around a kill.

RJ and Evan removed the rug. RJ's eye went to a stone pedestal stuck in a corner of the chapel that displayed more iconography of the Draculs.

"Evan. Give me a hand with this," said RJ, pointing at the pedestal. He removed the iconography from the top and placed it on the ground.

He and Evan lifted the pedestal. They waddled over to the stone covering of the burial site. The surface of the cover, blackened by years of mold and grime read "Vlad Tepes, 1431 to 1476."

"Can't the Romanians get anything right?" blurted Evan. "1428 to 1477! I won't lose any sleep smashing this."

They stood on top of the marking and caught their collective breath. RJ's face scrunched as he and Evan lifted, then dropped the pedestal. It struck the marker and cracked the surface of the stone. Evan walked to the middle of the stone.

"You wouldn't happen to want to have another go with the pedestal, would you, RJ? I have a feeling this—"

The stone collapsed. Evan's hands shot up in the air and his face contorted as he disappeared. The rifle, still slung over his back, slipped off, but followed Evan into the bowels of the chapel's mausoleum.

"Evan!"

RJ lunged for safer ground. But he waited too long to shout "Evan!" and plummeted down, down, down. He hit the ground on his rear end and bounced up like one of those old children's toys you punch but it never falls.

Evan hadn't fared as well. He lay motionless. RJ knelt to examine him, and found a pulse.

"You're going to be out for a while." RJ released his wrist.

RJ stood and brushed dirt from his hands. He searched his pockets for a flashlight. The Maglite still on the key chain, but the lens and bulb smashed by his fall.

"Damn."

He reached down to Evan's unconscious body.

"Please have a flashlight," he begged Evan. RJ searched Evan like he was frisking a perp, and when he finished, all he had in his hands was a penlight. Would have to do.

He flicked it on.

Empty. No skeleton lying next to an unconscious Evan. RJ moved the light across the floor. No sarcophagus on the ground, nor any evidence one had ever been there.

"I had hoped to find his headless skeleton wrapped in a decomposed shroud, lying at my feet," lamented RJ. "But that would have been too easy."

RJ's penlight landed on standing suits of armor, away from the center of the room.

He waved the thin beam of light back and forth over three standing suits, one of which did not have a helmet. It stood to the right of the other two.

Three generations of Draculs.

"Warriors in life and death, eh," RJ said, addressing the armor. "I'm going out on a limb. I'm guessing the one without the helmet is Vlad the Impaler. If we ever take you to America, we'll enjoy a trip to Sleepy Hollow, where you can, uh, discuss things with the Headless Horseman."

He cackled, laughing so loud and hard that he had to wipe tears from his eyes. RJ stopped when he heard a sound and wheeled around, gun drawn.

Evan rubbed the top of his head and groaned. RJ holstered Louise.

"How's the head?"

"Have to tell you, RJ. It hurts. A lot."

"I'm sure. Let me check you for possible concussion."

RJ kneeled, flashlight in hand, and Evan struggled into a sitting position. RJ checked Evan's pupils, and asked him a few questions.

"All right, Evan," he said. "Don't think you have a concussion. You are, however, going to have a nasty headache for a couple of hours. Wish I had something for it."

"Me too."

"Can you stand?"

Evan nodded and brought himself to his feet. When he stood, he noticed the triumvirate of armor. He focused on the suit missing the helmet.

"Can't be that easy, can it? Shouldn't there be some trickery where the obvious choice, uh, isn't the obvious choice?"

"One way to find out," RJ said. He walked over to the headless suit of armor and took it apart, starting with the breastplate. The shoulder and hip joints followed. The floor became littered with the armor piled high. RJ propped the torso against the wall.

"I'd say this is our man," said RJ, pointing at the headless skeleton. "Going to bring you home, Vlad. Let's get the skull fragments and get out of here."

"They're up on the chapel floor in my pack," said Evan, staring up through the hole in the ceiling. "I'm the bigger of the two of us. You'll have to get on my shoulders and pull yourself onto the floor."

"If you say so," said a grinning RJ. "I'm going to enjoy this."

They tried four times unsuccessfully. RJ just could not get close enough to the chapel floor to pull himself up.

They slumped to the ground. Evan's head pounded, and he leaned forward, holding it between his knees. RJ gave him some water and glanced at his watch.

"It's still light outside. It might be easier to escape the WolfThane if we get out now. Nocturnal animals and all that. Going to get dark in a couple hours," said RJ.

Evan grinned and looked up at RJ then stood, groaning the whole way to his feet. He walked to the pile of armor from Vlad III and pulled some of the larger pieces. He took down the other two standing Draculs, and began disassembling them.

"RJ!" he shouted. "Give me a hand with this. I think these other Draculs can help."

RJ caught on and piled armor on top of armor.

Evan secured the armor. The breastplates, stacked on the floor. Followed by the thigh protectors and then the shin guards. The combination of the metal parts might give the additional height for RJ to gain purchase to the floor above.

"Think this will work?"

"One way to find out."

Evan climbed on top of the pile. It swayed and crumpled, but held its structure. RJ climbed on top of Evan's shoulders, and steadied himself.

The armor collapsed.

Evan tumbled onto the dirt floor, but RJ hit the ground on his feet and fell backward against the wall where the armor no longer stood. The wall gave way under his weight, and he found himself looking down a tunnel.

"What the—?"

RJ righted himself and pointed his penlight at his accidental discovery. The beam illuminated the opening, and the first few feet of a tunnel.

"I'm taking a look."

RJ walked to the end of the tunnel. A ladder led to an opening in a floor above. He shined the light upward.

"Hey Evan! I found a ladder. I bet it leads to—"

"The belfry!" shouted Evan as best he could, his head pounding. "That tunnel leads from the mausoleum to the belfry."

He rubbed his forehead.

"Might have thought about adding a door to the mausoleum. Our way in isn't the best."

RJ held up a rusted hinge, once attached to the collapsed wall.

"That was the door. Doesn't look like our monk spent a lot of time in this family crypt," said RJ. "You stay. I'll take the ladder up to—fingers crossed—the belfry. From there, I'll cover the ground back to the chapel before the WolfThane can react, and when I get inside, I'll pull you up, somehow."

"Why don't we both make a run for the dock from the belfry?" asked Evan. "Catch the WolfThane off guard long enough?"

RJ walked back to Evan and placed a hand on the man's shoulder.

"We'd never make it. One step at a time. Got it?"

"Yes," he said, eyes down. The pain in his head increased.

RJ hurried back through the tunnel, climbed the ladder, and emerged inside the belfry. *Good call . . . so far.*

A gunk-covered window next to its door revealed the 30 yards he would have to run to return to the chapel. Midday had passed. The silence, save for the WolfThane's earlier howling, remained. They were nearby, but not in the open.

The WolfThane are still here.

With Louise in hand, he slipped out the door and sprinted toward the chapel. From the corner of his eye he saw two shapes, low to the ground, run from the monk's bungalow.

RJ turned, Louise lower in front of him.

"RJ!" shouted Evan. "Go! Go! *Go!*"

Evan had ignored RJ's plan and followed behind him down the tunnel. He now stood inside the belfry door. He fired his rifle at the WolfThane, no more than a couple of yards from RJ, as they thundered toward him. His shots hit both WolfThane and threw them off their mark. RJ pressed on toward the chapel.

The garnet wolf howled and sprang at RJ. His jaw clipped the back of RJ's calf and drew blood. Evan fired more rounds in that direction. He reloaded. The mottled wolf broke off from the attack on RJ and headed to the belfry. And Evan.

Evan slammed the door and dropped the cross-latch over it. The mottled wolf heaved its 275 pounds against it. The belfry shuddered. Its walls bent. The wolf went into a howling frenzy. The garnet wolf, now turning its attention to Evan, joined the mottled wolf and both attacked the belfry. Evan slid down the ladder using the sides of it as handrails. He sprinted to the mausoleum

With a violent crack, the belfry door cleaved in half. The WolfThane dashed inside just as Evan skittered down the ladder. They ran in tight circles, spittle hurling from their mouths, and crashed against each other in frustration. They shook themselves, and ran from the belfry back to their watch outside the chapel.

Evan arrived inside the mausoleum and yelled for RJ. He ignored the worsening pain in his head and shouted as loud as he could. No sound came from the chapel above.

"RJ!"

RJ Brancatelli lay strewn out on the floor above. Evan's second round had given RJ enough time to dive through the open door, but he lost so much blood from his calf wound that he drifted in and out of consciousness.

"RJ!"

Evan's last entreaty roused him from his stupor. RJ slapped himself.

RJ attempted to stand, but vertigo from loss of blood, now soaking into the dirt floor of the chapel, pushed him to his knees. He ripped off an arm from his shirt, and used it to apply pressure.

RJ grasped a shard of shattered stone from the top of Dracul's grave marker. He cut away the fabric around the rest of his calf, and applied a tourniquet.

"Evan," he rasped. "I'm all right. Give me a few minutes and I'll have you up here, but you'll have to restack the armor, or find something else to stand on."

"Great. In the meantime, I'll figure out how to get our pal up there." He hooked the skeleton of Vlad Dracul to his back by lowering one of its arms down inside his shirt.

RJ took off his belt, and removed his pants. He knotted the belt to one pant leg and dropped the lifeline down the hole into the mausoleum.

RJ wrapped his bare legs around a roof support column in the chapel. Evan assembled a tall but shaky mountain of armor, grabbed the pant leg and climbed, as RJ held the belt. Evan, head still aching, heaved himself and his passenger onto the floor of the chapel. The skeleton clattered to the floor.

"What do we do for our next act?" laughed Evan, seeing RJ wearing a shirt with only one sleeve and no pants.

"I'm working on it." RJ pulled on his pants and slipped the belt back through the loops. He tightened the tourniquet. The shirt, now more rag than anything, he removed and tied around his waist.

Evan and RJ smiled. Evan picked up the headless skeleton and set it in a corner. He pulled the largest of the skull pieces out of the bag.

As if he were crowning a new king, he gently placed the fragment onto the top bone of the spine. More than five hundred years had passed, but the fragment fit perfectly. He took more of the large pieces and balancing them, managed to place the lower sections of the skull together, along with part of the left side, up to the eye socket. Evan stepped back to admire his work.

Dracul's hollow eye socket stared at Evan, who ducked away, and took in RJ's condition.

Torn and bloodied leg with tourniquet. Shirtless. Pair of pants recently used as a rope. Cheek swollen to where he resembled the loser in a boxing match.

Evan had not fared much better, bruised and battered from the WolfThane. Headache worsening.

"Well, Sundance, next time *I* say we should go somewhere, maybe we should go somewhere," said RJ.

"Next time. And I don't think that's the actual quote." replied Evan.

"You should drink some of this," said RJ, handing Evan a water bottle. "I've had my fill."

"No, thanks. I drank a bunch of the holy water while you were putting your pants back on," Evan said, pointing to the baptismal font of the chapel.

"Guess that means the WolfThane won't be able to eat me?"

Evan threw back his head and laughed. RJ grunted and shifted his view back to the baptismal font.

"Holy water?" asked RJ.

"There's a huge basin of it back there. Maybe the monk believes that this isolated rock gets more visitors than it does."

RJ limped to the interior room. He sized up the basin and splashed some of the water on his damaged cheek. RJ returned to the outer room.

"What?" asked Evan.

"I'm taking a bath," he said as he untied his shirt. "And you're going to need one, too. At least your clothes are."

"I am? They are? They *are?*"

"Yep, the WolfThane *might* not come near *anything* sacred," answered RJ, "and this baptismal holy water qualifies. I think."

"You *think!*" shouted Evan.

"Right now, Evan, it is our best, no, hang on, yes, our *only* option."

RJ and Evan soaked their clothes and filled the empty bottle with the holy water. If their clothes wouldn't be enough deterrent, they might have one last chance if they sprayed the WolfThane with the liquid. RJ hoped it would not come to that, as the sport-top bottle didn't offer much distance or accuracy.

Evan hoisted the pack holding Vlad's skull onto his own shoulders, after dropping in the pieces he'd used on top of the torso. Evan re-rigged the skeleton of Vlad the Impaler to his back.

"Can't convince you to leave your ancestor here?" RJ asked. "Slows us down."

"Not a chance."

"Those WolfThane are concentrating on the chapel. I'll go to the belfry and run straight out the opening," said RJ. "No hesitation. We'll split our scent. Might buy us a second or two, and I want as much time as possible. Straight to the dock."

"Oh, bloody hell. Uh, the fall into the tunnel will probably kill ya," replied Evan.

"Not even close. Let's go."

"Hang on," said Evan. "*I'll* go to the belfry. It's further away from the dock, and you're on one wheel."

"Sundance," said RJ, clapping a hand on Evan's shoulder. "That might be the first sensible thing you've said today."

"Today ain't over yet. Aiming for two sensible things."

Evan walked to the shattered remains of Vlad's former gravesite marker. He removed the skeleton from his back and estimated the drop to the top of the armor pile.

"Me first. Then toss down the skeleton," said Evan. "I can make this drop, but don't want to break the skeleton. We came all this way."

"Copy."

Evan dropped into the mausoleum. He landed on the armor pile with a thud, and rolled off the side.

"Move, Evan," whispered RJ, and gingerly tossed him the skeleton. Evan placed it in his backpack.

"How do we time this?" asked Evan.

"I'll see you run out of the belfry, and be right behind."

The garnet and mottled WolfThane were but a few feet from the door of the chapel. As Evan ran down the tunnel, they heard his movement and moved away, providing RJ more of an opening.

Evan pulled himself up the ladder. The WolfThane stalked toward the belfry.

Evan exploded from the front door of the belfry, drawing the WolfThane further from the chapel. RJ ignored the pain in his calf. He flew out the open door, Louise drawn.

The WolfThane, distracted by the split in their adversaries, hesitated.

RJ and Evan made for the dock, the WolfThane in pursuit.

Kodiak — March 8

Doug Mackie sat, then stood, then paced, then read the signs in the waiting room of the hospital for the fifth time. He tapped his thumbs together. He repeated the same routine for the next hour. His back ached from sitting against the cheap plastic chairs in the waiting room.

The hospital staff rushed Kodiak into surgery two hours ago. Doug heard nothing since. The hospital only allowed cellphone use outside, but he did not go anywhere, not even to the bathroom, while he awaited word.

"Mr. Mackie?" asked Dr. Lapescu, now in scrubs.

Doug's eyes snapped open. He had drifted off to sleep. Lapescu untied and removed his surgical mask.

"We won't know for a few more hours. The dog has lost a lot of blood, but is stable."

Doug, his face worn, wiped fatigue and a couple of tears away. He could not speak but his face expressed gratitude, eyes shining, mouth smiling.

"You should go home. We'll call you when there's a change," said Lapescu, placing the mask in his gloved hand.

"No. I want to stay here. I'll wait," insisted Doug.

"Then I suggest you get something to eat and come back in a little while."

"Yes, of course."

Doug sat down and fell asleep.

At about the same time that the hospital staff wheeled Kodiak out of surgery, the white-headed, gray, and silver-white WolfThane, along with their blood-red leader, exited the Lair. The four entered the trail that would take them to the valley and then Poenari Castle.

Small shafts of light penetrated the forest canopy as they trotted along the hardpacked dirt, their paws leaving eerie footprints behind them. The air blew cold and damp.

The blood-red wolf broke into a run.

"You cannot battle the Nekredum and WolfThane without Kodiak," said Margaret, through her Zoom window. "None of you will survive the encounter without the dog. Even at that . . ."

Max, from the main floor of the castle, called Margaret to inform her of the visit by the Romanian police. He stared out through the shattered stained-glass window and watched the Romanian flags fluttering from the towers of the castle.

"The police cannot help you," said Margaret. "But let me assume that is not why you were visited by the local authorities."

"No, ma'am," said Max.

"What is it, Max?"

"We *do* need help," he continued. "And I've not heard much from RJ. Don't know where he is. And Kodiak? It's not looking good. He won't be back in time, *if* today is the return of the Nekredum and the WolfThane."

"They will be back today." Margaret stated with confidence. "They'll kill every darned one of you and then their Spawn will not be far behind. You could flee."

"And do what?" shouted Max. "Abandon Elizabeth? RJ?"

"Max." Margaret backed away from her screen.

"Alvin and Doug aren't going anywhere," he yelled. "Benjamin and Nate are out for blood revenge on those hellhounds. I want the Nekredum, or whatever they are, to give Elizabeth back, and I want to kill every single one of them."

Max turned sharply when Garrett marched in to the castle. Shedding his all-business attire, he appeared armed for war wearing fatigues and high-end weaponry—a Glock on his hip and a titanium nightstick, courtesy of RJ, in its scabbard. Garrett joined Max at the monitor.

Max turned back to Margaret.

"Our scant numbers . . . reduced today. Perhaps by two or three if Kodiak is gone and RJ cannot make it back in time with Evan English."

"I know, Max. I can only tell you what my research tells me. The United States Army could not stop Lucifer's minions if they gain Mors Aeterna."

"We know this, Margaret," said Garrett, his face tense with frustration.

"Do you?" asked Margaret. "Do you really? Do you know what you're up against, Garrett?"

"Now hold on a moment, Doctor. My sister is—"

"Yes, she's a prisoner of the foot soldiers of Satan, Garrett. At this very moment, they could be pulling her skin off her like an animal. Human beings will kill an animal before flaying it. The ritual of skinning used to be in Man's purview, but we're too civilized now. Make no mistake, the Nekredum are not."

Garrett stepped away from the monitor.

"I'm not done yet, Garrett. You can't call in the Army or the Marines. These are creatures that will slaughter anything in their path. The only reason they aren't out is because God, yes God, has put certain people in Poenari to stand against them."

Garrett moved closer.

"God put RJ Brancatelli there. He led you to me. I found Evan English, who might, let me reiterate, *might* be able to kill the leader of the Nekredum with Mors Aeterna." Margaret paused. "I would suggest you find it, and pray RJ returns with Evan soon, because the only way to stop Satan is to kill the leader of the Nekredum. If we fail, and I include myself in that 'we,' the Age of Man comes to an end."

The Hospital — March 8

Doug wandered around Curtea de Argeş to kill some time, but nothing distracted him. He checked his phone every few minutes. He finally gave up and returned to the hospital. When he arrived, he requested that the admitting nurse call for Dr. Lapescu.

Dr. Lapescu, now in street clothes, came to update Doug. Clean-shaven, and showered, the doctor appeared reborn.

"Kodiak will pull through, but must remain at the hospital for a few days. Blood transfusions for animals are not as common as for humans, but given the Astors' reach, additional supplies were rushed to Curtea de Argeş. With any luck, Kodiak will be up and about in less than a week."

"Not before?" asked Doug.

Lapescu looked him straight in the eye.

"No, sir. This dog has sustained severe injury. I don't know how he even survived surgery. When you brought him in, we thought his wounds were fatal. He is a remarkably fast healer, but it is going to take some time. We stopped the internal and external bleeding and had enough blood on hand to stabilize him. Until we replace his full capacity, Kodiak needs to rest, and let me emphasize rest."

Doug didn't respond.

"Is this a working dog, Mr. Mackie?" asked Lapescu.

"You could say that."

"You'll have to find another dog for a little while. I hope his duties aren't that specific. Can they wait for him to return to health?"

"First of all, Dr. Lapescu, there is no other dog like this, and second, I don't think *any* of us can wait for him to return to health. Call me if there's a change."

"Best thing for him, as I've said, is rest."

Lapescu shook Doug's hand and walked back to check on Kodiak. Doug exited the hospital, bound for Poenari. Nothing more could be done at the hospital. His friends needed him now.

As he waited for a cab, Doug called RJ. No answer.

RJ and Evan — March 8

The WolfThane, thrown off by RJ's change in tactics, recovered and sprinted toward the men, who passed the monk's hovel and closed on the dock.

RJ and Evan turned and opened fire. The garnet and mottled WolfThane flew through the air, shaking off what few times they were hit. RJ changed clips mid-run. The air thick with gunpowder. The WolfThane but yards away.

A couple shotgun blasts leveled the WolfThane, throwing them off the chase. The monk, his face a torn mask of blood, one eyeball hanging by a piece of connective tissue, lurched out of his doorway, shotgun at the ready. A breach-loaded weapon ejected shells.

"Run faster," the monk croaked, shoving shells into the breach. He aimed at the WolfThane and fired, hitting them again. They landed hard, then skidded along the ground.

The wounded WolfThane gained their feet, blood soaking their flanks and ribcages.

The monk fired again. The shotgun blasts smashed into the WolfThane once more, but before he could reload, the garnet wolf tore out the man's throat. The monk dropped to the ground. One eyeball in front of him. His other fixed on the chapel. The garnet wolf released the monk's throat.

The WolfThane, once more, closed on RJ and Evan.

RJ's well-aimed shots found their mark. One bullet ripped off the top part of the garnet wolf's left ear.

The mottled wolf sprang. He missed his target of RJ's wounded calf and hit the ground behind RJ and Evan. The mottled wolf writhed in pain and Evan fired into the wounds left by the monk. The garnet wolf grabbed the mottled wolf by the neck and shook it to its feet.

RJ and Evan arrived at the dock and headed for the raft, but stopped. Claw marks and matted fur covered the shredded remains. The WolfThane had destroyed it.

RJ touched his shirt. *Dry.*

The WolfThane were only yards from the dock. RJ emptied his clip, and pulled out the bottle of holy water.

Before he could use it, Evan yanked RJ away from the raft. RJ landed on his stomach with a thud at the bottom of the monk's outboard motorboat. In one smooth motion, Evan pulled the motor to life and engaged the gear. With his other hand, he loosed the frayed rope that held the outboard in place. They sped away from Snagov Island.

The garnet and mottled WolfThane howled. They tore down the dock and jumped into the water, but too late to be near the outboard that sped out of their range on its way back to shore.

The Spike — March 8, Late Afternoon

Nikolai squinted. He pedaled his bicycle toward the setting sun, the satchel swinging at his side. The closer he got to Poenari, the faster he rode. He had been in such a hurry to leave the bank, he neglected to pick up his cash.

"Doesn't … matter … now," he panted.

He rode the bike into the construction elevator with the satchel now tucked under his arm. He dropped the bike inside. When the doors opened, Nikolai made for the shack.

He ran inside and dumped the contents of his satchel onto the kitchen table. Nikolai lifted the leather sack and drew out the polished metal object. It reflected what little light penetrated the cabin's walls and windows.

He examined the gemstones on one side, and turned it over. In the far distance of the valley, he thought he heard howling.

Not the wind. The WolfThane are on the march.

Nikolai ran his hand along the etched Cyrillic inscription and brought it close.

He gripped the metal tighter, and lifted it to eye level. An electrical charge traveled up his arm and into his shoulder. Nikolai caught his reflection. His father's face stared back at him.

The Road to Poenari — March 8, Late Afternoon

The monk's boat crashed into the dock on the mainland side of Lake Snagov. RJ cut the engine, but momentum slammed the bow into the wooden structure.

The crash propelled both men onto the splintered dock. They collected themselves and ran for the safety of their car.

"Step it up, English! I'm not interested in finding out how fast those WolfThane swim. I got a taste for how fast they run."

They rounded the bend from the ramp and hustled to the side street where they parked.

Gone. The vehicle stolen or towed.

"Of course," said Evan.

They turned back toward the island and spotted the WolfThane moving through the water.

"How much of a head start do you think we've got?" asked Evan.

"Not enough," said RJ. "Come on! Over there!"

He pointed to an old truck parked in the driveway of one of the nearby homes. No activity at the house, but RJ pulled out Louise as the two of them closed in on the truck.

"Older vehicles are easier to hotwire," said RJ. "But if anyone comes out of that house, be prepared to shoot. It will be a nicer way to die than getting mauled by those WolfThane."

"You have no idea how much I agree with that statement." Evan exhaled. He took out his sidearm.

RJ opened the driver's side door. He crawled into the front seat and shoved himself under the steering wheel. The old truck had a stick shift, so RJ not only needed to bypass the ignition but had to get the vehicle rolling to jumpstart it.

The WolfThane shot out of the water and tore up the boat ramp to the side street. The scent of the men lingered. They lifted their noses to the air.

"They're out of the water!"

Evan opened the passenger door. He gripped the door jamb. RJ released the emergency brake and slipped the truck into neutral. It didn't budge. He opened the driver's side door and stepped out. At the same time Evan spotted a gray blur at the end of the street. He fired in its direction. Next to him, RJ grunted as he shoved the truck backward. It moved slowly and then stopped.

"On three?" RJ asked.

"Shut up and push!" shouted Evan, who leaned into the passenger side door jamb and bellowed. RJ followed on his side and the truck lurched backward. They jumped inside and RJ engaged the clutch and the transmission. The engine turned over.

RJ shouted into the air, as the truck accelerated down the driveway. The garnet and mottled WolfThane lunged at it and left several dents in its side, forcing it up on two wheels on the driver's side at one point. Evan grabbed RJ and pulled himself over to push the vehicle back onto all fours.

"Why Evan, you old flirt." RJ laughed.

After a few backfires, the old pickup made its way down the access road toward the main highway that would take them to Poenari.

The Gathering Forces — March 8, Late Afternoon

The blood-red wolf stood in front of the semicircle formed by the WolfThane at the base of the foothills. The last stop before the assault on the castle.

He shook his head, hinged back on his haunches, and let loose a howl that reached the walls of the castle and spun into the cold night air. The other WolfThane joined, and the sound rang through the forest and reached, once more, to the Nekredum Hive.

The WolfThane marched up the hill next to the sheer drop and on to Poenari Castle.

The ultrasonic howling of the WolfThane hit Kodiak's ears. The Sentinel of Poenari still lay on his side at the hospital in Curtea de Argeş. He picked up his head and cocked it in the direction of the castle.

The WolfThane are on the move.

Animarus also stirred in response to the howling of the WolfThane. Its reptilian wings unfolded and pushed it from the cove in which it slumbered. It passed a four-taloned claw over its face and chattered. The cicada-like rhythm echoed down the Hive. The Spawns' cocoons pulsed.

Young claws pushed at their webbed enclosures. The edges of a number of wings showed greenish against the white of the cocoons. Animarus chattered louder.

The Spawn returned the chatter. They shoved their claws inside their cocoons with more force and frequency.

Animarus' serpent tongue flicked out and tasted the air. It ceased chattering.

The three Nekredum drifted down to the floor. Animarus walked to Elizabeth, and lifted her head to look into her face.

"DraCH-CHul!" It chattered; grabbed her by the throat; and unlashed her.

Elizabeth, released from her bonds, balled her hand into a fist and struck Animarus in the middle of its face. It blinked and tightened the claw around her throat. Animarus lifted Elizabeth off the ground and dangled her over the point of a stalagmite.

"CH-ah! DraCH-CHul!" It chattered to the Nekredum. It dropped Elizabeth onto the point of the stalagmite.

But caught her with its wing.

And the Nekredum chattered.

On the Road to Poenari — March 8, Early Evening

RJ stood at the ready next to the pump while they refueled, Louise drawn. Customers pulled into the station, but sped away when they caught a glimpse of an armed station attendant.

The sun set on Romania. Slivers of white light flickered through the wooded western side of the highway, cold and weak.

An hour from Poenari, RJ noticed flashing blue and red lights in his rearview mirror. He checked the speedometer. Below the limit. RJ choked out a breath.

"You couldn't outrun a dog with this truck," said Evan. "I know we aren't speeding."

"Look in the cop's passenger seat. Anyone there?"

Evan adjusted the streaked rearview mirror.

"Nobody there, unless he's really small."

"Good. This guy's alone."

RJ saw Evan shift uneasily as the truck eased onto the shoulder.

"I'm not killing anyone, but you will have to knock this guy out," said RJ. "I can't leave the truck. If I do, he'll call it in, if he hasn't already, and I'm not taking any time to talk to the local authorities."

He slid his titanium nightstick into Evan's hands.

"You're going to have to be fast," instructed RJ. "I'll say 'Canadian,' and become agitated. That should distract him for a few seconds. Hit the officer over his left collar."

Evan sat frozen. RJ slapped him across the top of his temple.

"What the—?"

"We have a narrow window of opportunity here, Evan. If you don't do this, *our* friends are going to die. Got it?"

"Ah, why don't you shut the—"

The officer rapped on the truck window. RJ cranked down the pane. The officer wasn't talking and reached down for his weapon.

RJ flew out of the truck and clamped down on the officer's arm. Evan thought he heard the word 'Canadian' and some shouting. He bolted out of the truck and ran to the driver's side.

RJ locked his right hand down on the policeman's forearm, but the officer, the size and strength of an NFL linebacker, gained the advantage. RJ had no leverage. He lost his hold on the man's arm and saw him grasp the handle and trigger of his gun. An instant later the muzzle of the gun pointed at RJ's face.

RJ released his hand from the officer's arm.

The officer collapsed to the ground with a loud thud after Evan delivered the necessary blow.

RJ and Evan gasped for breath.

"I told you! A *narrow* window of opportunity," said RJ.

"Are … you sure you … said 'Canadian?'" panted Evan.

They cuffed the officer to the grill divider in the backseat of his vehicle, removed his weapons and gagged him.

RJ drove the police car to another service station, waited for the lone customer to leave, and parked it behind the building. Evan followed in the truck.

"How long before they check on him?" asked Evan.

"Doesn't matter," said RJ, as he pressed forward on the gas pedal. "At this point, the Red Army ain't stopping us. We're getting to Poenari, now."

Kodiak — March 8, Early Evening

Using his nose, Kodiak repositioned the IV tube in his leg. Then with bared teeth he bit down on it and pulled it out of his leg. His tongue pressed the restraining tape that covered the puncture mark.

He lay down and panted until his heartbeat slowed.

Kodiak lifted his head and moved to a sitting position. He dropped to the floor and moved to the closed door. It contained a simple latch-style handle, same as some of the rooms at the castle. Kodiak lifted his right paw and pressed down. It opened.

He shoved the door open with his nose and stuck his head through the opening. Kodiak didn't pick up his own scent anywhere, so he could not follow it to the exit. He shook himself and moved out of the room.

The Nekredum darkened the sky as they passed over the WolfThane. Their wings shadowed the moon, cutting off light to Poenari. The wind generated from the beating of the Nekredums' wings filled the air with a foul stench. To the innocent residents of Curtea de Argeş, it appeared a storm had blown in from the west. The people of the town looked skyward for clouds, but saw none. Many retreated to the safe confines of their homes.

Animarus chattered. Ahead of them, Poenari Castle crested above the trees of the Carpathian foothill.

Kodiak picked up his scent. He had not come in through the front of the hospital, but the Emergency Room entrance in back. He turned around and passed by the door of his hospital room. Kodiak spotted someone inside. An orderly examined the removed IV tube on the empty table.

Kodiak shoved a chair from the hallway to underneath the latch. The dog wedged it tightly so it blocked the orderly's exit. Kodiak heard the footsteps of the orderly, who pounded on the door, but the dog trapped him inside.

A light flashed. People shouted. The hospital-wide emergency button had been pushed.

Kodiak shot down the hallway and followed his scent to the admitting desk in the Emergency Room.

Empty. No waiting patients. Not even hospital staff. They'd left to find the source of the emergency.

He surveyed the area and his ears perked up when he heard footsteps the length of the hallway behind him. The dog sprinted into Admissions. He shoved his body underneath the main desk and pressed himself up against the wall. And caught his breath.

Two people entered the Emergency Room. One of them stuck their head into Reception. More talking. Kodiak heard the security bar slide across to open the door.

Kodiak threw his body from underneath the desk and sprinted across the floor of the waiting room. He coiled onto his haunches and fired himself at the opened door.

An orderly who had exited the waiting room to search for Kodiak outside returned, blocking the dog's way.

That was the idea, anyway, until Kodiak's bulk and speed met him head on when the orderly stepped inside. The two of them crashed through the door and both tumbled onto the driveway of the entrance ramp. He tried to grab Kodiak. With one swipe of his paw, Kodiak delivered a blow to the man's nose, breaking it. The dog sprinted from the hospital.

RJ and Evan turned onto the access road that ran around the perimeter of Curtea de Argeş. RJ floored the gas pedal, but the truck maxed out at 65 mph.

"Do you want to get out and run?" asked Evan, only half joking.

"If I thought it would get us there faster, I would. I think this is the best we're going to do," answered RJ.

He called Max during the drive. No answer.

The winding road to Poenari slowed their progress. Just before they hit a straightaway, RJ slammed on the brakes. Evan's chest thumped against the much-too-close dashboard. He shot back in his seat and shouted at RJ.

"What are you doing!?"

"We just passed Kodiak."

"Kodiak?"

"The huge dog guarding Poenari. I told you about him."

"I would have remembered that."

"You were knocked unconscious, Evan."

"RJ. I—"

"Hang on," said RJ, and he twisted around in his seat to look behind the truck.

"Are you sure *we* passed *him*?"

RJ cocked his head and exited the car. A golden blur shot past the car.

"Kode-yak!" shouted RJ.

Kodiak heard a familiar voice. The dog turned and headed back. In one move, he bounded into the payload behind the cab and the three of them continued to Poenari.

The Caretaker of Poenari Castle — March 8, Night

Another bloodcurdling wail, primitive and unholy, echoed as darkness shrouded Poenari.

Nikolai shrank back from his barricaded window. He turned and walked to the kitchen table. An envelope lay next to the sack. It had his name on it . . . in his father's handwriting.

Nikolai had discovered it in the sack after pulling out the metal object.

My son,

I will be brief.

When you were a little boy, you held the Spike of the Dragon in your hand. I am sure you do not remember. And it stands in front of you, as it had for centuries before you were born. It is your birthright, and is tied to Poenari Castle. You have been entrusted with much, and the instrument you hold in your hand now is the key to that which was forged by the Draculs. You, my son, are bound to that great line of Wallachians.

Keep it safe. It cannot fall into the wrong hands, and those may be revealed to you when you become a man.

I will always love you,

Papa

The sound of a crash caused the ground to rock under him and nearly knocked him off his feet. He steadied himself, but the next crash made him slip.

Nikolai struck his head on a corner of the table. The last images he saw were the mannequins swaying in the wind at the walkway to the castle's footbridge, and then, blackness.

The Breach — March 8, Night

Lucifer's army of Nekredum and WolfThane descended upon Poenari Castle. The WolfThane ran up the foothill from the valley floor, then to the front of the castle. The Nekredum, led by Animarus — Elizabeth clutched under his right wing — dropped through the roof, not yet repaired from their previous attack.

The WolfThane increased their pace and launched themselves at the front door of the castle. It had been replaced in the past few days, but the sheer force of 1800 pounds of WolfThane splintered the wood and the pieces rained down onto the stone flooring. Construction dust and shards of stone flew up in the air, landing in a musical rhythm, orchestrating an overture to their arrival.

The blood-red wolf led the pack onto the empty main floor of the castle. The WolfThane panted, breaths echoing through the room. The blood-red wolf pricked up his ears and lifted its nose into the now quiet air.

It howled a warning, and the WolfThane fled the castle floor, but not before gunfire from scaffolding that surrounded the floor unloaded on them. Their attack rained bullets down from above. All save for the blood-red wolf were hit.

Doug drew his sights on the white-headed wolf, the last to make it out of the door. As he prepared to fire, a Nekredum flew down from above and grabbed Doug. His shot sheared off some of the fur on the wolf's right flank, the damage minimal.

The Nekredum lifted Doug high into the air and chattered to Animarus. The Nekredum flew even higher and dropped Doug.

Doug relaxed into a crash position, his body limp, hands under his head, in an attempt to survive the fall.

Doug's body, unbalanced by his gear, turned just before impact. Doug's backpack and ammunition belt met the floor first. His torso jackknifed. His head smashed into the stone with a skull-fracturing crack. A death rattle escaped his body, loud enough to reach his fellow soldiers above. His gun, which flew out of his hand when he was dropped, landed nearby and skidded across the floor and came to rest a few feet from one of Poenari's brave soldiers.

Alvin cried out for his partner.

The planned ambush failed.

The WolfThane regrouped outside the entrance. The blood-red wolf brought them through the shadows and they slipped inside through the opening they'd made. The silver wolf eyed the scaffolding where the men, now exposed, reloaded. It growled at the white-headed and the gray WolfThane.

Nate and Benjamin fired in their direction. It did nothing more than keep the WolfThane at bay. Benjamin pointed to the ceiling. His night-vision goggles searched the cluster of Nekredum and he spotted Elizabeth Astor.

Elizabeth, bound and trussed by Animarus, dangled by a single four-taloned claw. She struggled against the grip, smashing her captor repeatedly in the torso with her legs. The other Nekredum hovered above, chattering, their beating wings moving the air of the castle, thick with the smell of the battle.

"They could kill us all in a minute," said Nate to Benjamin. "Why don't they just do it?"

"They're waiting for Garrett," replied Benjamin. "I believe they want to exchange Elizabeth for that spike RJ talked about. Sending the WolfThane in was just a ploy to get us to expose ourselves. Max was right to keep Garrett away at the beginning. Let's see what happens. We're just getting started."

"You think they know who Garrett is?"

Benjamin turned to his colleague.

"They know exactly who Garrett is."

The evening fog rolled into Poenari. Max and Garrett lay hidden in the gully underneath the footbridge covered by the white vapor. The WolfThane scurried out of, then returned to the castle.

"We need to get inside, Max," said Garrett. He started up the embankment.

"Still waiting for confirmation that they have Elizabeth and she's alive," said Max, grabbing Garrett by the arm and pulling him down.

"Spread out! Form a triangle!" shouted Benjamin. Alvin slid away to Benjamin's left, and Nate crouched and moved to Benjamin's right.

The WolfThane charged the scaffolding, bending it. The metal supports buckled, but held. Wooden platforms bent, then cracked, but flexed back into place.

Not for long.

Another charge by the WolfThane snapped the supports. Alvin, Nate, and Benjamin held onto the vertical pipes and rode them to the floor, avoiding the crush of wood and metal, as they landed on their feet and vacated the immediate area.

The silver and white-headed WolfThane got caught in the collapse, which allowed the men to regroup. The WolfThane shook off the pile of scaffolding and charged out, looking for the men. But their vision became obscured by a combination of smoke from the gunfire and fog that settled around the floor of Poenari Castle.

The fog rose to the level of the crouching men and obscured them from the WolfThane's field of view. The WolfThane raised their snouts and sniffed the air. Nothing, save for the powerful odor of Nekredum and the smell of gunfire, that further covered the scent of the men.

The fog thickened and rose higher.

Animarus chattered. With his free claw, he pointed to the fog.

"Where the hell are Max and Garrett?" asked Benjamin, over the walkie. He waved the hand holding the walkie-talkie at the fog. His breathing alternated between shallow and hyperventilation. The low cloud cover so thick, the walkie disappeared into it as Benjamin cleared his vision looking for Nate and Alvin.

Silence at first, then Alvin's voice.

"Doug was tasked with telling Garrett and Max that Elizabeth was with the Nekredum!" shouted Alvin into the fog. All three opened their walkie channels, and spoke at the same time. The crosstalk drowned out any coherent instructions to RJ and Max.

"Alvin! *You* call them. NOW!"

Above them the chatter of Animarus continued, now joined by the two other Nekredum.

"CHA!" spat one of the Nekredum, who dove down into the fog. His counterpart followed and they flapped their wings not for flight, but to clear the fog and the vision of the WolfThane. It worked—the clouds drifted away exposing Alvin, Benjamin, and Nate.

"Na-KHAH!" screamed Animarus. The Nekredum flew up, as the sounds of gunfire filled the main floor again, the men also taking advantage of the reveal to attack the WolfThane.

Max's walkie squawked.

"Elizabeth is here and alive!" Alvin shouted into the walkie. Then he reloaded his weapon. "Repeat. Elizabeth is here and alive!"

Max flipped down his night-vision goggles, pulled out his Beretta 9mm, and patted the handle of his titanium nightstick, a gift from RJ. He scrambled up the gully, Garrett close behind.

"Mr. Capitanou!"

Max spun around, gun drawn.

And saw Nikolai.

"This is no place for you, Nikolai," shouted Max, and he stood in front of Nikolai, blocking his way into the castle.

"Mr. Capitanou! I know where the spike is!"

"What? Where is it?"

Nikolai did not reply. He turned and ran in the opposite direction. Max yelled after him to stop.

"Let's go, Max!" yelled Garrett. "That man is useless, and we need to get inside."

"Garrett—"

Garrett charged ahead of Max, who had no choice but to follow him to the front of the castle.

RJ drove Evan and Kodiak into the parking lot. Kodiak bolted from the truck into the foothill leading to the castle.

"That's a shortcut we won't be able to take," observed Evan.

They sprinted down the tunnel to the elevators, entered, and hit the button for the castle level.

As the elevator ascended, the lights dimmed. Then it stopped dead just above the lower level. They heard the power surge when the emergency backup generator kicked in. Bulbs flickered and shone. RJ and Evan exhaled in sync and waited for the car to move.

The elevator didn't budge.

"Of course," said RJ, exasperated, pulling his nightstick out of its quiver. He jammed it between the doors up to the hilt and pried them open.

"Lend a hand, Evan. We're climbing out of here."

"We seem to be doing a lot of that."

RJ and Evan had extricated themselves from the construction elevator and ran down the hall to a stairwell.

Evan charged toward the door to the stairs, but RJ stopped him mid-stride. The chaos coming from the main floor of the castle—the efforts of Benjamin, Nate, and Alvin—had stopped.

"Hang on, Evan," hissed RJ. "Nothing worse than silence."

Stillness hung over the main floor of the castle. The WolfThane had not moved. The men held their positions. Nate wiped sweat from his forehead. Above him hovered the

Nekredum, their wings treading the air, the sound and wind in rhythm with the breath of each WolfThane.

One beat. One breath. One beat. One breath.

Animarus held Elizabeth, exhausted but continuing to struggle in the Nekredum's grasp. Animarus' wings moving in synch with his compatriots.

Nate shifted his position. The WolfThane, their bodies clear of the fog, stood on all fours in a diamond-shaped position. Fur stood on the backs of necks, and down their spines. Posture forward. Their focus at the entrance. The blood-red wolf's head turned as Kodiak arrived on the main floor of Poenari Castle.

Three of the WolfThane from the phalanx fanned out, and the blood-red wolf stepped from the phalanx and turned to face Kodiak directly. A low rumble escaped the dog's throat. It stepped forward. Kodiak confronted his foe.

Miles away, in the Hive, the Nekredum Spawn increased their chatter. It now sounded as though a single harmonious voice.

RJ and Evan pressed up against the doorway to the stairwell.

"We need to talk to someone," said RJ, his voice low. "The walkies are on chargers in the room where we were sleeping, second door on the left."

"Be right back."

Evan returned with two walkies. RJ switched his on.

"This is RJ. Evan and I are on the lower level. Ready to engage. Report?"

"No movement," whispered Max. "Doug was killed in the fight with the Nekredum. A few of the WolfThane wounded, but able to fight. Kodiak is inside."

"Aw, shoot. I really liked Doug." RJ sighed and stared down. When he regrouped, he asked, "How many WolfThane?"

"Four."

"There may be a couple more shortly," said RJ. "Two of them followed us from Snagov Island to here."

"Any more good news?"

"I have Evan English with me," said RJ. "Does that help?"

"Actually, mate," said Evan. "I think you should know something."

"Now?" RJ hissed. "We're going up. You can tell me later."

RJ flung open the door. They took two steps at a time and hit the main floor. Both skidded through blood, and drew their weapons.

Snarling and growling started again. Max slipped inside and trained his weapon on the three WolfThane who formed a line in front of Kodiak. He blasted away, clearing them from the battlefield, then turned his attention to the Nekredum and Elizabeth. Kodiak advanced on the blood-red wolf.

Animarus chattered and one of the Nekredum dove toward Kodiak. A storm of bullets drove the Nekredum off its mark and it crashed onto the floor and skidded across the stone until it landed in a heap against a wall. It righted itself and screeched into the night. The sound carried through the unfinished roof and out into Poenari. RJ fronted the creature, who stood on its muscular legs and spread its wings. RJ pulled the nightstick out of its quiver.

"*How about some more of this!?*" he shrieked at the creature, who cocked its head and screeched at RJ. "Say, you look familiar. You were the one that grabbed my cart!"

Max, joined by Garrett, continued firing into the WolfThane, when they approached Alvin, Nate, and Benjamin.

The dog squared off, and paced back and forth in front of the blood-red wolf. Kodiak bared his canine fangs only, but his growl, low at first, increased and he showed all his teeth and pinned back his ears.

The WolfThane retreated as Kodiak and the blood-red leader crashed their chests into one another.

Kodiak, half the size of the blood-red wolf, gave no ground and pushed the leader of the WolfThane back. Both reared up on their haunches. A shell casing hit the floor, a tinny echo bouncing off the walls. Alvin, Doug, and Nate were out of ammunition. They each pulled their knives.

The other WolfThane advanced again, but the blood-red wolf growled and chased them back. It charged, as did Kodiak, and they smashed into each other, chest first, more tissue and bone cracking. Kodiak got the worst of the exchange. He hit the ground, but regained his footing and stared at the blood-red wolf. Blood poured from his mouth. He shook his head from side-to-side.

Kodiak howled, strong and defiant. The result was a shower of blood on his opponent, who backed away from the dog.

The blood-red wolf and Kodiak stalked each other. They waited for one of them to resume the fight. The other

WolfThane moved into the fray, eager to end Kodiak's life. The blood-red wolf growled, but not to back them off.

Chattering increased in intensity from above.

The three WolfThane, hides and heads riddled with bullets, their black blood coating the castle floor, charged. Fangs bared, jaws slack, they launched themselves at Kodiak.

Nikolai Asilimov stood in front of the mannequins along the trail leading to Poenari Castle. The metal grip in his right hand. He yanked both spikes that skewered the mannequins out of the ground. After cutting the rope that secured the bodies, tossed the Ottoman "soldiers" aside. He picked up the one closest to him and placed the grip into a notch about two-thirds of the way from the barbed tip of the spike.

A perfect fit.

He turned to head to the castle.

Wait!

He took the second spike. Nikolai removed the grip from the first spike and, just as the first attempt, placed it into this second spike two-thirds from the barbed tip.

Another perfect fit, but something was off. He felt it, but held onto the spike. He switched the grip back to the first, and prayed his decision correct.

He knelt. Nikolai looked up and raised his arms to the starless sky.

"Tell me what to do!" he implored. He looked at the gripless spike. He held one in each hand and sprinted to Poenari.

Kodiak bared his teeth, pinned back his ears, and took on the three WolfThane charging toward him. They never arrived.

From their positions, Benjamin, Nate, and Alvin, their ammunition exhausted, charged the WolfThane from behind. Each man drew his knife. They leaped onto the backs of the WolfThane, who had no time to react. The three men plunged their knives several times into the WolfThane's necks and eyes. The three WolfThane, wounded but not incapacitated, turned away from Kodiak toward their assailants.

The WolfThane shook off the men, who skidded away on a floor covered in black and red blood.

"Back-to-back-to-back!" shouted Nate. The three of them, bleeding from gouges in their arms and legs, took a stand in the middle of the floor.

Garrett and Max moved toward the doomed men, but Animarus swooped down from the ceiling, still with Elizabeth in its grasp. Garrett backed away. Max ducked under the attack of Animarus, and continued toward the triangle of Nate, Benjamin, and Alvin. Just a few feet from his compatriots, Max pulled his nightstick. The other Nekredum dove from above and knocked Max backward, breaking the bodyguard's cheekbone. Max landed hard on the side of his head and collapsed unconscious.

WolfThane blood flowed onto the floor of Poenari Castle. As did the blood of men. Alvin, no longer able to stand, dropped to one knee. He held a long knife in front of him as his adversary, the silver wolf, blinded, sniffed for its prey. The gray wolf, its head more exposed skull than fur, and with Nate's KA-BAR knife jutting out of its front right shoulder, limped and then threw itself on top of its tormentor, Nate, who collapsed under its 350 pounds.

Nate freed an arm under the bulk of the gray wolf, pulled the knife from its shoulder, and severed the wolf's throat. Viscera and neckbones exposed and its lifeforce pulsing out of it, the animal bellowed but kept its feet. It crashed its bulk against him, driving the man's ribcage of splintered bone through Nate's heart.

Alvin, valiant to the last, stood in defiance of the silver wolf, who caught Alvin's scent and charged. Alvin attacked, a living corpse of screaming rage. He flew through his own red blood, mixed with the black of his opponent both on the ground and shooting through the air from severed arteries. He landed a final thrust of his knife through the vestiges of the silver wolf's right eye and deep into its brain. Both dropped to the floor, the last of their lives running out onto the stone of Poenari Castle.

Benjamin, a long raking claw mark bisecting his chest, drove his KA-BAR knife through the skull of the white-headed wolf. The dying man spotted his former IDF partner only yards away, lying next to the now-dead silver wolf.

Benjamin took one step and fainted from lack of blood, but lifted his chin a second later. Using it, and the ebbing strength from his arms and legs, he crawled to Nate. Benjamin pushed himself between Nate and the silver wolf, and died next to his former IDF compatriot.

RJ backed into a corner, parried the wings of Animarus, determined to help what remained of the castle's, and Mors Aeterna's, protectors. His Nekredum opponent frustrated his every move to get past it and help.

Max had not moved. The other Nekredum turned its attention to RJ. It raced across the floor to engage RJ, who found himself outflanked.

Kodiak feinted away from the blood-red wolf and latched onto the Nekredum by its wing. Once again, the dog's signature move hurled the Nekredum across the castle's floor and smashed it against one of the walls with such force that several pieces of stone dislodged and rained down on the Nekredum, cracking its skull. It shook off the blow, but before it could rise up again, Garrett sprinted to the struggling Nekredum. He lifted the stone, and took one last look at his sister.

The Nekredum tried to block him with his wings, but Garrett bellowed and delivered the stone with such force it crushed the Nekredum's gray skull. Black blood shot from its head and its brains followed, coating the floor with a green viscera.

Kodiak turned back to the blood-red wolf, but found his attack blocked by the mottled wolf, just returned to Poenari.

Nikolai closed on the front door of the castle, still carrying both spikes. He stopped just outside the opening.

Evan English had fled the main floor, and stood there. Gun in hand.

He heard a familiar sound, the beating of wings and chattering, which grew louder, then dropped to silence. The battle between Man and WolfThane had stopped. Evan looked at Nikolai and then back toward the main floor, his face a road map of conflict. And now a man stood in front of him holding two long spikes.

Nikolai offered them to Evan.

"You are the descendant of Vlad Dracul, yes?" asked Nikolai, now offering him only Mors Aeterna.

Evan hesitated before taking the spike *without* the grip handle.

"I am not Evan English, mate," he admitted. "My name is Aloysius Sloan, but that doesn't matter now. Our friends need our help."

"B-but—" Nikolai protested, as he slid his hand into the grip, the color drained from his face. "I am not a Dracul either."

"Tonight, we are all Draculs," replied Aloysius Sloan, lowering the spike in front of him and facing the abyss of the open doorway. "To our friends!"

Both swung around when they heard the growl. A low constant sound from the throat of the garnet wolf, which stood no more than ten feet from Aloysius and Nikolai

The growl continued. Teeth bared. Hair rising on the back of its neck.

Evan swallowed and coughed a dry and fearful cough. It caught in his throat, as the wolf paced back and forth. It dropped its head and pulled its ears back. The wolf's slaver dripped onto the ground.

"Lower your spike in its direction," said Aloysius.

"It'd have to run right onto it," replied Nikolai.

"It won't. If I'm right, it'll avoid it," said Aloysius. "And us."

"How do you know?"

"Educated guess."

The garnet wolf slowed to a stop and growled at the spike Nikolai held. Nikolai, his hands unsteady, lost control of the spike. It seesawed his hand. Aloysius reached over and righted it.

Nikolai wrapped his hand around it once more.

The garnet wolf trotted to the right of both to avoid the spike. Now, Mors Aeterna only protected Nikolai, and not Aloysius who held the grip-less spike. The garnet wolf reared back on its haunches.

"Go!" shouted Aloysius to Nikolai and shoved the man through the doorway of Poenari Castle. The garnet wolf leapt at Aloysius, still holding on to the gripless spike, as Nikolai skidded onto a Jackson Pollack spatter of black and red blood against white and gray stone.

Animarus' chatter increased. Its lone compatriot, squared off with RJ, now turned its attention to Nikolai, who slid into the fight. Garrett remained frozen in place as he stared up at his sister in the claw of Animarus. The leader of the Nekredum had done nothing since Garrett dispatched one of the Nekredum.

The mottled wolf, also back from Snagov, skulked to the side of his blood-red leader.

"CHA! CHRA-CUL! CHA! CHRA-CUL!" chattered Animarus and it took its free arm and pointed a talon at Nikolai, who held Mors Aeterna in front of him. The other Nekredum flew high enough over RJ to avoid the parries of his nightstick. It unfurled its wings as it landed and screeched at Nikolai. The Nekredum closed on Nikolai and snatched at Mors Aeterna.

RJ spun around when he saw the mottled wolf turn toward Kodiak. RJ headed to the pile of dead WolfThane, and slid through a still-slick river of blood until he crashed into Nate and Benjamin. He removed Nate's night vision goggles, put them on, and scanned the room.

The mottled and blood-red WolfThane increased their pace. RJ pulled a KA-BAR knife out of one of the dead WolfThane and launched it at the mottled wolf. A perfect shot, it shivved the wolf's shoulder, knocking it off course. The wolf stumbled through blood and viscera before slamming into the wall below one of the fractured stained-glass windows.

The Nekredum grabbed one end of Mors Aeterna, just beyond the barbed tip, and pulled to free it from Nikolai's grasp, but RJ smashed the creature's arm, cracking some of its hide, with his nightstick. Animarus dove to the floor toward RJ.

Nikolai buried Mors Aeterna into the other Nekredum's midsection. It screeched a stream of blood from its maw and fell forward, driving the spike up through its torso and its heart.

Nikolai lost his grip on the handle, but regained it when he yanked it from the torso of the dead Nekredum. Nikolai squared up to Animarus.

Animarus stood and held Elizabeth in front of him by her thin, fragile neck.

"CHA! CHRA-CUL!" Once again, Animarus pointed at Mors Aeterna.

"Give me my sister!" screamed Garrett and charged at Animarus, whose face appeared to split in half with a smile.

The blood-red wolf and Kodiak slammed into each other once more, the dog landing hard on his side. Kodiak gained his feet, charged, opened his maw, and latched onto the blood-red wolf's neck. The dog dragged the blood-red wolf toward Animarus. The mottled wolf reared back and attacked Kodiak. The three on a dead sprint toward Animarus.

Garrett whipped his head around as Nikolai shrieked. Kodiak, the blood-red and mottled WolfThane slammed into Animarus, causing the leader of the Nekredum to release Elizabeth. She fell to the floor, all dead weight. Nikolai arrived a split second later, driving Mors Aeterna into the torso of Animarus.

Kodiak, both WolfThane, Animarus, and Nikolai crashed through the stained-glass window, landed on the thin plateau at the top of the sheer wall drop in front of the castle. Their momentum took all over the edge and they plummeted more than a thousand feet onto the parking lot below. Nikolai, crying out in terror every foot of the way.

RJ, a second behind, vaulted through the opening in the stained glass. He pulled up short of the cliff, and searched the plateau for signs of anything or anybody.

He engaged the night vision goggles. He strained with the distance, but through the trees, made out a pile of remains on the parking lot below.

And movement.

Animarus, its wings badly broken, but still alive.

RJ hung his head.

Kodiak and Nikolai killed in their valiant attempt. Doug, Alvin, Nate, and Benjamin sacrificed. Max gone?

"RJ?"

RJ pulled off the goggles. The voice belonged to Max.

"Animarus lives, Max. Same as you," said RJ. "But he has Mors Aeterna now, and I'm sure the Spawn—"

"RJ. Let's get—"

RJ reached his arm back and grabbed Max's right wrist.

"Something else is down there, Max. . . ."

The Apocalypse — March 8, Late Night

Animarus stopped crawling just past the construction trailers. It rose to its knees, screeched, and pulled Mors Aeterna from its torso. It drew out cleanly until the spike's barb caught a piece of the Nekredum's leathery hide. Animarus sucked in his breath and clamped both taloned hands around it and pulled. The hook tore off the protective skin, followed by a torrent of black blood, that shot across the valley floor. Animarus tilted back its green and blue head, opened its maw of jagged teeth, and loosed a scream. It screeched again, and ground its fangs down so hard on its jaw that it drew more blood. It dripped in front of Animarus as it half-walked/half-limped. It left the carnage and headed for the safety and sanctuary of the Hive.

Animarus clenched Mors Aeterna in its right claw, using it as a cane to support its broken strides. Its damaged wings slowed its pace, but the Leader of the Nekredum pressed on to the Hive.

There, at the Hive, the Spawn, newly awakened, waited. There, Animarus, with Mors Aeterna and an army of Nekredum, would summon the darkest of Lords. The Age of Man would end with Lucifer by its side.

RJ and Max ran along the plateau and back to the construction elevators.

"We need to find Evan and get to the parking lot."

"No!" shouted Max. "Animarus is headed back to the Hive. We need to get to there while it is wounded."

RJ threw his arm in front of Max, and both stopped. They leaned over, hands on knees, to catch their breath. When they stood, their eyes widened and they moved back. RJ stumbled, but kept his balance. Max hacked out a breath.

In front of them, skewered on a pole, the body of the last WolfThane, its blood dripping down. But at the base lay the body of Evan English. His throat ripped out. Somehow the man had hoisted the 300-pound wolf onto the pole.

"Evan!" yelled RJ, who drew in his breath and dropped to his knees.

Evan lay on his side, claw marks shredding his clothes and torso. RJ rolled him onto his back and closed the man's eyelids. RJ bowed his head and crossed himself, and clasped his hands in prayer. Max placed his right hand on RJ's left shoulder.

"RJ," Max whispered, "we have to go."

RJ nodded and got to his feet.

"It looks like our last descendant of the Draculs is dead."

RJ gripped Louise, before holstering it. Max turned his nightstick over in his hands, and stuck his Beretta into his belt.

"It's all we've got RJ," said Max, who spun around, nightstick still in hand.

One of the construction elevator doors opened and a slim, broad-shouldered man stepped out. He wore a brown flight jacket. His jeans and work boots black in the darkness. The man spotted RJ and Max.

RJ trained Louise on him, but all the man did was walk. His face with all the emotion of a winning poker hand with all the tells in check. RJ now recognized the man who had introduced himself as Aloysius Sloan back in London.

"You won't need that, RJ." His voice carried through the night air. He approached, and held out his hand.

"I'm—"

He stopped mid-sentence and pulled back his hand.

"Oh no. Aloysius," said the man quietly, a sob catching in his throat. *What have I done?*

He stepped toward the body, wiping a tear from his eye.

"No time for a proper burial now. We'll do that later. At home." The man abruptly turned his attention from Aloysius back to RJ and Max.

The man squared up to them. "Gentlemen, my name is Evan English," and finished shaking their hands. "Should you wish to help me save mankind, I suggest we step it up."

RJ opened his mouth, then closed it.

"RJ Brancatelli. We meet again." Evan pointed at RJ, who nodded. "Take down that abomination and when it hits the ground, pull up its head, please."

RJ made no movement toward the pole topped by the wolf.

"All right, Mr. Capitanou," he said turning to Max. "Will you oblige me? At least lend a hand?"

Max and the man pulled the pole out of the ground. Max grabbed the wolf by the scruff after it slammed into the ground. Evan stepped forward and in one motion pulled a short sword from a scabbard at the back of his left hip. "This is for Aloysius," he said as he slit the creature's throat. The blade, so sharp it passed through the wolf's sinew, cut all the way to the vertebrae. Max's grip caused the head to lever like a Pez dispenser.

"No sense in taking chances," declared Evan. He removed a handkerchief from his jacket and wiped the blade before sheathing it in its scabbard.

"Now, Mr. Capitanou, while Mr. Brancatelli recovers from surprise, let's remove the spike from that creature."

"Like removing a fish hook," said Max. He and Evan levered the spike out of the underside of the wolf.

"Hold on to that spike, Mr. Capitanou."

RJ shook his head like a wet dog.

"Just a minute, Evan. If that's who you are," he said. "Animarus has Mors Aeterna. What good is *this* spike going to do us?"

"Ah, Mr. Brancatelli. No time to explain. To the Hive of the Nekredum."

Evan turned and hustled back to the construction elevators.

"Chop chop," said Evan, holding the construction doors open.

RJ and Max, caught off guard, stumbled before falling into a dead run.

RJ reached over and grabbed Evan by the sleeve of his flight jacket. Evan blinked hard.

"You want to explain this, Mr. English? I just spent two days on the road with your partner and assumed he was you."

"Yes, I know," admitted Evan. "Aloysius kept me well informed. Thank you for retrieving the skull and body of my dear, departed ancestor. Once this is over, we will bury him on the premises. I am sure your boss, Elizabeth Astor, will not object."

"All right, Mr, English. I'll bite," said RJ, releasing his grip. "What's your plan?"

"Simple. We pursue Animarus back to the Hive of the Nekredum. Wrest Mors Aeterna back from him by sowing doubt in his mind as to which spike is the correct one. Kill him with Mors Aeterna. And watch as the Spawn, their life force tied to Animarus, shrivel up and die."

Evan never broke verbal stride.

RJ stared at Evan in disbelief until the elevator stopped.

"That sounds a bit flimsy, Mr. English."

"Chop chop! Presto! Andiamo! Mach schnell!" Evan prompted, noticing RJ's reluctance to exit the elevator. "Mr. Brancatelli, I've studied the Nekredum longer than your mythocologist friend, Dr. Margaret Barnes."

"And?"

"We might have to be a little clever in our divesting Animarus of Mors Aeterna."

"And?"

"*Please*, Mr. Brancatelli," Evan pressed, turning in the direction of the valley floor. "If you can keep up, I'll be happy to fill you in on the way. I hope you and Mr. Capitanou have some semblance of cardiovascular conditioning? You are going to need it."

RJ, arms crossed at his chest, glared at Evan.

"Let's go, RJ," said Max, his hands wrapped around the middle of the spike. "Unless you have a better idea?"

The three passed the construction trailers, increasing their speed as they approached Poenari Forest. Evan, surprisingly fit, led the way, while Max and RJ struggled to keep up. They fell further and further behind. Evan turned around and shouted at them as he ran backward.

"You will be much happier facing Animarus *without* an army of thousands of Nekredum Spawn. I'd pick up the pace."

"What the hell? Sure, you weren't a part of that last fight against evil forces…" RJ grumbled, but increased his speed.

Animarus arrived at the edge of the forest. It walked quicker now, but still with effort, dragging its feet and digging Mors Aeterna deeper into the ground with each stride. It stepped into the forest, its wounds still weeping black blood, falling freely on the path.

RJ and Max increased their pace to catch Evan. They didn't catch up until they reached the trailhead, all within a few seconds of each other. While RJ and Max dropped to the ground to catch a second wind, Evan reached into another pocket of his bomber jacket and produced a flashlight. He pointed the beam down at the trailhead.

"Yes," he confirmed to the supine RJ and Max. "Black Nekredum blood. The Hive should be about a kilometer further in from here. Let us proceed. Animarus is definitely wounded, thank God. It's not far ahead."

"How do you know all this about the Nekredum?"

"Once again, Mr. Brancatelli," said Evan. "I have studied the Nekredum forever. A description of their Hive lay hidden in diaries and texts Charlemagne and Pippin kept. The Draculs also identified it when they re-entombed them in 1430."

"But how —"

Evan set off down the path in a run, following the trail of blood.

RJ and Max doubled their already doubled effort and followed.

Evan followed the trail of blood. Max and RJ kept him in sight. Evan slowed when the path, no more than a yard wide at its inception, narrowed to a foot wide.

He moved the light over the area. Evan stopped when it landed on some brush, tree roots, vines, and branches grown over each other like a cancerous tumor. He switched off the flashlight and turned to RJ and Max.

Evan wiped perspiration from his neck with the same handkerchief that caught the wolf's coagulated blood, leaving a smudge. He grabbed each man by their forearm and squeezed, demonstrating to RJ and Max incredible physical strength.

"If you follow me in here," he started, his voice gritty and worn, "you may not come out. Are you willing to do that?"

His light green eyes penetrated the darkness that surrounded them.

"Let's go, Evan," said RJ. "Five of our brave friends have died tonight. We owe them."

"Six," said Max. "Kodiak."

Evan dropped his right hand from Max's forearm and extended it toward the tumor.

"I will need that spike, Max." Evan released RJ's arm and pointed at the spike with the finger of his left hand. "And both of you follow me *at all times*."

With his right hand, he drew out the short sword and slashed an opening in the tumor.

Once they cleared the growth, a pathway that sloped downward greeted them. Evan descended, RJ and Max close behind. After a minute of running, they dropped into a chamber so large that the ceiling and the wall at the far end vanished into blackness.

Chattering greeted their ears, but not from Animarus.

Evan led them into the blackness, stalagmites halting their progress.

A stalagmite moved, and defined itself.

Animarus, the wounded Nekredum, its wings useless, hanging in shreds at its side. It walked with a limp and came within a spike's length of them. It raised Mors Aeterna to chest level using its right claw, as did Evan with his spike using his right hand.

"CHA-DRCHUK-LA!" spat Animarus.

"You see me, Animarus," said Evan, glancing at his spike. "You still searching for Mors Aeterna? I'd have thought you would have located it by now."

"CHA!" Animarus shook Mors Aeterna at Evan. Behind him, from the darkness of the chamber, Animarus and the others heard more chattering, which sounded like a plague of locusts. Taloned claws stuck out through the webbing of their spawning cocoons. Activity from the cocoons increased. More talons pushing out from behind the ghostly cauls. The outline of more wings shoved against their temporary white covers. Chattering. Always chattering.

Evan slashed at Animarus, catching the open wound. Animarus knocked away Evan's spike, but it caught in the shreds of its left wing. Evan took the opportunity to pull more viscera from the slender bones holding what little of it remained.

Animarus screeched and thrust Mors Aeterna at Evan, catching enough of his left forearm to open a half-inch wound in the muscular flesh.

"You will not defeat me, Animarus, traitor of God!" thundered Evan. RJ ran to Evan's side, but Evan shoved him away and roared. "Stay where you are! I will settle this with Animarus!"

Evan thrust his spike at the battered creature.

The first of the hatched Spawn dropped onto the inner cavern's floor. It unbound its wings from the cocoon webbing and bodily fluids which restricted them. Behind it, more Spawn cut their way out of their cocoons.

The Spawn on the ground chattered, a sound that drew the attention of Animarus, who, once again, appeared to smile, despite his crippled condition.

"CHA! Draaaa-Cul! DeCH-ead!" Animarus lunged forward with Mors Aeterna's barbed end tearing Evan's bomber jacket. Evan returned the thrust and drove his spike into Animarus' open wound, but he pulled back. The hole in its torso grew large enough to allow Evan's spike to come out with no further damage.

"HA-AH! DRA-CHUL! DIE!"

Animarus brandished Mors Aeterna.

From the recesses of the cavern, several more Spawn freed themselves from their cocoons and unfurled their wings. They gained their feet after a few stumbles and marched forward to the sound of Animarus' chattering.

Animarus lunged again, missing Evan, who had moved to his right.

The sound of taloned feet marching on the cavern floor drew closer. RJ and Max turned to face an onslaught they could not imagine.

The first young Nekredum emerged from the shadows. Evan remained on the right side of Animarus, avoiding a forward parry by the creature.

"Evan!?" shouted RJ as he made out the shapes of the marching Spawn, already dozens strong. Behind them, the chattering of hundreds more dropping from their cocoons.

"I will return you and all of Lucifer's Spawn back to hell, Animarus!" growled Evan. Blood flowed down his left arm. He tightened his grip on his spike.

Animarus moved in front of Evan, who again stepped to the Nekredum's side.

"Dra-ACHUL! De-EAD!" chattered Animarus, and lunged again at Evan.

The first line of Spawn approached the shadows of the cave and quickened their pace. RJ and Max fired into the group, but their bullets did not slow them.

"Evan!?" shouted RJ as he smashed his nightstick against the skull of one spawn, but soon five of them had him by the arms and legs, and carried him toward the top of one of the stalagmites. The same fate awaited Max, who fought them barehanded until one of them latched onto Max's right wrist.

The Spawn grabbed Max's bicep and bent his arm until his wrist almost met his shoulder. The cracking and shattering of the joint was drowned out by Max's piercing cry of agony.

Shards of bone pierced his skin. Blood flowed and spurted onto the stalagmite meant to impale Max.

"Meet your end, jackal of Satan!" screamed Evan, who dropped his spike.

Animarus lunged once more at his now-unarmed opponent. Evan drew his short sword and severed the Nekredum's right hand at the wrist in one clean slash. Mors Aeterna flew into the air and clattered to the ground, landing facing the Nekredum. Animarus, showing no sign of pain, reached for it with its left hand and snatched it up just below the metal grip.

The Nekredum smiled, but before he made another move toward Evan, Evan rushed at it and plunged the barbed end of Mors Aeterna deep in its torso.

Evan bellowed and propelled Animarus into the air. He used the Nekredum's body weight to drive the un-barbed end of Mors Aeterna into the ground. Animarus screeched as Evan levered the creature higher and higher toward the ceiling. Animarus twisted and fought against the spike. He tried to beat his useless wings, first against stalagmites, then stalactites.

He screeched again and then no more as a stalactite pierced his back and met the tip of Mors Aeterna in the heart of the now vanquished leader of the Nekredum.

Animarus, like so many of Vlad Dracul's victims, slumped over the spike, its black blood coating Mors Aeterna from the wound created by the barbed end, down to the ground where it pooled and reflected the death of Animarus.

RJ and Max saw the stalagmites looming below them. As the Spawn lifted the men to a position over the top of the cavern's death formations, Animarus, with the horrific cry of a dying animal, screeched his last.

The Spawn halted, some still marching forward crashed into their compatriots. As one, all cried out in a voice of fear and destruction. It echoed with the grinding sound like a bone saw working its way through a corpse.

They released their victims, and collapsed to the ground, shrinking into pulpy masses of viscera, unformed bone, and cartilage.

Max, the site of his compound fracture bleeding, landed on top of one pile of Spawn and bounced down. RJ, however, too close to a stalagmite to avoid significant injury, caught his right shoulder on the very top of the point and hung onto the structure like a fly in a spider's web.

The ground shook with the force of a million jackhammers. The walls cracked and dislodged stone which avalanched to the floor.

Evan had fallen onto all fours. He lifted his head, and gasped for air.

"Unless you would like to be entombed with these foul creatures—" he half-shouted, half-choked out above an increasing rumble and grinding, "—I would suggest we find our way out of here!"

Max pushed himself onto his unbroken arm. He spotted RJ.

"Evan!" screamed Max. "We need to lift RJ off that stalagmite."

"Why, yes we do!" yelled Evan, who sprinted to the stalagmite where RJ's right shoulder hung. The point had pierced it between the blade and the top shoulder bone. Max joined him, but both men were jolted by an even stronger tremor, which knocked them down.

Max's eyes narrowed and searched for the cave opening

"Lucifer's portal is also gone with Animarus' death! Get up, Max!"

Max scrambled to his feet as quickly as he could, and placed his left arm under the middle of RJ's back. Evan did the same with his right arm.

"Don't count to three on my account," said RJ. "No reason to—"

He screamed until he spat blood from his damaged vocal cords. He tumbled off the top of the stalagmite and ripped another wound in his bicep. RJ slammed into the ground, but gained his feet, and ran toward the pathway exit.

"Uh, before we bleed out?" RJ shouted to the men behind him.

An even stronger tremor tripped them and jagged pieces of lime crumbled off the stalactites and rained on the men as they dodged the spears. The three headed up the path toward the cave opening.

Behind them a series of ground tremors so fierce they caused every stalactite to crumble to the floor of the cavern, covering the remains of the Nekredum and their Spawn forever.

Animarus' body survived several storms of stalactites, until a last tremor loosed a 100-square-foot chunk of the cave ceiling itself. The massive stone landed directly on his impaled body, driving it toward the floor where it crushed the leader of the Nekredum, sealing him up in a stone sarcophagus for eternity.

Aftermath — March 9, Morning

They raced up the pathway, fragments of the ceiling dropping in their way and several times one of them tripped, but they helped each other up and along. As the entire structure behind them collapsed, the three men dove out of the cave opening and rolled onto the ground.

RJ, Evan, and Max took turns fashioning tourniquets for each other's wounds. Max's shattered arm defied any field first aid they knew. He held the appendage as they trudged miles back to the bottom of the foothill in front of Poenari Castle. They found Nikolai's badly crushed remains and those of the blood-red and garnet WolfThane. RJ only saw half of the other Nekredum's armor-plated hide until he realized the rest of it had driven itself through the black-top tar of the parking lot on impact.

"I'm afraid I do not see Kodiak," sighed RJ, sporting deep cuts around his eyes, a shoulder that would take a year to heal, and a broken nose.

In the silvery morning moonlight, Evan looked up the foothill at the area where the shack would have been, obscured by the trees.

"Nikolai," began Evan, as he bowed his head. "Thank you . . . and your father."

RJ noticed Max had moved away from Nikolai's body. Even with the pain of a broken arm, Max searched the parking lot.

"Max!" shouted RJ, who ran toward him. "We'll find Kodiak! We need to get you serious medical attention!"

Max wheeled around, his eyes red rimmed. His jaw trembled. His face a bruised and bloody mess.

Max's right arm, in addition to his destroyed elbow, a part of either the ulna or the radius pushed toward the surface of his forearm, a compound fracture that would get worse if not tended to quickly.

Max dropped onto the ground. And then collapsed. RJ kneeled next to him and put his arm around Max's heaving shoulders. Max had found Kodiak's collar on the lot. He held it as tightly as he could grasp anything. RJ gently took it and touched the aluminum nameplate.

"If not for that dog, who knows what would have happened, Max." RJ paused, his eye half closed, but this time to hide a tear. Max sobbed.

"Max, Kodiak had a mission. This is what he had to do." Evan placed his hand on Max's good shoulder and squeezed.

RJ pulled out his cell and phoned 112 for the EMTs. From the corner of his open eye, RJ saw Poenari Castle, bathed in the cold amber light of the rising sun.

Inside Poenari Castle rested the broken bodies of Doug Mackie, Benjamin Saperstein, Nate David, and Alvin Chen. The dead WolfThane lay scattered, heaps of bones covered in black blood-soaked fur. One of the Nekredum lay crushed under an avalanche of stone. The other in a heap, a broken wing, a hole in its torso, and a pool of black blood.

Elizabeth awakened, but for the moment she had no memory of her incarceration in the clutches of the Nekredum.

"Glad to have you back, Sis," said Garrett, hugging her gingerly.

"You don't *really* want to build DracuLAND, do you?"

Garrett could only laugh.

An EMS vehicle sped toward the parking lot, Teomer Turrik's police cruiser in pursuit. The police car screeched to a halt and he flew out of the vehicle. Evan, RJ, and Max ignored him. Evan and RJ ran to join the medical technicians.

Two techs loaded Max onto a gurney and wheeled it into the ambulance. Turrik stood by his cruiser.

The two EMTs left behind tended to Evan. RJ also received medical attention on the spot, including dozens of stitches and staples. Once the EMTs had stabilized RJ, they moved to the castle, though they were informed by Evan that there might be no survivors.

RJ and Evan watched the ambulance pull away.

A reddish band blanketed the front of the towers and foundation wall. The new morning dawned.

RJ and Evan looked up at the castle.

"DracuLAND, huh?" asked Evan.

"Needs work."

Epilogue

Two months later, Max Capitanou walked the grounds of Poenari Castle. Work on the theme park continued. The authorities completed their investigations into the deaths of the several workers.

Then DracuLAND opened.

Elizabeth recovered from her injuries and returned to work less than a month after the final battle.

Per Margaret Barnes, Elizabeth dispatched several helicopters to flood the Hive of the Nekredum and the Lair of the WolfThane with holy water then Dead Sea salt. When asked, Elizabeth said she thought it wise to be considerate and proactive to mitigate drought conditions that could contribute to wildfires.

Evan English changed his name back to Erik Van Helsing. He buried the remains of his ancestor, Vlad Dracul III in a crypt in the basement of Poenari Castle. Visitors could only visit the gravesite through special arrangement. Erik moved to South Africa to assist Dr. Margaret Barnes in her continuing research into the somewhat questionable science of mythocology. The remains of the WolfThane and Nekredum were spirited out of Romania and sent to them to study.

RJ Brancatelli returned to New York City, left the employ of Astor Holdings, and disappeared.

Max remained in Romania to serve the same security detail for which he was hired. He made daily rounds around Poenari Castle. Max allowed himself a sad smile each time he walked along the path to the reconstructed footbridge. He rubbed Kodiak's collar, which he kept in his jacket pocket.

One day four months later, Max stopped on the footbridge just before heading up to the castle. Movement behind him. He heard a low, growl, gutteral in its tone. His still-compromised right arm drew his gun and he spun around.

Max laughed, then put his gun away.

Another Romanian stray.

A breath caught in his throat. He sprinted to the dog.

A puppy, about the biggest puppy Max had ever seen. Its coat appeared whitish, but he thought it would turn golden-red as the dog got older.

It will be the same color as the dark tips of its ears.

The dog's blocky head dominated its body. Enormous paws supported already strong and muscular long legs. A few flecks of black shot through its tail.

But the eyes had drawn him — slightly tilted in a feline way, translucent brown with black pupils.

The puppy shoved its nose into Max's hands.

Max knelt to pull the dog in for a hug. He pressed the dog's nose into his chest. He inhaled, his breath catching. When he settled, Max drew back and looked into its light brown eyes.

"Let's go, Kode-yak," he said, his voice quaking. "I found this a while ago." He slipped the too-large-for-now collar around the dog's neck. "I'm sure you've been looking for it."

The puppy fell into a trot beside Max as they headed into Poenari Castle.

"That's right, boy. I have a castle to guard, and I can use all the help I can get."

George W. Young
Bio

George W. Young started his professional life as a dancer in New York City in 1979, where he worked in summer stock and way-off-Broadway in musical theater, and he performed in some of the earliest music videos with Diana Ross, The Pointer Sisters, and Louise Robey.

He switched over to the other side of the camera in New York City in 1984, where he worked on national and international TV commercials for Fortune 500 companies. Directors on his credit sheet include Bob Giraldi, Joe Pytka, and Steve Steigman. He moved to California in 1988.

George spent the next 30 years working on a variety of projects including feature films such as *The Nightmare Before Christmas, Junior, Serendipity,* and *The Internship.* He also produced three video games for George Lucas based on the Star Wars canon, Rebel Assault, Jedi Knight, and Force Commander.

He worked with Larry Page CEO of Google on several projects including the launch of Google+. He collaborated with Apple's Steve Jobs on many of the company's advertising campaigns, and the introduction of QuickTime as the standard for computer-based digital video.

In 2017 he turned his attention to writing novels. *The Google Earth Murders*, a serial killer reboot; *Kooktown, USA*, the tale of how San Francisco became the Liberal Mecca of America, and two non-fiction books, *Try Not to Annoy the Kangaroo: A Lifetime of Putting Up with Creative People in the Film Industry*, and *I'm So Far Gone, I'm Back*, an actual funny travelogue about Covid-19.

His time-travel baseball novel, *TIME Blinked*, was released in October 2021. *DracuLAND*, the story of a NYC real estate mogul who buys Dracula's Castle and possibly lives to regret it, was released on Hallowe'en 2022. Both were published by Celestial Echo Press.

Other publications from Celestial Echo Press

George W. Young's debut novel, *TIME Blinked*, was released in 2021.

Just like Dorothy in the Wizard of Oz, college athlete Bobby spends his days with those he loves and stays close to home. But unlike Dorothy, when Bobby's "tornado" bushwhacks his world, it doesn't move him into a fantastical realm of color and delightful beasts. He is propelled into a complicated past, where his dreams come true through a somewhat mystifying, somewhat terrifying wrinkle.

TIME Blinked is available at Barnes & Noble, and other fine bookshops, and online on Amazon.

"Twins are said to share special bonds, understand each other's unspoken communication, speak their own languages, even possess powers of ESP. Their double-ness continues to fascinate the rest of us. Adored or abhorred, sheltered or shunned, twins have universally and perpetually aroused attention and curiosity. It was that fascination that inspired this collection of twin-themed stories. In them, you'll find all matter of twins: the good, the bad, the fantastic, the fearsome, the magical, the envious, the secretive, the devious, and more. Being a twin. Fun, right? Think about it. *What could go wrong?*"

--Merry Jones, from the Foreword

The Twofer Compendium is available at Barnes & Noble and other fine bookshops, and online on Amazon.

French novelist Honore de Balzac once wrote, "Behind every great fortune lies a great crime." And we believe him. Some of the stories you will read in this anthology include criminals motivated by riches and fortune. Some of the stories have perpetrators with more pure agendas. But as Jacques Barzun quipped, "The danger that may really threaten crime fiction is that soon there will be more writers than readers." We don't believe him. We know you, along with millions of book lovers, will continue to enjoy reading stories throughout the ages. It's because crime stories evoke the "bad boy" in all of us, the hidden, mysterious desire to vicariously commit the crime – and get away with it. And we love to read about those criminals. "We don't give our criminals much punishment, but we sure give 'em plenty of publicity." Thanks, Will Rogers. We agree, and we promote.

This murder mystery anthology is dedicated to Sam Spade, Hercule Poirot, and Dick Tracy, as well as to all the writers of hard-boiled detective stories of years past, many of whom formed the basis for the crime mysteries we read today. Enjoy this wide variety of storylines, each of which include criminals, victims and trench coats.

The Trench Coat Chronicles is available at Barnes & Noble and other fine bookshops, and online on Amazon.